THE MALL WALKERS

R. BRIAN HOWE

SOMEWHAT GRUMPY PRESS

Published by arrangement with Somewhat Grumpy Press Inc. Halifax, Nova Scotia, Canada.
SomewhatGrumpyPress.com
The Somewhat Grumpy Press name and Pallas' cat logo are registered trademarks.

ISBN 978-1-998555-01-7 (paperback)

ISBN 978-1-998555-02-4 (eBook)

March 2025 v6

To my family,
Katherine, Tim, and Chris.

Gathering Clouds

June 2020

1

Inside Wolfville Mall, the mall walkers are doing their usual morning rounds. Some are chatting about the number of steps they do in a day, others about the warm June weather, and others about the horror and rising death count from Covid-19.

At ten, the stores open. A booming female voice from the PA system echoes through the mall. "Mornin' folks. Happy June the third. The mall's now open for business. For your safety, it's recommended you wear masks. And kindly observe the guidelines for social distancing. You have yourself a great day at Wolfville Mall, and God bless America."

Michael McQueen, the manager of the mall, is on his way to the Starbucks coffee shop to grab his first coffee of the day. As he always does in the mall, he's wearing a mask. He figures it's important that he and the mall staff set a good example. He hears a ping on his phone, indicating a text. A couple of minutes later, another ping. It's probably nothing important, he assumes. It usually isn't, this time of the morning. He'll look at it when he gets back to his office. He joins the long lineup at Starbucks, and finally gets his espresso macchiato.

On his way back to his office, he hears a commotion and some yelling coming from a side hallway. He goes for a closer look and is shocked by what he sees. Two paramedics are pushing a body on a gurney out of a unisex washroom. They come out into the hall, turn toward the back exit door, and leave the mall. A handful of people are standing around watching, including two uniformed police officers and a security guard who Michael knows.

Looking alarmed, Michael approaches the guard. "What's going on, Jim?"

"Horrible thing just happened, Michael. I sent you a text, but I guess you didn't get it. I got a report earlier of an old bald man lying on the washroom floor. I rushed over and found the man lying on his back in front of one of the toilets. He was in an awkward position and his eyes were open wide, extremely wide, with a look of absolute terror. Couldn't believe it. It was as if … as if … he was being attacked by some kind of demon or monster. It was a really awful sight."

The guard shudders. "The old man seemed to be dead. I checked his pulse and breathing. Nothing! And so, I phoned 911. The next thing I know, the paramedics arrive, then the police, then our own doctor—you know, Dr. Cortez from here in the mall."

"Good God!" says Michael, worried about how this is going to affect the mall's image. "This is awful, Jim, just awful. Sorry it had to happen on your watch. Did you know the man?"

The guard takes a deep breath. "Yeah, as I told the police, I knew him. At least, I knew him a bit. He was a nice old guy, in his seventies I think, who worked as a part-time clerk here at the mall bookstore. He just got the job. We sometimes talked. He told me he was a retired bus driver but had to take on this job because he was broke. Didn't have much of a pension. And whatever savings he had, he lost most of it through online gambling. So sad. He told me he lived alone. His wife died about a year ago, and his only family was a sister who lives out on the coast, somewhere in Oregon. He was a great guy, always polite, always cheerful. He was also so careful to wear a mask, just like we always do. Thought it was his duty. Had a blue one on his face all the time."

A police detective and the two uniformed officers interrupt. They ask Michael and the security guard to move back. They explain they'll need to seal off the washroom and the surrounding area for a full investigation, should it be determined later there was foul play. If that happens, they'd be back with a forensics team and more questions.

The police then leave. Michael and the guard walk back to Michael's office and continue their conversation. "You were saying, Jim, that the old man was always wearing a mask."

"Yeah, he was a believer. He really believed we should all be wearing masks in the mall. But you know, it was really strange … really strange. After I phoned 911, I noticed something funny inside his mouth. I didn't know what it was, and I didn't think I should look any further. But after the ambulance crew came, while they were trying to resuscitate him, they pulled a mask out of his mouth, a blue surgical mask that he always wore. Weird or what! Anyway, then Dr. Cortez came over, did an examination, and declared the man officially dead."

Michael scratches the back of his head and looks puzzled. "Yeah, Jim, that's weird stuff. So, did the mask have anything to do with his death? Maybe some kind of choking? What did Dr. Cortez say?"

"Well, the police asked the doctor about it. Dr. Cortez said he couldn't imagine the death was caused by asphyxiation, that it was more likely a major seizure, maybe an epileptic seizure or a massive stroke. The mask, he added, could have fallen into the man's mouth while he was struggling with whatever it was. But then, with a very serious expression, the doctor said it also could have been a homicide, a strangling, where the perpetrator shoved the mask into the man's mouth after the fact.

"A strangling! Good God! But wouldn't there have had to be marks on the man's throat?"

"Michael, the police asked the doctor the same question. Dr. Cortez said that while there were no visible marks, there didn't have to be. Only in about half of strangling cases are there marks. He also said while he's only speculating, that the exact the cause of death, whether it was a health condition or a homicide, will have to be determined later by a medical examiner down at the morgue. There almost certainly will be an autopsy."

A homicide? Good grief, Michael thinks. Could this have actually been a homicide? What a disaster this would be, for the mall, and for him. "Hmm. Thanks for the information. Jim, can you just keep this whole thing quiet for the time being? At least until we know more. I realize there'll probably be some gossip. It's not every day we have a body carried out on a gurney and we have the police asking questions. But we really don't know what happened, do we? If anybody asks, just say you know nothing. And please ask the rest of the security staff to do the same. We don't want to alarm our shoppers unnecessarily. Be bad for the mall's business. Okay?"

"You got it."

2

Later that morning, a crowd gathers for a rally in front of the main front door of the mall. The voices are getting louder and angrier. Merle Haggard's song *The Fightin' Side of Me* is playing as Marv Hammar, leader of a local anti-government and anti-masking group, jumps onto a platform to give a speech. He's heard that the mall is contemplating a new policy of mandatory masking to replace the earlier one of only recommending masks.

Marv is furious. Skilled at organizing rallies and marches, and in using social media to help do it, he has mobilized hundreds of people in the local area to fight what he thinks the mall intends to do. His plan is to fire up the crowd and lead them in a march around the outside of the mall, sending out the message that a mask mandate won't be tolerated.

Marv is a colorful and charismatic figure around Wolfville, a medium-sized city in a mountainous region of the Pacific Northwest. Unshaven and wild-eyed, Marv sees himself as a patriot in the tradition of those who fought in the American Revolution. He is inspired by revolutionary heroes such as Patrick Henry. He is especially stirred by the famous words attributed to Henry, "Give me liberty, or give me death!" In Marv's eyes, just as Henry fought against the wrongs committed by the British, he is fighting against the injustice of current American policies, particularly the taking away of individual liberty. For him, forcing people to wear masks is a case in point.

Fueling Marv's speeches are feelings of anger and bitterness. Growing up in a small town in southern Idaho, his father, a low-wage sanitation worker with a drinking problem, was often cruel and abusive to him. Frustrated by poverty and his precarious financial situation, his father took out his inner rage and resentment on people around him, including Marv. He bullied Marv and Marv's two brothers, he disparaged immigrants and foreigners, and he expressed a deep hatred of government, who he blamed for many of his problems. Marv swore he would never be like his father. In some ways, this turned out to be true. He never had a problem with alcohol. But in other ways, Marv was much like his father, especially in his being filled with anger and grievances and in his anti-government and anti-immigrant feelings.

The music ends. Marv, wearing the black cowboy hat he always does, lifts a bullhorn. "Fellow patriots," he says in a thunderous voice, "this is a bloody outrage. Bad enough the mall recommends we wear masks. Now, the tyrants want to *require* us ... actually want to *require* us ... to wear the bloody things before we can enter their holy premises. Imagine that! Damn it, we'll not stand for it! Back in the day, our patriotic ancestors had to fight the British and their disgusting policies. Our ancestors had to seize their lousy tea, throw it into Boston Harbor, and then go to war in the name of liberty. Today, we'll continue the fight for liberty. If we choose to wear a face covering, so be it. But if we choose not to do it ... if we don't want to wear the damn things ... in a mall, or in a store, or in a sports arena, our choice should be respected. We need to be respected! Down with tyranny!"

The crowd cheers wildly. Marv smiles. His practice sessions, and his courses in public speaking and elocution, have paid off. But there's more to it than that. Marv connects with his audience. He connects because he can channel his own anger and resentments into the delivery of his messages, and tap into the feelings of people who also have grievances and animosities. They see in him a vehicle for expressing their anger and their dislike of outsiders, immigrants, and elites, telling them how to think and what to do. They like him because he genuinely speaks for them. He is their voice and their agent of protest.

Marv relishes the adoring crowd. In the front row, he sees his girlfriend, Tina Morellato, now in her early thirties, clapping loudly while furiously chewing her gum. She is dressed, as she usually is, in a skimpy blue crop top and black yoga pants, an outfit that accentuates her curves. Marv appreciates her look—not just the curves, but her long jet-black hair, multiple ear and nose piercings, and Goth tattoos, including a large skull on each arm.

Beside Tina are Marv's two closest pals, also clapping. Tall and sturdy, they serve as his bodyguards and are known around Wolfville as his black coats. The reason—they wear identical black jackets, summer or winter, rain or shine. They look much the same except that one has short reddish hair and pointed ears, almost like Spock in the *Star Trek* series; the other is handsome and wears long black hair and a Hitler-style mustache. He's always gazing at Tina and offering to assist her. She seems to enjoy his attention.

Behind Tina and the black coats are Marv's large group of supporters. Some of them yell "freedom" and "no to masks," others hold up signs: "fuck masks," "down with tyranny," and "we love Marv." Some wave the American flag, two hold up a 1776 banner, and one waves the old Confederate battle flag, an oddity in the Pacific Northwest. Behind them, at a distance, are the Wolfville Police. They do not expect trouble. But they are there, just in case.

Marv jumps down from the platform. With the help of Tina and the black coats, he prepares his followers for the march. As he does, he's greeted by the mall manager.

Michael McQueen and Marv Hammar are both in their forties but otherwise quite different. Michael drives a white Tesla as his bit to protect the environment; Marv drives an old gas-guzzling pickup, spewing purple smoke. Michael lives in a middle-class house in the suburbs; Marv rents a dilapidated one-bedroom apartment in the downtown. Michael has a university degree and is a corporate manager; Marv failed to complete college and works as a dispatcher for a local taxi company; Michael is well-dressed, clean-cut, and refined in his language; Marv dresses like an old-time cowboy, has scruffy long brown hair, and speaks simply and bluntly.

"Good morning, Marv," says Michael, still thinking about the mysterious death of the bookstore clerk. "You've got a sizable crowd here. Must be over three hundred people. Listen, we've talked about this before. But let me remind you about the rules for your rally and march. This is private property, and the mall has the right to regulate what you can do here. We have chosen to allow you to have your rally and then lead a march around the outside of the mall one time, and disperse by the east door. We want to accommodate you and your supporters as much as possible. You can express your political views. But keep in mind—and I can't emphasize this enough—make sure it's orderly. You have permission to protest, but it has to be kept peaceful. If things get out of hand, you'll have a hard time getting our permission again. Do you understand?"

"Sieg Heil!" barks the handsome black coat, sarcastically.

"Sieg Heil!" yells the other one.

Michael shakes his head in disbelief. "Look Marv," he says, "we're not, to use your language, tyrants. We don't intend to simply declare a new policy of mandatory masking. We're only considering it as a means of keeping people safe from a deadly virus. But before we make a final decision, we'll be doing our homework. We'll be looking at the rates of people getting Covid in the area, at the latest research on the effectiveness of masks, and at what people around here think about the issue. You can be confident we won't be making any quick or arbitrary decisions. We're going to be consulting with everybody—shoppers, business operators, workers, plus the public health professionals. And you can rest assured, your views will be considered."

"Why in the hell," shouts Marv, grabbing back the bullhorn, "would you even consider such a harebrained scheme? Think about it, man. If you force us to wear masks today, you'll be forcing us to salute you tomorrow, to goose-step in front of you the next day. This is bull, pure and simple. It's just one more step into getting American people into an obedience frame of mind, getting us compliant, getting us psychologically prepared for a police state."

Marv stops to take a drink of water. "Look, back in March, your pal the Governor hit us with a lockdown, forcing many of our businesses to close. And also our schools. Many folks lost their jobs and their livelihoods. And now you've got the audacity to bring in mandatory masking. You'll say it's for our own good... our own good! We'll not be gaslighted, man. We'll not stand for it! Down with tyranny!"

Hearing this, led by Tina, the crowd breaks into roaring applause. A chant begins. "Down with tyranny, down with tyranny." My God, Tina thinks, it's no wonder I fell so madly in love with this dude. The man is so strong, so passionate, so patriotic, so principled. Even though we haven't been together that long, there is almost nothing I wouldn't do for this guy and for the cause.

Marv then tosses the bullhorn to one of his black coats, the one with the pointed ears, and yells, "let's march!" Although Marv is confident the march will go well, he's also worried about violence. He knows that while most of his followers are peaceful, there is a racist and aggressive element. He has sympathy for them, but worries that violence or an incident of racism will turn people off his cause. The march has to be free of any disturbances or altercations.

Michael steps off to the side, watching the crowd go by. He prays the march will be without incident. The last thing he wants is for the image of the mall to be tarnished by scenes of violence or racism.

This would be bad for business and, along with this, for his chance of getting a promotion. Worse, if things really got out of hand, he could lose his job.

Michael's thoughts turn back to the old man on the gurney. Was he murdered? If he was, how would this affect the mall? Would it mean a loss of business?

3

Walking in the mall the next morning are Richard and Mary Barker, both wearing masks. Among the regular mall walkers, they're getting in their steps before it gets busy. They intend to go once more around the mall before the stores open.

Retired now, they like to get their exercise in through mall walking, despite the pandemic and the risks of being indoors. They love the social life of the mall and, for Richard, the benefit of protecting himself from allergies and the asthma he gets from outdoor walking.

The Barkers have been married a long time. Before retiring a year ago, they were both teachers at Wolfville High School in the city's north end. Tall and slim, and wearing a goatee, Richard taught social studies. Mary, short and somewhat overweight—she has a hard time resisting desserts—was a math instructor. Although they often tease each other, they have a close relationship. They've always been happy together, despite their different outlooks on life. For Richard, the glass is half full and people are ultimately good; for Mary, the glass is half empty and people, at their core, are selfish and instrumental.

"Richard," says Mary, "don't you think this mall is getting to look a bit run-down? Floor tiles are cracked and paint is peeling from the walls. I guess I didn't notice it so much before. But now, with Covid and with fewer people in the mall, I'm noticing it more."

"Your eyes aren't the best, that's for sure," replies Richard, with a grin. "But you make a good point. The mall needs some sprucing up. We should mention it to the manager. See what Michael says. I know he's got his hands full dealing with Covid, but he needs to do something about this."

Wolfville Mall, one of the city's two main shopping malls, was built back in the 1960s. It is a large, rectangular-shaped, two-storied building, with a gray and white exterior. It has over three hundred stores and services, plus all kinds of kiosks cluttering up the hallways. At one end, there is a big pharmacy; at the other, a multiplex theater and a gym, both closed because of Covid. In the middle of the mall, at the lower level, are two restaurants, also closed due to Covid, and a row of administrative offices, one for the mall manager, another for customer relations, and another for security, with a door to a monitoring room where security staff can observe video from the surveillance cameras. On the upper level, there is a food court with over thirty eateries and a large Starbucks, exempt from the Covid closing order. There are escalators and an elevator to connect the lower floor to the food court.

Richard remembers when the mall opened. It was busy and considered upscale. But now it is losing its luster and with it, some of its business to a newer shopping center, Sunrise Mall, four miles down the road. So yes, Richard thinks, the time has come for the mall to get an upgrade. Hopefully, the manager has a plan.

As they walk along, Richard waves to a group of mall walkers he knows. Some of them are wearing masks, but others aren't. He thinks about the overall situation of masks in the mall, and the different ways stores have responded to the state department of health's recommendation that face coverings be worn indoors. Some stores now require masks inside their premises, others remain silent on the issue, and others post notices that masks are recommended or encouraged. The mall itself recommends masks for entrances, hallways, and common areas.

Richard also reflects on the different responses of people in the mall. All the mall staff—security guards, customer relations people, and cleaners—wear masks. Most of the managers and office workers do. But among customers, only about half wear them. The other half either don't wear them or, if they do, wear them in a useless way, around their necks or on their chins or on one of their ears. Least likely to wear them are older people, construction workers from nearby building sites, and unhoused people, who increasingly frequent the mall.

"Lucky the march yesterday didn't get out of hand," says Mary, interrupting Richard's train of thought. "There could have been violence."

"Yeah," replies Richard, "but there was that one nasty incident ... remember ... that horrible disgusting chant from Marv's supporters at the tail end of the march: 'You will not replace us, you will not replace us'."

"Of course I remember it! I'm not like you, showing signs of dementia," she says, with a wicked smile.

"Cut it out, Mary. Be nice for a change. Anyway, I keep thinking about the incident. And I keep thinking about the reporter from *The Wolfville News* who asked Marv about it. She asked him why he allowed racists in his group. Marv said to her, and I could hardly believe it, but he said she must have misheard. Marv said—and I think these were his exact words—my people are good people, sensitive people, the least racist people you'll ever meet."

"What a laugh!" says Mary. "No way. The reporter heard it exactly right. We were standing right there outside the east door. It was the white nationalist chant: 'You will not replace us'. It was disgusting, absolutely disgusting. Sad to know there are people who think this way, right here in Wolfville. Makes it clear that some of the anti-maskers—not all but some—have feelings of racism and hatred in their hearts. It's a horrible state of affairs."

The Barkers stop in their tracks. A handwritten note on the community bulletin board, outside the pharmacy, has caught their attention. The note is scribbled on dirty and stained paper.

This is a warning. To you who wear masks and demand everybody wears masks, stop it. If you keep it up, I may have to throw sulfuric acid into your face. Ever seen a face after acid? Not a pretty sight. The face is ugly and it'll be ugly for life. So, stop it. Keep it up and you'll really need a mask, a full-size one, to cover up your face. I'm really tired of seeing masks in the mall. It makes me sick. They're creepy. I hate them and I hate every one of you assholes who wear them.

Richard and Mary are stunned. They look at each other in disbelief.

"Richard, this is incredible. What do you think? What should we do?"

"I really don't know. You have any ideas?"

"Well, at the very least, I think maybe we should take the note down, keep it for the time being. Might cause alarm in the mall. Besides, it's so obnoxious."

"Good idea. Let's take it down, get some coffee, and try to figure this out."

They finish their walk, take the escalator up to the Starbucks, and look for a table, which is harder to find these days because of the Covid restrictions on seating. Playing in the background through the PA system is the Fats Domino song *Blueberry Hill*. Years before, customer relations had decided that playing popular songs from back in the day—golden oldies—was a good way of getting aging baby boomers, a good chunk of their demographic, into the mood for serious shopping.

They find a table. Richard says he'll get them the usual—two cups of cappuccino. Mary asks if he could also get her a piece of banana loaf.

"Really?" he replies, with a sly smile. "You wouldn't want to lose your sexy figure, would you?" She thinks about it, then tells him to skip the banana loaf. He leaves and comes back with the cappuccinos.

"This note is beyond the pale," he says, sitting down and taking off his mask. "In all my years of teaching, I've never seen anything like it. Not even my most delinquent student would say or write anything like that. It's nasty, so full of venom. Can't believe it. I can't believe somebody would write such disgusting words. Hard to imagine anybody around here coming up with the idea of throwing sulfuric acid into somebody's face. I've heard of acid attacks in places like India, usually men against women for refusing them sex or turning down a marriage proposal. But I haven't heard of it, or even the threat of it, here in the United States."

"I keep telling you, Richard, and you need to get it through your noggin, there are some pretty nasty people in the world, including here in America. We always have to be aware that people everywhere are capable of some vicious things. But imagine it ... imagine some twisted human being purposefully disfiguring somebody in the mall. For what! Just for urging people to wear masks."

Richard sips some of his coffee. "But as I think about it, Mary, I wonder just how serious this threat really is. The writer says I *may* throw acid, not I *will* actually do it. Maybe this person is not being that serious. Maybe the guy's just an oddball or looney tunes, who went over the edge for a minute. Look at the reason for the guy's rant, that masks are creepy. These are the words of a wackadoodle, not a serious person."

Mary looks puzzled. She puts her hand under her chin and ponders the situation. "Maybe. But who could have done it?"

"Might have been one of those homeless people ... sorry, unhoused people, I keep forgetting the new language. Anyway, we see more of them in the mall these days. Some are drunk or on drugs, some have mental problems. And many of them are dirty. If you look at the note, you see the paper is dirty, and the writing is almost illegible. Doesn't it make sense to you it was one of these folks?"

"It's possible," replies Mary, sipping some of her coffee. "But there's other people too. Could have been Marv. He's got the motivation. But, as I think about it some more, Marv's a high-profile guy and well known around the mall. He's smart, and it'd be risky for him to put up such a note."

"I see what you mean. But others could have put it up on Marv's behalf. Marv could have paid one of his idiot followers to do it, or he could have paid one of the unhoused people."

"Or," says Mary, "one of his followers could have been inspired to do it, without Marv even knowing. You know how devoted they are to him. Could have been one of the black coats. Could have been Tina, his weird girlfriend—the one with those disgusting tattoos. She'd do almost anything for him. Or it could have been one of the workers or security guards here in the mall, with a secret admiration for Marv."

"It's all possible, Mary. Many people could have done it. But what now? We have the note. What should we do with it?"

Mary ponders what to do. "Well, I think we better take it to the mall manager. Get the responsibility off our shoulders, put it on his. Michael should know what to do."

"Yeah, I think you're right. Let's go home, get some lunch, feed our lazy cat, then we'll come back and see Michael."

"Okay, let's get to it."

4

The Barkers miss Michael by ten minutes. He had to leave his office early, having a dental appointment downtown, which is going to take more time than usual. Then he has to get a haircut and pick up some groceries on his way home.

During his drive downtown, Michael turns on the car radio and listens to Ray Charles' classic song, *Georgia on My Mind*. The song reminds him of the girl from Georgia who became his wife some fifteen years earlier.

Michael had wanted to become a college professor and teach English literature or philosophy. But, after getting his BA at Wolfville College, he saw that jobs in that field were scarce. He decided to be practical. He enrolled in Duke's highly ranked School of Business, where he met Cornelia. They fell in love, got married after graduation, and then moved to the Pacific Northwest. Michael had applied for, and accepted, a job as a junior manager at a large insurance company in Wolfville, the city where he'd grown up. He was thrilled to come back home. Cornelia was happy to accompany him, in love and looking forward to building a family.

Michael worked his way up in the company. He changed companies and got a middle management position with Pacific Gold Corporation, a large real estate and investment company in Wolfville.

His primary job was to be the manager of Wolfville Mall, though he had other tasks, including being the property manager of three condominium towers surrounding the mall.

Michael now earns a good salary with Pacific Gold, though not nearly as good as Cornelia would like. His hope is that after he proves himself, he'll be able to negotiate a promotion and a much larger salary. Now that he and Cornelia have two girls to raise, he has to move upward.

Cornelia, now in her mid-thirties, grew up in a wealthy southern family in Macon, Georgia. She is short and looks, from certain angles, like movie star Reese Witherspoon. Her mother died when she was young, so she hardly remembers her. But she's close with her father, a retired judge who still lives in Macon. Despite the distance, her father is enmeshed in Cornelia's life, always advising her, and wanting the very best for his darling daughter. For her last birthday, he bought her a brand-new black BMW SUV. She adores him and still calls him Daddy. They connect regularly by phone or text or email. The first thing he always asks is how she and her twin daughters—eight-year-old Bobbie and Brandy—are doing. He rarely asks about Michael but when he does, it's usually to express disappointment in him. The man lacks drive and ambition, he always says. He's too easy-going, lacking the killer instinct to do well in the business world.

Michael pulls up in the driveway and parks beside Cornelia's SUV. As he plugs in his car, he admires their house, as he often does. It's a stately, two-story home with three bedrooms and a big backyard. It's professionally landscaped and on a quiet street. Couldn't ask for anything more than this, he thinks, as he takes in the groceries. He decides that, until he knows more, he won't mention anything to Cornelia about the weird death of the old man, something he's been worried about ever since he found out about it.

"I'm home, princess," he says, coming in a side door.

"How did it go at the dentist?" she asks, her blond shoulder length hair in a perfect bob.

"Well, it was a complicated root canal. So it took longer than expected. But I got through it okay."

"Good," she says, putting away the groceries. "How about we sit down and have a nice glass of wine before dinner. The girls are still playing in the backyard. I've got a bottle of French Sauvignon Blanc in the wine cooler. It's a premium white from the Loire Valley, so it should be good. We had it before and we liked it. Remember? It had that nice bright acidity and those sublime aromas of grapefruit and freshly cut grass."

Michael is puzzled. Freshly cut grass? "Hmm. Oh yeah," he says, with a grin. "I think I remember it now. Yes, yes, let's have it. But let me get changed first."

After getting into his shorts and a tee-shirt, Michael gets the wine and joins Cornelia on a sofa in the family room. He's still thinking about the smell of freshly cut grass.

"Cheers," they say in unison, clinking their glasses.

"But let me taste it first," says Cornelia. "Make sure it's up to scratch."

Cornelia treats her glass of wine like a sommelier. First, she holds it up against the light to observe the clarity of the wine. Then she swirls it around in her glass, releasing the bouquet. She then sticks her nose into the glass, taking a full sniff. Finally, she has a small sip, moving it around vigorously in her mouth as she would mouthwash.

"It's good, sweetie, it really is. Got that taste of passionfruit and green apples."

Michael grins again. Green apples? "Yeah, I like it too, princess. I'm impressed. You know your wine, don't you? Good thing you took that wine tasting course a couple months back. It really paid off."

"Yeah, it did, sweetie. With Covid and with so many places shut down, I had to find some hobby to keep me occupied, something interesting I could do. The online course filled the bill."

"How did it go with your yoga session today? I think you said you were meeting over at Alexandra's house."

Cornelia recalls how the sessions started. Before Covid, she had been going to yoga classes at the local community center. While there, she had developed good friendships with women in the area. But the classes got canceled in the early days of Covid. She decided, with six other women, that they would organize their own sessions at their homes twice a week. They would take turns in hosting the sessions and they'd perform their exercises with the help of a great video they were familiar with.

"Yeah, it went well. Everyone showed up. And lots of good juicy gossip."

"About anybody I know?"

"No, you wouldn't know them. They're high-powered people out on the west side."

Michael looks out the window of their family room and sees the girls playing with their Barbies.

"I guess that's right, I wouldn't know them," says Michael, with a touch of sarcasm in his voice.

"Well, if you really must know," she says, detecting the sarcasm, "it's about a messy love triangle. But I don't want to get into it now. How about you? How'd it go at the mall today?"

"I saw someone on the board of directors this morning. Asked her what the corporation thought about the masking issue, about what I should do in terms of policy. She told me it was my call. She said the board had great trust in my judgment."

Michael stops for another splash of wine. He looks out the window and sees the girls yelling at each other. Wonder what that's about. They rarely fight.

"But I'm not sure what to do," he says. "I thought I had come up with a reasonable policy in the first place—to recommend but not require face coverings. I had to do something about Covid. The number of cases were climbing, deaths were increasing, and the department of health had recommended masks for all indoor settings. The most sensible thing to do, I figured, was to follow the department of health and have a middle-ground policy of recommending—but not requiring—face coverings in the mall."

"Seems sensible to me, Michael. But what happened? How did it ever get to be such a big deal?"

"It became an issue," he explains, "because I came under pressure, lots of pressure, to do more than just recommend masks. I got emails and phone calls from people almost every day, urging me to have mandatory masking. And it wasn't just medical people who pressured me, it was also many of our customers. In response, I said that a change would be considered. And word got out somehow that the mall was intending to bring in mandatory masking. It's not surprising what happened next. Marv and his wild gang of anti-maskers got wind of it, and they had their damn rally. So now I have pressures barreling in on me from both sides."

"Michael," says Cornelia firmly, "this is not rocket science. It's simple. You need to make the right decision for your career and for your family. Up to now, you've got yourself a good reputation with Pacific Gold. You earn a decent salary, and you do a fairly good job as the mall manager. But as Daddy says, you can't stand still. It's important you get a promotion and a raise, that you move up in the corporation to upper management. Maybe you can get a job as one of the senior managers. You told me it pays lots of money."

"Yeah, it does."

"To make it happen, you'll need to make a decision the corporation likes, one that benefits your customers and businesses."

Michael rolls his eyes. "It's not so simple, princess. I have to figure out which policy on masks is most beneficial. This means assessing not only the percentage of people who feel a particular way about the issue but also how deeply they feel. One side might be in the minority but feel intensely they are in the right. The other side might be in the majority but feel relatively indifferent to what happens. I have to figure out not only how people feel but also how intensely they feel. And I also have to assess the trend in local public opinion."

Cornelia is looking impatient. "Okay, okay, I can see it isn't easy. But you can figure it out, Michael. You *need* to figure it out."

"And on top of this," adds Michael, sipping some more wine, "I have another problem. Business at the mall is down. Part of this, obviously, has to do with Covid and the shutting down of our movie theaters, the gym, and the two restaurants. We've had fewer people coming in. But another part of it is we've been losing business to Sunrise Mall. From what I hear, the new manager at Sunrise—Brenda somebody—is a real go-getter. She's been working hard to improve their business and she's been having success. I have to do something to turn our mall around and get our customers back. Plus, I've got to get it right on the masking issue."

Cornelia stomps her feet, like a child having a tantrum. "Yes, yes, you *do* have to get it right, Michael. You listen to me. Our family depends on you. When we got married, you told Daddy you'd provide for me in the style I grew up in. You need to keep your word to Daddy. You need to be successful, and we need to be moving up in the world. Later, when the twins are older, I can go back to work and help out financially. But right now, you *need* to be making more money."

"But—"

"Look, Michael, I want a better life. I want to move into a bigger house. I want us to be living in a more upscale neighborhood where there is a better class of people and better schools for our girls. And I want our girls to be in good private schools, so they can get a better start in life. This requires money. So, Michael, you've got to—you've simply *got to*—make the right decisions."

"I hear you, Cornelia," says Michael, feeling miffed about her little sermon.

Cornelia abruptly finishes her wine and goes out to get the girls for dinner.

Michael wants to please Cornelia and prove her daddy wrong. Despite her snootiness and tendency to be bossy, intrusive, and uncompromising, he loves Cornelia. He admires her spirit and her determination, as well as her good looks and skills in bed. She's been a great mother to their two girls, showing affection and patience, and providing effective guidance. Besides that, she had agreed to move with him to Wolfville, far away from her family and friends in Georgia. She has sacrificed a lot and given him support. So, he owes her. He wants their relationship to succeed and he wants to please her. To do this, he realizes, he'll need to buckle down, be more pragmatic and aggressive.

But he also thinks about his late father, a church minister and a humanitarian, who Michael deeply loved. It wasn't that his dad was a heroic guy and a fantastic role model. He sometimes lost his temper for little reason and occasionally drank too much. But Michael admired him a lot. What he most admired was not his dad's religiosity but his strong ethical sense. His dad repeatedly said to him it's important to do the right thing, even if it's not always in your own interests. Do what's practical, he said, but put your moral principles first. And his dad did try, though not always with success, to practice what he preached.

Michael also recalls that when he went into the world of business, although he initially tried to follow his father's advice, he gave up. It was unrealistic, he came to believe. Business requires that, in the pursuit of profits and success, people sometimes need to cut corners and compromise their ethical principles. As the old slogan says, nice guys finish last. His dad, admirable though he was, was out-of-touch and just didn't understand the world of modern business. So Michael figured he needed to be pragmatic, put his moral principles on the back burner. But now he wonders if he's gone too far. Maybe his dad was right.

Michael wishes Cornelia would be more satisfied. They have a nice lifestyle, the girls are doing well, and he has a good job. Why can't she be more pleased? Why can't she be more supportive of him? Why does she always want more and more? At the beginning, when he first met her, she wasn't like this. She was easy-going and happy with things in the moment. She wasn't a social climber. What changed? Maybe it was the long-term influence of her upbringing and her father. But he can't change her. She is who she is. Maybe one day, she'll return to the person she was. In the meantime, he has to be loyal, and he has to be patient and understanding.

That night, Michael dreams he is being chased around the mall by two huge and aggressive gorillas, each clutching a bullhorn. One screams into his bullhorn, *Put yourself and your family first, screen out everything else. If you don't help yourself, no one else is going to.* The other one shouts, *Help yourself, yes, but help others too. Be compassionate, think of your community. We're all in it together.* Joining these gorillas running after Michael are other gorillas who scream, *You will not replace us, you will not replace us.*

5

It's Monday morning, just after the stores have opened. Michael is cleaning his hands in a small washroom inside his office, and considering his next step. He wants to get a sense of what shoppers at the mall think about the masking issue. He decides he'll talk to a handful of customers. It won't be a fully accurate reading of public opinion, but it'll give him a rough sense of what's on people's minds. He aims to not let his own views on the subject get in the way.

He puts on his mask, leaves his office, and walks through the mall and up the escalator to Starbucks. There are fewer shoppers and fewer tables because of the Covid restrictions, but there is a sprinkling of people drinking coffee, some of them with bakery items. Michael gets himself an espresso macchiato. He then picks a table, goes over, and introduces himself to an elderly couple.

He explains that he is doing an informal survey about wearing of masks in the mall. He asks the couple which of the three options they favor: no policy at all on masks, continue the current policy of recommending masks, or introduce mandatory masking in the mall.

"That's something we've talked about," says the woman. "We're in favor of masks being mandatory. We're both in our seventies now. I've got a heart condition, and my husband has diabetes. We're in the group they talk about all the time on TV—older people with underlying conditions, at high risk of getting Covid-19. We understand many people don't like wearing masks and they don't like being told what to do. But until vaccines come along, we all need to be wearing masks indoors. People need to understand we're *all* at risk, all of us, to different degrees. It's not just us old folks. We all have to protect ourselves and protect others from this dreadful virus."

"Couldn't agree more," says the man. "My wife is spot on. We need to protect each other. We're all in the same boat."

"Thanks very much, says Michael, "I appreciate your input. Have yourself a great day." He goes over to a young couple at another table and asks the same question.

The man replies. "I don't think the mall should get involved at all. Shouldn't require masks, shouldn't even recommend the damn things. It's none of the mall's bloody business. I tried wearing a mask once. It made me puke. I tried it again later and it fogged up my glasses. Plus, it made it hard for me to breathe. I've talked to other people; they feel the same. Masks aren't needed. Why should any of us have to wear them?"

A harrowing image flashes into Michael's mind: the old man lying in front of the toilet with a blue mask jammed into his throat. Why did he have the look of terror in his eyes?

The voice of the woman brings Michael back from his thoughts. "I read online the other day that Covid's not that big a deal. It's exaggerated. It's sort of like the flu. Comes and goes. If anybody is going to be getting it in a serious way, it's going to be old people. They are going to be dying off anyway. Why should we have to sacrifice our comfort and our freedom just to protect them? It's not fair!"

"That's right," says the man, "it's not fair. Best to forget about it."

"Many thanks," says Michael, trying not to show his disgust. "You've been a lot of help." As he gets up to leave, he wonders how these people got to be so selfish and unthinking. Was it their parents? Was it a lack of education? Who knows? He surveys the tables again.

He sees three middle-aged women sitting at a table on the other side of Starbucks.

"Masks aren't right," says one. "If I'm going to get Covid and die, so be it. It's God's will. Nowhere in the Bible does it say that God wants us to wear face coverings. They had plagues and diseases back in those days too. It's in the Bible. But God didn't say anything about wearing masks. We shouldn't be interfering with the will of God. The mall shouldn't be requiring, or even recommending, masks."

"For me, it's not a matter of religion," adds another. "But it is a matter of my body, my choice. It's me, it's not anybody else, it's me who gets to choose what's on my body or in my body, whether I get a tattoo or not, whether I wear earrings or not, whether I wear a mask or not. The mall shouldn't be able to dictate to me, or to anybody else, what to wear. I'm okay with just encouraging masks. But a mask mandate is completely, and absolutely, out of the question."

"I agree with my friends," says the third, "but for a different reason. I was a history major when I went to college. My teacher always said, 'Remember the lesson of Munich!' Chamberlain appeased Hitler, and by appeasing him, allowed Hitler to become more and more aggressive, and we had that horrible war. The lesson—we need to stop bad things in their tracks before worse things happen. If we allow the mall or any authority to dictate to us today, where will it lead tomorrow? We might think masks are no big deal. But if they force us to wear masks today, they might force us to get brain implants tomorrow. I hope you get my point."

"Yes, and thanks, you all have been most helpful," Michael responds, finishing his coffee. "You've obviously given this issue some deep thought." He gets up, puts on his mask, and turns away from the women, his eyes rolling. Going down the escalator and heading back to his office, he wonders how anybody can possibly suggest a mask mandate might lead to brain implants. Where does this weird kind of thinking come from? Maybe it's the internet. They tell me there are an incredible amount of ridiculous conspiracy theories on social media. That could explain it.

6

Michael goes back to his office, creates a Word file, and summarizes the responses to his survey. Maybe he should talk to more people. His thoughts turn back to the mysterious death of the old man. Obviously, the death will be extremely upsetting for the man's sister and friends. But it could also be bad for the mall. If there's a lot of publicity, and especially if it turns out to be a homicide, shoppers could be wary about coming in. Business could suffer and so would his chances of getting a promotion. It's best, he figures, to keep the matter as quiet as possible.

As Michael reaches into his mini fridge to get out a sandwich for lunch, he hears a knock on his door. He opens it and sees it's Mary and Richard Barker. "Well, if it isn't the mall walkers. Come on in, have a seat. Can I offer you something, maybe a fresh chocolate brownie?"

Mary is tempted. But she recalls what Richard said earlier. "I'd better pass," she says, looking over at her grinning husband.

"Not for me either," Richard adds.

Michael knows the Barkers well. He sometimes joins them, as well as some of the other regular mall walkers, on their early morning rounds. Apart from enjoying their conversations, he figures it's a good way of getting information about what's on people's minds.

If he gets alerted to any problems in the mall, he can act quickly to fix them before things escalate. The mall walkers also enjoy having Michael on their walks. He's empathetic, engaging to talk to, and pleasant to be around. Liking his company so much, they gave him the nickname of mall walker-in-chief, later shortening it just to chief.

"Well, what's up?" says Michael.

"Listen, chief," says Mary, "something important has come up. Since you're the mall manager, we thought you should see this note."

Mary hands the note to Michael. "No one's seen it except us. We came across it on the bulletin board yesterday morning, shortly before the stores opened. We thought it might cause some anxiousness in the mall, so we decided to take it down and show it to you."

Reading it, Michael is stunned, just as the Barkers were. This is unbelievable, he thinks. First, we have a possible homicide and now a threat of violence. Something weird is going on here. Getting nervous, Michael fidgets with a pencil on his desk. But he stops himself, figuring he needs to appear calm and collected. He doesn't want to alarm the Barkers and have them spread fear in the mall.

"Listen, thanks for reporting this to me. Looks like we have another nutbar on our hands. I'll tell you what. Give me a couple days on this. I'll check it out with our security, see what they have to say. We'll also check out the video from our surveillance cameras, see what it shows. In the meantime, please don't say anything about this. We don't want people in the mall to get worried. I'll get back to you as soon as I can."

"Okay, chief," says Richard, "we'll leave the note with you. Don't worry, we won't mention it to anybody else. But please don't tell anyone it was us who gave it to you. We don't want some psycho coming after us with acid. Okay?"

"Yeah, I promise," Michael replies. "It'll be our secret. By the way, on a different topic, I've been asking people in the mall what they think about the masking issue. What do you folks think the mall should do?"

"Mary and I are on the same page," says Richard. "We both think you should have a mask mandate. For me, it's the morally correct thing to do. I agree, I certainly do, that our rights and freedoms are important. This is in our constitution. But our responsibilities are also important. Many people forget this. They forget that responsibilities are the flip side of our rights. If I have a right, you have a responsibility to respect that right. In the case of masks, we all have a responsibility to wear masks so others can enjoy their rights, including their right to be free from unnecessary sickness and death. And this means that authorities—such as you, Michael—have a responsibility to protect people under their watch, which includes requiring masks, so that our rights and freedoms can be enjoyed. People are not free when they get the virus and end up sick or dead. So, in the mall, it's imperative that you—"

Mary cuts in. "Richard could go on like this all day. He should have been a philosopher. For me, it's not a matter of abstract moral principles. It's self-interest, pure and simple. Call me selfish, but I'm sure I'm right about this. This virus is deadly and it's spreading. In the coming months, it's going to spread more. So, until we get vaccines, we need to contain it. As the doctors say on TV, wearing masks indoors is an important way of doing this. Yes, we could just recommend people wear masks. But I'm afraid some people, out of stupidity or laziness or ignorance, aren't going to do it. They're going to put other people in jeopardy. We need everybody in the mall to be wearing masks. We need it to be required. Until we get vaccines, and maybe even after that, this is the best way of containing Covid."

"You come at it from different angles," replies Michael, "but you ultimately agree with a mask mandate. Thanks for your input."

A thought pops into Michael's mind. He wonders if the note is connected to the strange death of the bookstore clerk. Whoever wrote the note is obviously a hater of masks. The old man had a mask stuffed into his mouth, which could have been done by a hater. Coincidence?

"One more thing, chief," says Mary, interrupting Michael's thoughts. "We've been noticing how run-down this mall is looking these days. It needs some fixing up. We know how busy you are with the Covid issue. But isn't there something you can do? Friends we know don't come here anymore. They say it's getting to look dingy. They're shopping at Sunrise. So, we're hoping you can do something. We love this mall and want it to be successful."

"We're aware of the problem," responds Michael. "And I've spoken to our corporate heads about the need for renovations. I haven't got anything definite back from them yet, but they said they'd look into it, see if they can set aside some money for a major upgrade. I think they may do it. When I hear back, I'll let you know."

"Okay, thanks," replies Mary.

The Barkers leave Michael's office. Finally, Michael can have his lunch. As he bites into his tuna sandwich, he glances at the note, still on his desk, and worries. Questions flood into his mind. *Who could be responsible for the note? How serious is the threat? Should I tell the police? But if I tell the police, won't word leak out to the public about the threat, causing anxiety in the mall, and maybe loss of business? And if there's less business, there'll be less chance of me getting a promotion. If that happens, Cornelia will not be pleased.*

Michael decides he'll hold off deciding about the note. He'll first consult with mall security.

7

Two days later, in the early afternoon, Michael walks over to the security office. Marvin Gaye's classic *I Heard it Through the Grapevine* is playing in the mall. Michael hums along.

Waving him into his office is Wally Waller, head of mall security. He is wearing a mask, as all security personnel are required to do. In his late twenties, Wally is tall, rough-looking, and athletic in build. He has a big and ugly scar above his right eye, caused by a bottle thrown at him in a bar fight. After high school, Wally had tried to get into the Wolfville Police Department. Not making it past the interview stage, he wondered if it was because of his wild lifestyle. He decided he'd try again after a few years. In the meantime, to gain relevant experience, he'd try to get a job as a security guard. He applied for and received a job in a company under contract to provide security for Wolfville Mall. He worked his way up and is now head of security at the mall. Perhaps later, he'll apply again to the police force.

Michael is suspicious of Wally for many reasons. For one thing, Wally seems to have an anger problem, evident by the fact he has explosive outbursts for what most would consider minor irritants. For another, he's rumored to be a late-night boozer. It's also rumored he is a secret member of a white power group, who attends the regular meetings of the group and goes on their marches. If it was up to

Michael, he'd find a way of letting Wally go. But Wally is good at his job and often provides sound advice on security matters. He also has good relations with the security staff and with other staff in the mall. More than that, through family ties, Wally is well-connected in his company and with the senior management at Pacific Gold. That is how he got his job. Michael has to be careful.

"Hey, man, what's going on?" asks Wally, taking off his mask to munch on a chicken wing. "Have a seat."

"Thanks. I've got a few things I'd like to discuss with you, Wally."

"Shoot, bro."

"First off, I assume you know from your security guy, Jim Hill, about the bizarre death of the bookstore clerk a couple mornings ago, just before the rally."

"Yeah. I heard about it. Understand it happened over in the new unisex washroom. Heard he had a mask stuffed into his mouth. Weird or what! I really didn't know him, but Jim did, and so did some others in security. They're blown-away."

"Yes, a lot of people are blown-away. Apparently, the medical people don't know yet what caused his death. Possibly it was a homicide of some kind."

"Well, maybe, but let's hope not," says Wally, finishing the chicken wing and flinging the bone into a garbage container. "That'd be horrible, man. And it'd be horrible publicity for the mall!"

Michael nods. "Wally, can you do me a favor? Can you check with the morgue and the police from time to time, find out if it actually was determined to be a homicide, and let me know? I hope to God there's some other explanation."

"Yeah, I can do that."

"And Wally, let's keep this to ourselves for the time being. Please emphasize to your staff they do the same. I know word is going to leak out anyway. But let's try to keep a lid on it, tamp it down as much as we can, at least for now."

"Gotcha."

"Thanks, Wally. A second thing on my mind is this note." Michael hands the note to Wally. "This was pinned up on our bulletin board yesterday morning. Someone brought it to me. I'd like to get your take on it. And how do you think the mall should respond?"

Wally reads the note and looks puzzled. He thinks about it for a few minutes.

"Hmm. Looks like we've got ourselves a problem here, don't we, bro. I just don't know what to say."

"It's strange, that's for sure. Do you think, Wally, there could be some kind of a connection between this note and the possible homicide in the washroom?"

"Nah, I can't see it. The dude who wrote the note is a real sicko. Look at what he says about masks—they're creepy. What a laugh! He must have some kind of mental problem. He's written a note, yes, but I doubt he'd be capable of murder, if it really was murder. He's just blithering."

Michael raises his eyebrows. "Or she. The person could be female ... it is possible. Same thing with the old man's death. If it was a homicide, the killer could be female. It happened in a unisex washroom. So, we can't just assume things. But back to my question: how do you think the mall should respond to the note?"

"Well," says Wally, "in my humble opinion, it's best to ignore it. As I said before, it looks like it was written by a sicko, a whack job, probably one of our demented street people. You can hardly read the writing, and the paper is dirty. Looks like it was slobbered on. It's gotta be one of those homeless freaks. I'd say it's an idle threat, written by a street person, probably drunk. I think you should just ignore it. If you make it public, and if the police get involved, there could be an investigation, which'll draw a lot of attention. People would get worried and we could lose business in the mall."

Michael nods his head. "You could be right, Wally. I'm inclined to take your advice."

Michael asks Wally about any possible legal implications. Is it legal to ignore a threat of physical harm? Is threatening to attack people with sulfuric acid a crime? If it is a crime, does the mall have a legal obligation to report it?

After thinking about it for a few moments, Wally suggests to Michael there's nothing to worry about. First, nobody—including the police—would blame the mall for dismissing the note and assuming it was written by some nutty street person. Second, the mall is under no legal duty to report the threat of an attack, even if it is a crime. People *can* report a criminal act to the police, but they don't have to. But to be on the safe side, Wally adds, mentioning nothing specific, he'll check with one of the corporation's lawyers to make sure all of this is correct.

Michael thanks Wally for his thoughts. He asks Wally to talk to his security guards, find out if they saw anything odd the morning the note was found. And have them check out the video recordings from the surveillance cameras, especially between the opening of the mall and the opening of the stores. Maybe the camera above the bulletin board will confirm that the writer of the note was an unhoused person on drugs, who didn't know what they were doing.

Wally agrees. As Michael gets up and is about to leave Wally's office, he thinks of something else. He wants to know Wally's view of a possible mask mandate for the mall.

Wally polishes off another chicken wing and tosses the bone into the same garbage container. He then tells Michael it's a terrible idea. He says he's been talking to the guards about the possibility. They're not comfortable with it. They're happy to catch an occasional shoplifter or throw out a homeless idiot. Gives them something to do and it can be exciting. But to have to confront good people, regular people, who refuse to wear masks and who feel strongly about it—that's too much. Many of our guards are young dudes not long out of high school. Some of them are young gals. They're okay confronting bad people, but they don't want to get into conflict with good people, not for the low pay they get. Bottom line, it's a bad idea.

Wally notices his nose is dripping and wipes the mucus onto his shirt sleeve. "Besides, I hate masks myself. Wish we didn't have to wear them. They're a bother and they're not really needed. But listen, boss, I've gotta question for you."

"Go ahead," says Michael, looking at Wally's shirt sleeve with disgust.

"Well, you know as well as me, we've got a lotta street people in here these days. I'm sure it's bad for our business. A good part of the problem, I figure, is our soft approach in dealing with them. We just politely ask them to leave if they're causing trouble, and gently escort them to the door. But this only encourages them more. They come back into the mall and there's more of them. As a deterrent, I think we should use a tougher approach."

"What do you mean by tougher, Wally?"

"Ideally, being able to use pepper spray. Nah, I'm just joshing ya, Michael. I know that's not in the cards. What I mean is an approach where the guards would confront these people in a more combative way, be harsher with them, throw them out more aggressively. None of this politeness bullshit! They'd think twice about coming back. Would you be okay with this?"

As Michael mulls over the suggestion, he thinks about Wally's insensitivity and authoritarian outlook. No wonder the guy didn't make it into the police force. "Well, I agree, Wally, it's a problem. But this new approach of yours could cause other problems too. Many of our shoppers wouldn't like to see our unhoused people being treated in such a rough way. While they may not enjoy encountering them in the mall, they also have some sympathy for their plight. They see them as having problems in their backgrounds—mental health issues, drug addiction problems, family problems, and so on. I really don't know what the answer is. But I'm inclined—at least for the time being—to leave our current approach in place. But I'll give the issue some more thought. Maybe we can revisit it at a later point."

Wally looks disappointed. "Yeah, okay, boss."

Michael gets up and goes back to his office. Thinking about the meeting, his suspicions about Wally linger. Why is Wally so hostile to our unhoused population? Why is he so opposed to a mask mandate? Why is he so adamant about ignoring the note? Maybe, just maybe, Wally agrees with the hateful message in the note. Maybe he's a quiet supporter of Marv and the anti-maskers.

8

The following morning, Grumpy Bill is rushing about. Wearing a mask, like many of the business operators in the mall, he is hard at work putting up a new display in his sporting goods store. Slim and medium height, he is in his mid-sixties and looks a bit like Hollywood legend Humphrey Bogart. He has short gray hair and is known for using old-fashioned language like "gee" or "golly"—language he learned from his folksy grandfather.

Grumpy Bill is proud of his store and his business accomplishments. Growing up in poverty in a town ten miles north of Wolfville, he had to work his way through high school and college. Eventually, after years of saving money, he acquired this store, and later, two branch stores, one in downtown Wolfville and the other in the northern suburbs. Due to the success of his stores and his shrewd real estate investments, he has become quite wealthy. He lives by himself in an upscale neighborhood—Blue Mountain Heights—and has never married.

It's rumored that Grumpy Bill, or GB for short, had a tragedy in his past which made him permanently grumpy. The reality, as Michael McQueen knows, is quite different. Grumpy Bill developed a tic around age five, a neurological and muscular condition where his head would suddenly jerk to his side, sometimes a couple times, sometimes multiple times. He found it highly embarrassing. Boys teased him without mercy and girls would have nothing to do with him. So, to avoid unpleasant encounters with people, and to keep people away, he developed a habit of being grumpy. His tic hasn't prevented him from being successful with his business, although his sudden jerks have scared away more than a few customers.

Grumpy Bill looks at his watch. It's time for his meeting with the mall manager. Michael had called him earlier that morning to arrange it. The reason, Michael had told him, was to see what the business association thought about the issue of masks. It was logical for Michael to do this since Grumpy Bill was head of the mall's business association. A key role of the association is to advise the mall manager on common business concerns.

Grumpy Bill alerts his assistant that he is departing. He leaves the store and heads for Michael's office. Along the way, he notices an old Indigenous homeless man. With a crutch under one arm and wearing torn clothes, the man is looking inside garbage containers to see what he can scrounge up. He's finally able to grab a discarded pop can and half a bagel with cream cheese. As he wolfs down the bagel, Grumpy Bill looks at him in disbelief. "How doggone awful is that," he mumbles.

Grumpy Bill's thoughts shift from feeling sorry for the old man to feeling sorry for himself. *I'm not eating from the garbage, but I'm lonely. I've often wanted to be with somebody special, share my life with somebody. But I held back. It wasn't just because of my tic. I grew up seeing my parents bickering and unhappy. I saw my friends getting married, then fighting and getting divorced. So, I chose to remain alone. I put all my energy into building up my business and making money. But by golly, I've paid the price. I ache for a partner, but I don't have one. And I probably never will.*

Michael welcomes Grumpy Bill into his office and offers him a chair and some coffee.

"Not that fancy stuff, is it?"

"No, just regular drip coffee. I only have my macchiato when I'm out somewhere."

"Okay, then, chief, I'll have some."

Michael gets him a cup of coffee. In spite of his gruff manner, Michael likes Grumpy Bill. He knows that underneath the grumpiness is a soft-hearted and sensitive person. Michael also sees him as a man with sound judgment, which is why he likes to consult him.

"So, how are you doing these days, GB?"

"Just dandy, Michael. Thanks for asking. By the way, do you mind me calling you chief? I notice some of the mall walkers do."

"No, not at all. At first, I thought it was a bit weird. They originally called me mall walker-in-chief, then shortened it to chief. But you know, I got used to it and now, well, I actually like it. Even some of our other managers and the doctors and staff over in the clinic call me chief."

"Okay. So, chief, before we get into your issues, can I ask you a couple things?"

"Sure thing."

"For one thing, what are you going to do about all those hobos in the mall? Heavens to Betsy, there's more of them around these days and I'm sure they scare away our customers."

"You and my head of security think alike. But as I said to Wally, while many of our customers don't like to see these unhoused people in the mall, they're also sympathetic to their plight, and sad to see them down on their luck."

"Fiddlesticks," says Grumpy Bill. "Sure, some of our shoppers might be softies. But most aren't. Most aren't that keen on seeing them around. Besides that, shoppers complain about the smell. Michael, I've got friends who live near our competitor, Sunrise. They go in there all the time, and they tell me there's hardly any of these derelicts. They say Sunrise has a new female manager—Brenda somebody-or-other—and she's been cleaning house, clearing out the bums. They don't know how she's doing it, but these dang people don't go in there so much anymore. And Sunrise seems to be getting more shoppers. You might learn something from her."

Michael puts his hand under his chin. Maybe Grumpy Bill's got a point. "Interesting you say this. I may have one of our security people go over to Sunrise, poke around a bit, and see how they're handling the issue."

"Make sure you do," says Grumpy Bill, lowering his mask and sipping some of his coffee. "I've got another question for you, chief. When in the world are we going to get this mall back into shape? Starting to look run-down, don't you think? Have you heard anything back yet from the big shots upstairs? You said they might provide some money for renovations. Well, they need to get on it."

"I don't disagree with you, GB. But no, I haven't heard back from them yet."

"As I told you, Michael, the manager at Sunrise is busy improving things. My friends tell me that apart from clearing out the riffraff, she's initiated a slick advertising campaign to attract more shoppers. And she's also managed to bring in some new stores to appeal to the younger crowd—stores with sexy underwear, tattoo shops, tattoo removal shops, that sort of thing. So, you've got to do something. Prod our big shots, tell them to get moving on the upgrade."

"I hear you loud and clear, GB. I'll go see them again and explain the urgency."

"Yup, make sure you do. One more thing—any news yet about the bookstore clerk? Have they figured out what happened to him? I heard it might have been a murder."

"A murder? Good God, no, GB. No, no, no! That's just a wild rumor. Listen, I'll let you know when I hear something definite."

Michael wonders if other business managers have been talking about murder. Have shoppers been talking about it? Have the security staff been spreading gossip? *I told them to keep it quiet. Why can't they keep their mouths shut?*

"Anyway, GB, the reason I've got you here is to get your read on the question of face coverings in the mall."

Grumpy Bill explains to Michael that he's talked with almost all the business operators. Although they agree there should be a policy, they're divided on what it should be. Half want a mask mandate. They say shoppers would feel safer and more comfortable in the mall, which will spell more business. The other half want to keep the current policy of just recommending masks. They say shoppers would be given the impression the mall actually cares about their well-being, without anybody actually being forced to wear masks. They claim this would be better for their bottom line.

Michael looks up at the ceiling, wishing there was more consensus. That would make his job a lot easier. "What do you think should be done?"

Grumpy Bill's head suddenly jerks to his side for a couple of moments, startling Michael. "Sorry about that, Michael. It happens when I least expect it. The issue of masks is a tricky one, it really is. But from a strictly business point of view, I'd say you should stick with our current policy of recommending masks. It's not perfect. But it's better than the other options. It's a compromise most people can live with. Besides, and this is my own personal view, I have doubts about the effectiveness of masks. One day, the research says masks have not been shown to be effective, the next day, they are. It's a mixed picture. It doesn't make sense to me to mandate something which may or may not work."

Grumpy Bill stops to blow his nose, then continues. "There's one other thing to keep in mind, chief. It's my understanding that our competition, the people at Sunrise, are opting for a policy of simply recommending masks. If we were to adopt a mask mandate, and make some people mad, we'd likely lose more of our business to Sunrise."

"Never thought of that."

"You should, you really should. Mind you, if Covid gets worse and deaths keep rising, I can see public opinion getting on board a mandate. Pressure would build and our Governor would have to bring in a mask requirement. We'd have to comply, and the public would understand this. And if there is resistance or a backlash, it wouldn't be us taking the heat—it'd be the Governor. In the meantime, it seems to me, the wisest thing to do is just to recommend masks, not require them. This is my advice."

"Thanks very much, GB. What you say makes sense. I'm inclined to act on it."

"Yup, I hope you do, chief."

Grumpy Bill gets up, finishes his coffee, and leaves. Michael feels his advice is reasonable. After all, in the world of business, one has to put sentiment aside, put ethics aside, and simply calculate what's most practical and advantageous. Who can quarrel with that?

Michael then thinks about his dad and what his dad would tell him: be practical, yes, but put your moral principles first. His dad would say there are times when you have to do what's right, even if you might suffer from it. Michael scratches his head and puts his hands under his chin. He wonders if he's being overly sentimental about his dad. He loved his dad. But his dad was a church minister. He didn't have to contend with the rough and tumble world of business and economic competition.

I'm a business manager, not a minister or a rabbi or an ethics professor living in an ivory tower. I have to live in the real world. I have to do what's most practical and what gets me and my family ahead.

9

THE WOLFVILLE NEWS

Monday, June 15, 2020

SURGE IN COVID DEATHS—REFRIGERATION TRUCKS ON STANDBY

Deaths from Covid-19 are surging in the Wolfville area and across the state. Following a steady rise of Covid cases, hospitalizations, and ICU admissions during March, April, and May, the numbers of deaths are spiking, putting pressure on the three hospitals in the city.

In the first week of March, the number of deaths in the city stood at 30; in the first week of June, the number rose to 122, over four times greater. Nursing homes have been hit hard. A third of the residents of Southside Wolfville Manor have died in the last two months.

Due to growing case numbers, hospitals are full and the doctors and nurses are working long shifts and under enormous stress. The stress has been taking a toll on their own health.

Particularly revealing is that there is now little room left in the hospitals for severely ill patients or in their morgues for the dead. As in New York City, hospital administrators have ordered refrigeration trucks on standby to serve as makeshift morgues.

The crisis is putting more pressure on officials to take stronger action against Covid. At present, masks are recommended for indoor settings by the state department of health. As well, masks are encouraged by many stores as well as some hotels, theaters, and shopping malls. But more people are saying a voluntary approach is not enough. They are urging mandatory masking in all indoor settings.

10

N ext to the pharmacy and across the hall from Grumpy Bill's store is the medical clinic. There are three doctors, all general practitioners. The oldest and most popular of them is Dr. Juan Cortez. Wearing a mask, he sits in his office going over notes. It's early morning and the day after Michael's meeting with Grumpy Bill. Dr. Cortez's phone pings, indicating a text from Michael.

Michael: Got a few minutes to talk?

Dr. Cortez: Glad to, chief. What's up?

Michael: See the paper this morning?

Dr. Cortez: Yes, big story on deaths from Covid! Like NYC.

Michael: Lots of nervousness out there. Like to get your thoughts on mall masking policy.

Dr. Cortez: Okay. Had a cancelation. Over in about half an hour.

Michael: Great. See you around nine. I'll have coffee on.

Dr. Cortez is in his late fifties, tall and graying. He wears owl-shaped glasses and is dressed, as he often is, in a tweed sports jacket and a black turtleneck that matches his distinguished manner. He has been a family doctor in the clinic for nearly twenty years.

Born in Santa Fe, New Mexico, his father was an immigrant from Guatemala and his mother, a member of the Navajo nation. After taking some wrong turns, he decided to do something positive with his life. This led to medical school at the University of Washington in Seattle. He graduated and moved to Wolfville, where he established a successful medical practice.

Dr. Cortez walks out into the hall and heads to Michael's office. Along the way, he notices some of the regular mall walkers. He passes by Richard and Mary Barker, who he hears arguing. Richard tells Mary not to worry so much, that Covid will probably be over by the fall. Mary tells Richard to get real, he shouldn't kid himself. It is going to continue for at least another year, maybe two or three years.

The doctor catches sight of Marv's girlfriend, Tina, up ahead. Wearing skin-tight jeans with huge, ragged holes and a revealing low cut black top, she is talking with her mother, Sofia Morellato, who is struggling mightily with her walker. As he gets closer, he overhears them talking. Sofia asks Tina, chewing gum at great speed as usual, why she can't wear a mask when she's around her. "You should be more thoughtful," she says, "and realize your mother is an older woman now, vulnerable to the virus." Tina tells her mother to get a grip, not be such a big baby, not to listen to the mainstream news propaganda.

Nodding to them as he passes by, Dr. Cortez remembers when he first met the Morellato family. Sofia had become a patient of his about ten years earlier. He was happy to have her as a patient—she was so warm, sincere, and giving. After a few years, she developed problems with balance, and tremors. He referred her to a specialist, and she was diagnosed with Parkinson's disease. The disease was controlled for a time with medications, but now it's getting worse. It shows in her face. She looks like she is always under stress.

The doctor recalls when Sofia told him she wanted to get her daughter and granddaughter, Brianna, to see him in the clinic. Tina needed a new doctor, and all agreed it would be convenient to have Dr. Cortez as her doctor, since she lived so close to the mall. But it didn't happen. As Sofia had explained it to him, Tina had started to go out with Marv Hammar, and Marv couldn't stomach the idea of Tina having a Latino doctor.

Marv Hammar was not his first encounter with racism. It was a common thing. And it was hurtful, deeply hurtful. But over time, the racism lessened, or at least it seemed to.

"Come in, Doctor," says Michael. "Some coffee?"

"Yeah, that would be great, thanks."

Michael admires Dr. Cortez. He reminds him of his own dad—earnest and sincere. Although Dr. Cortez is not Michael's doctor, he's the person Michael goes to for public health advice, as it concerns the mall. It's understandable Michael would do this, since the doctor is knowledgeable about public health, keeping up with the latest medical research and writing health columns in *The Wolfville News*. He's also well known in the city for his advocacy of preventive medicine, appearing regularly as a guest on local radio shows and TV news.

Dr. Cortez is a forceful advocate of preventive medicine due to the death of his wife, a decade before. As the doctor had told Michael in confidence, she had developed a serious case of bacterial pneumonia, which was not diagnosed. She thought it was seasonal allergies. She was coughing and had shortness of breath, as she often did in the spring. As this was happening, Dr. Cortez was preoccupied with his ailing father, often going to see him in New Mexico. While he was in Santa Fe, his wife's condition worsened. She was rushed to the hospital but died.

Dr. Cortez never forgave himself. He asked himself why didn't he insist she get checked out, get a chest X-ray, get a CT scan, get antibiotics, get a pneumococcal vaccination? Why didn't he prevent this from happening? To make amends, he became a champion of preventive medicine.

Michael served the coffee. "Dr. Cortez, as I mentioned earlier, I'd like to get your thoughts on the masking issue. I've already talked to some people about it—shoppers, our head of security Wally Waller, and Grumpy Bill, speaking for the business association."

The doctor slips his mask down and sips his coffee. "What did Wally and GB tell you, as if I didn't already know?"

"Both argued against a mask mandate. Wally said it would be too hard to enforce. GB said it would be bad for business."

"These are vested interests speaking to you, chief. Those in security think about what's easiest for them. Those in business think about what's best for their profits. But what about the health and well-being of people? You read the news. You see the crisis we're in."

The doctor takes another sip of coffee. "Michael, I strongly urge you to have a mask mandate. This is based on principle, not self-interest. I have no stake in this. Although I appreciate the mall has to consider the profits of businesses and the concerns of the security folks, at the top of the list has to be the health and safety of the people in the mall. It seems obvious to me, and I hope to you, that to ensure public health, we need to prevent diseases, infections, and other conditions that threaten health."

"We can't prevent Covid-19 until there are vaccines and widespread immunity. But until we get vaccines, we must contain the spread of the virus through the wearing of face coverings, especially indoors. This is demonstrated in the research. You must be aware of this. And for masks to work, we need virtually everyone to wear them, not just some people. This means a mask mandate."

"I hear what you're saying, Doctor. Your complete focus is on public health, and this is understandable. But surely you have to acknowledge there are other values in our society. Ask Marv and people like him. They insist that freedom is more important than anything else. This is what America is all about." As Michael says this, an image of a refrigeration truck loaded with the bodies of Covid victims pops into his head.

"Well, I agree freedom is important," replies the doctor. "But think about this. If you have Covid and refuse to wear a mask indoors where there's lots of people, if you infect me and I get sick or die, you are robbing me of my freedom ... aren't you? I won't be able to exercise my rights. Freedom, Michael, has to apply to everybody, not just to Marv and his ilk."

The doctor finishes his coffee and puts his mask back on.

"Can I pour you more, Doctor?"

"No, I'm good. Let me finish with this, Michael. A mask mandate is the principled thing to do. But it's also, I suggest, the pragmatic thing to do. Public opinion is changing. Pressure is building for masks to be required indoors. I can see it coming. I can see the Governor and the department of health mandating masks. But before this happens, if you introduce a mask mandate here in the mall, you'd be ahead of the curve. You could be seen as an influential leader. You could be seen as a progressive figure in this city, ahead of the Governor.

"Hmm. I'm not so sure."

"Remember, Michael, some years back, we had the issue of banning smoking indoors. At first, people resisted, people like Marv. But then it all changed. Now, we see hardly anybody smoking indoors. Again, Michael, you don't need to play it safe. You could be a leader. You could introduce a mandate and take credit for protecting public health."

"Thanks, Dr. Cortez," says Michael. "You make a persuasive case. I'll think about it. Any news yet about the bookstore clerk, about the cause of his death?"

"Nothing yet. I understand that the pathologist downtown is going to be doing an autopsy soon. Her report could take months to complete. But if it's a clear-cut case, we could get preliminary results in a few days."

"Thanks, Doctor. Please let me know when you hear. I'm worried about the outcome. If it was a homicide, apart from anything else, it'll be bad for the mall's image."

The doctor smiles, recognizing Michael's concern. "I get it, chief."

As the doctor leaves, a thought creeps into Michael's head. Should he tell Dr. Cortez about the note? If the threat is real, if there actually is an acid attack, the doctor would be a prime target. No one has been more outspoken about the need for masks than he has. But then Michael has another thought. The threat couldn't, it really couldn't, be all that serious. The note had to have been written on the spur of a moment by some delusional nutbar. There is nothing to be gained by alarming the doctor needlessly.

11

That evening, after dinner and after the girls go to their rooms, Michael opens a bottle of California Pinot Noir, grabs a couple glasses, and invites Cornelia into the family room for a chat. He's got a cheerful fire going in their stone fireplace.

"Here's some Pinot for you, princess, the one you really like from California."

"Thanks, sweetie," says Cornelia, taking a sip. "Yeah, it's really nice. Got that subtle cranberry aroma and the velvety mouthfeel. And the complex flavors of cherry and raspberry. We really need to get some more." She takes another sip, then says "Daddy called today."

"What's new with him?"

"Nothing much, sweetie. But he said he's getting a lot of golfing in. Tomorrow, he's going over to Savannah to meet with one of his old buddies, a retired prosecutor. He's really looking forward to it. They're meeting, he said, at one of those old fancy golf clubs, a beautiful antebellum building surrounded by live oaks."

"Love the live oaks down there, and the Spanish moss. Brings back memories."

"Yeah, I really miss Georgia sometimes. Listen, I told Daddy about your masking issue at the mall. He said if you were wise, you'd leave masks as optional. Otherwise, if you go for a mandate, it would be divisive, and you'd lose some business."

"Really?"

"Yeah, that's what he said. And Michael, I think Daddy is right. He's almost always right. You should listen to him."

Michael looks upward and grits his teeth. *Daddy's almost always right? Why doesn't she drop the 'almost' and just say he's always right? But I've got to be calm, I've got to keep my cool.* "Well, I talked about it with some people at the mall. Shoppers were divided, Dr. Cortez urged a mask mandate, as you would expect, and Grumpy Bill said, from a business point of view, we should leave the current policy in place, masks as only recommended."

"GB is absolutely right," Cornelia replies, speaking with total confidence. "He's got sound judgment, just like Daddy. Look at how successful his business is. He's one of the wealthiest people around. And look at where he lives—in Blue Mountain Heights. Dr. Cortez is a nice man, I grant you that, but he's a bit extreme. Always holier than thou. And he isn't that successful, if you think about it. Look at where he lives. In the city's east end. Not very impressive. I, for one, would take the judgment of GB over the doctor any day of the week."

Michael raises his eyebrows. "Isn't this over the top, Cornelia? Equating a man's judgment with his wealth?" Michael's mind again goes back to the refrigeration trucks on standby outside the hospitals.

"All I'm saying, Michael, is you'd be wise to take the advice of GB. It's practical advice and it's in the best interests of the mall. Which means it's in your best interests and the best interests of our family." Cornelia gives Michael a stern look. "You've got to think about me, you've got to think about our family."

"Cornelia, it's more complicated than this. Let me show you something." Michael heads for their bedroom, gets the note out of his suit jacket, and returns. He hands her the note and explains it was found pinned up on the bulletin board a couple of days ago.

Cornelia reads it and is taken aback. "Wow, this is incredible! Why didn't you show it to me before?"

"Uh, well, I wasn't sure what to do. And I'm still not sure what to do. I go back and forth."

"Did you show it to anybody else?"

Michael stops to sip some more wine. "I showed it to only one person, Wally Waller, head of security. He said he was certain it came from, to use his words, some deranged street person. We get them in the mall all the time. He also said we should just ignore it, keep it quiet. Otherwise, people in the mall will get nervous or panicked, and the mall will lose business. I thought about it and agreed it's the best move, at least for now."

Cornelia finishes her glass of wine. "Amazing for this to happen. But as I think about it, your security guy is probably right. Had to be written on impulse by a whacko. Best to ignore it. I'll talk to Daddy though. He might have some thoughts."

Cornelia leaves the room and goes upstairs to check on the girls. Michael continues to sip his wine in front of the fireplace. Why, he wonders, does she always have to bring up dear old Daddy? What could the old guy say that would be of any value? He's light years away. She doesn't mean it, but Cornelia's habit of deifying her father is a way of putting me down. I don't understand it and I wish she wouldn't do it. I could call her out on it, but this would just create more conflict. What I need to do is be more patient with her. After all, she misses her father and he's thousands of miles away from her. Hopefully, one day, she'll realize what she's doing and stop it.

Michael recalls seeing a counselor a couple of years earlier about their relationship. He'd been so frustrated with Cornelia's demanding behavior, and with his failure to stand up to her. He was afraid he was going to blow up some day and say things that would tear their relationship apart. The counselor had been helpful in identifying a source of his difficulty—his dad as a role model, his dad's gentleness, and his dad's accommodation of his wife, Michael's mother. Michael had internalized his father's approach.

The counselor also had been helpful in providing advice: recognize that you are not in the same situation as your dad, recognize that Cornelia is much different from your mother, and speak honestly about your feelings. Practice saying no, don't always back down, anticipate what she'll say, and practice what you want to say to her beforehand.

Michael had tried to put this advice into practice. But he couldn't do it consistently. It didn't seem to be in his nature. He went back to being patient and understanding, allowing Cornelia to get her own way most of the time. He figured it would be more peaceful that way. He'd save his energies for advancing his career and dealing with the challenges at the mall.

12

Mary and Richard Barker are walking in the mall. Ahead of them is another one of the regular mall walkers, Sofia Morellato, the mother of Tina. They walk faster to catch up to her and exchange greetings. Richard suggests they get together and have coffee at the Starbucks upstairs. Sofia agrees and they walk together, slower, toward the elevator.

Up ahead, they see a tall man in a hoodie rushing out of a high-end clothing store. He's clutching a bunch of leather coats. A clerk runs out after him but stops as the man disappears around a corner. She makes a phone call. Observing this, Richard says the guy will eventually get caught. Mary tells Richard to stop being so naive. "Check the police statistics," she says. "Most of them get away with it and it's us who have to pay for it with higher prices."

The Barkers help Sofia get into the elevator, and they go up to Starbucks. They find a table and Richard gets their coffees, cappuccinos for the Barkers and a vanilla latte for Sofia. They sit down and take off their masks.

The Barkers admire Sofia. They know she's been battling Parkinson's disease. And they know she's been fighting depression since the death of her husband a year ago. He'd been the love of her life. Despite her struggles, she rarely complains, always tries to look on the sunny side of life, and is deeply interested in people and the world. She speaks her mind on social issues and has a special passion for animal rights and child welfare. She could easily be withdrawn or miserable or self-pitying. But she is not.

"Sofia, what did you think of that march we had a while back?" asks Richard, sipping his cappuccino.

"Well, when I went outside to watch, they almost ran over me. As they rushed by, one of them, the one with the Confederate flag, clunked my walker and knocked me sideways. I wasn't hurt. But frankly, I'm embarrassed by the whole thing. I'm embarrassed that Tina—my own daughter—has got so involved. What an example to set for her daughter, my sweet three-year old granddaughter, my little Brianna. I also feel bad that Tina is going out with that Marv character. I don't like to say this but ... well, he's really a terrible person, more terrible than you think, so much hate inside him. But Tina thinks he is a god! How can she think that!"

"Hard to fathom," says Mary. "I can't understand how any woman, any woman at all, would be attracted to hate-filled Marv."

"I can't either. He carries around so much anger. And he swears a lot. Call me old-fashioned, but I don't like people who use foul language. Shows poor character." Sofia recalls her parents. They came to California from Milan when she was only a toddler. Deeply religious, they dressed up and went to church every Sunday. And they hated swearing. Sofia didn't agree with them on much. But she did see eye to eye with them on the abhorrence of foul language.

"Sofia," says Mary, taking a sip of her cappuccino, "what do you think about Marv's opposition to a mask mandate?"

"I think it's nonsense. I'm strongly in favor of a mandate. I speak out about it all the time. I'm always talking to the chief, urging him to make masks a requirement in the mall. Mind you, Tina gets mad at me. Says I should keep my mouth shut. Says I might get into trouble. But it's just too important. We've all got to protect each other."

"We think so too," says Richard. Switching the subject, he asks about her health. "How are you feeling these days, Sofia? We see you walking in the mall almost every day. You must be in good shape."

"Well, I sometimes get tremors and I sometimes have problems keeping my balance. I live in an apartment across the street, not too far from Tina's, and I often have a hard time crossing the street to get to the mall. At least for some of the time, I do feel pretty good. I get in my exercise, my nine thousand or so steps a day, by walking around the mall. The walking helps me out a lot."

Sofia stops for a sip of her latte. She hears a crying baby in the distance. "But to be truthful, though I sometimes feel good, I'm gradually going downhill. The pain from my Parkinson's is getting worse, and so are my tremors. To control it, I take L-dopa, but it's not helping as much as it did before. Dr. Cortez has been very supportive, but there's only so much he can do."

The Barkers both nod their heads in sympathy.

"Oh, but I'm sorry. I'm so sorry to be going on about all this. I know I should keep a stiff upper lip, as they say in England. But it's hard. It's really hard to keep it all in."

"Sofia, you must get some comfort, some support, from your daughter Tina," says Mary.

Looking grim, Sofia puts her latte down. "No, I'm … I'm afraid not," she replies, her voice cracking. "She doesn't … well, she simply doesn't have much time for me anymore." Sofia stops to calm herself down, then continues. "When she's not with Marv, she's wrapped up with her new job, working from home for a special events company. She's busy designing and printing custom invitations for weddings, birthdays, that sort of thing. So I don't see her much and I don't get to see my granddaughter much either, my little Brianna. Oh, how I love my sweet Brianna. You know, I took care of her almost every day for the first year of her life, when Tina was working on the other side of town. But now I hardly see her. It really hurts me."

"Sorry to hear that," says Mary, with a look of concern.

"Well, it gets worse. Tina gave me a real jolt the other day. She said if I kept on insisting she should wear a mask when she's around me, she'd make sure I'd never get to see Brianna again, at least until the fuss about Covid is over."

"That's a real shocker," says Richard, finishing his cappuccino. "Hard to imagine she'd threaten you that way. She obviously knows you have Parkinson's, knows you are at high risk of Covid."

Sofia sighs. "I'm afraid she just doesn't get it." Sofia pauses for a moment and is on the verge of crying. "Tina keeps saying, keeps telling me over and over again, Covid is a hoax, masks are a hoax. I really worry about her. She's always on the internet, getting more and more into conspiracy theories, getting a warped view of the world. I wish it were different, I really do. I wish we could get more connected. And I wish I could see my granddaughter more often. This is eating me up."

Sofia stops to clear away some tears from her eyes. "Tina," she continues, "was not always like this. Back in the day, she was a thoughtful young woman. She was sensitive and had lots of compassion. Never mean, never cruel. But shortly after Brianna was born, her partner left her. Classic case. He left her for a young blonde he'd met at work. Tina became extremely bitter. For weeks, she played the old Ray Charles song *Hit the Road Jack*. And I kid you not, his name was—and is—Jack. And for a long time, she wouldn't even let Jack—Brianna's father—see his own daughter. Vengeful or what! But you know what, once in a while Tina reverts back to how she used to be—kind, gentle, considerate. She sort of goes back and forth."

"Sorry again to hear about this," says Mary. "Must be extremely difficult for you. But any time you'd like to talk, as you know, we're always in the mall."

"Thanks," Sofia replies, looking at her watch. "I've got to get home. Before I do, though, I'm going to go over and see Michael, pester him again about bringing in a mask mandate. He's just got to listen. So, goodbye, arrivederci."

The Barkers watch Sofia put on her mask and slowly walk over to the elevator. Richard has a horrible thought. If the threat in the note is genuine, if the writer is serious, Sofia might be a target. She speaks her mind about the need for masks and she'd be so easy to attack.

13

Sofia gets out of the elevator and heads for Michael's office. It's late morning, and the mall is crowded with shoppers.

Racing up behind her, not wearing a mask, is a power or speed walker. Tall and gangly, he's a friendly man in his late twenties, known for his charm and warm smile. No one in the mall knows his real name, and he has not offered it. So, they call him Power Walker, which is fine with him.

His walking entertains the other walkers. He zips along, dodging people in the way. Suddenly, he'll fling his arms from side to side and up and down. He then stops and squats several times, followed by some tai-chi moves. After that, he quickly walks backward, with his arms flailing. Some days he does this routine at Wolfville Mall, other days at Sunrise, where his aunt is the mall manager.

As Power Walker gets close to Sofia, a shopper comes out of a store without looking. Power Walker sidesteps to miss him and clips Sofia, knocking her and her walker flying. She screams as she glances off a wall and hits the floor. A crowd gathers. A security guard, who witnessed the incident, sends a text to Michael and Dr. Cortez. Michael and the doctor come rushing to the scene. The doctor examines Sofia, who has blood on her forehead and face.

"Sofia," says Dr. Cortez, "you've got a nasty gash just over your left eye, and a bruise forming on the side of your head. Do you feel pain anywhere else?"

"No, I seem to be okay. I'm dazed, but I'm otherwise alright."

"Do you think you can get up?"

"Yeah, I think I can."

The doctor and Michael help her up. The doctor cleans her blood and the gash, and puts on a large bandage. Michael retrieves the walker and gets it ready for Sofia to use.

"Okay, let's get you over to the clinic," says the doctor. "We'll check you out more fully. Can you walk okay?"

"Yes." As she grabs hold of her walker, Power Walker comes up beside her.

"I'm so sorry this happened," he says. "I apologize. I sincerely apologize. I should have been more careful. God damn it, I can't believe I was so reckless. I'm so pissed off with myself. So sorry. So very sorry."

"It's okay, Power Walker," replies Sofia. "I know you didn't mean it. The doctor's going to check me out. I'm sure I'm fine. But please watch your language, you don't need to use swear words. It's not a good image. And you should be wearing a mask!"

"Oh," he says, taken aback. "Sorry."

Sofia and Dr. Cortez head for the clinic and the crowd disperses. Michael and Power Walker remain at the scene.

"I'm Michael McQueen, the mall manager. I don't think we've met, but I see you in the mall all the time. Listen, you need to slow down in your walking, especially when it gets more crowded. Sofia's probably okay, but it could have been much worse. And it could be worse the next time."

"I apologize. I'm really sorry this happened. It's all my fault. It won't happen again. I'll be more careful, I swear."

"You must be from Canada. You're so apologetic, eh."

"Eh, what did you say?" Power Walker says with a big smile. "No, I'm not from Canada. One of my grandparents, though, came from Vancouver—beautiful city—but that was a long time ago. I actually grew up in Seattle. But I've lived here in Wolfville the past couple of years. I work nights as a bartender down the road, and I live with my aunt, Aunt Brenda, who's the manager of Sunrise Mall. I also do some of my walks over at her mall, Sunrise."

"Oh, that's interesting. I hear she's a real dynamo. Works hard to build up her mall."

"That's right. She's a hard worker. And she's also a really nice person, caring and generous."

"Why is it you walk so incredibly fast? Some kind of exercise regime?"

"I try to keep fit, that's for sure. But when I was in my teens, a doctor said I had a heart murmur. He said that walking, fast walking, is a good way to strengthen my heart. Plus, I sometimes get soreness in my muscles. So, for a long time now, I've been doing fast walking and stretching exercises. It's been helping me out a lot."

"Good this works for you. But again, try to keep the speed reasonable. And also, I see you're not wearing a mask. Any reason for that? A health condition, maybe?"

Power Walker frowns for a moment. "You know, I just don't think people should be wearing masks in public. I worry about people getting away with crime. Think about it for a second: if people who commit crimes have masks on, how can they be identified and charged? It wouldn't be so easy, would it?"

"You've got a point. I guess I didn't think about it that way. Have a good day."

Michael walks away, reflecting on what Power Walker has said. Odd way to think about masks, but the guy could be right, at least from the standpoint of crime control. Masks certainly would be a big help to criminals. But surely he knows that this is more than outweighed by the public health benefit of wearing masks. How can he, or anyone, think this way? People like him need to be educated about how masks protect the public.

Michael's mind goes back to the threatening note. If people in the mall are wearing masks, he thinks, and if they get acid thrown in their face by some twisted weirdo, they are going to get at least some protection by having masks on their faces. Maybe he should tell that to Power Walker.

14

The Barkers are doing their usual morning walk in the mall. Earlier, while getting their coffee at Starbucks, they had heard from a barista about Sofia's accident the day before.

"Let's hope," says Mary, "that Power Walker has learned his lesson. The guy needs to slow down, think about others' safety."

"He's an interesting guy, a likable guy," replies Richard. "But you're right, he needs to decelerate. Good thing Sofia had only minor injuries."

"Well, she's not out of the woods yet. As the guy at Starbucks said, she has to go back and see Dr. Cortez for a follow-up. There still could be issues. You know what it's like when you get older."

"For sure. The more they poke around, the more they find."

Their conversation is interrupted by an announcement through the PA system. "Shoppers, can I have your attention please? Would the owner of a white Honda Accord return to the south side parking lot. The last three digits of your license plate are HGB. You've left your lights on. Thank you."

"Sounds like something you'd do, Richard."

"At least I don't leave the stove on, like you do."

"C'mon, stop it now, Richard."

The Barkers walk in silence for several minutes. They pass the bulletin board, and talk about the note and wonder what Michael is going to do. Up ahead, beside the main entrance, Michael is greeting his head of security, Wally Waller.

"Michael," says Mary, as they approach, "sorry to cut in but can we talk to you for a minute?"

"Sure but—"

Michael's is interrupted by a shabby middle-aged woman who enters the mall and pushes between them. Smelling of alcohol, she tries to keep her balance as she walks. She is talking to herself, wearing dirty and ripped clothes, and carrying a grubby green knapsack on her back. She has a blue mask around her chin, her hair is unwashed, and her teeth are yellowed.

"Can you just wait a second?" Michael replies, eyeing the woman.

"Would ya look at that?" says Wally. "Look at what the cat's dragged in!" He steps up behind her.

"Isn't it a bit early in the morning to be into the rubbing alcohol, lady?"

"Fuck off, rent-a-pig," she mutters, spitting on the floor.

Wally's face turns red, and he looks like he is about to explode. Michael wonders if he should intervene. Mary and Richard take a few steps back.

"Look ya clueless asshole," he says, "get your mask on properly and get the hell out of here. You're drunk and we don't want you harassing our customers." Wally turns her around and escorts her to the door. She resists and he gives her some pushes, nudging her along. He finally shoos her out the door.

Wally returns. "Michael, there are a couple things I need to tell you. I just heard back from—"

"Can you excuse us for a few minutes," Michael says to the Barkers.

"Of course, Michael. We'll go over to your office and wait."

Michael nods.

Wally continues. "I heard back from the pathologist's office earlier this morning. I'm afraid it's bad news about the bookstore clerk. The preliminary results from the autopsy say it was a homicide. The old man was strangled and then a mask was stuffed into his throat."

"Oh, no! Jeez, not what I wanted to hear," says Michael.

"No, it's not good. The police are going to be checking it out. They'll be bringing in a forensics team to look for prints, clothing fibers, hairs, that sort of thing. And they'll be checking out our surveillance cameras. But I don't know how much they'll find. I know the camera by the unisex washroom hasn't been working for months. Plus there's an exit door by the washroom which the perp could have used to get away undetected. There's probably not much for them to go on, in terms of identifying who did it."

Michael wonders why Wally has not had the camera fixed. He'll have to ask him about it later. "Thanks for letting me know about this, Wally. The police might not have much to go on, but it's a bad look for the mall. Any thoughts on who might have done it?"

"Nope. But ya know, from what I hear, the old guy was self-righteous about wearing a mask. Apparently, he looked down on people who didn't. My guess is that—and it's only a guess—somebody got annoyed with him, followed him into the washroom, and choked him to death."

"Interesting theory, Wally. Could this be connected to the note? I know we talked about this before and you dismissed it. But isn't it strange we have these two events happening at around the same time?"

"I just don't know, man. It's a mystery. Could be a coincidence, I suppose."

"Yeah, I don't know what to think either. In any case, knowing it was a murder will be a terrible thing for the old man's family. I think he had a sister. And I'm afraid it'll also be bad for the mall. Bad publicity that we can do without."

"Ya know, bro, I've been thinking about this. For sure, there's gonna be some publicity, but I don't think a whole lot. My buddy at *The Wolfville News* tells me that while they're aware of the pathologist's report, they're not going to make it into a big story. There's a lot of political news happening right now, and news about forest fires and a big oil spill out on the coast. And the autopsy results are preliminary, not final. So, my buddy says they'll put it somewhere in the back pages. I also haven't heard a thing about it on the radio or TV. Same thing, I guess, a lot of other news going on. I'm pretty sure we won't have that much publicity, at least for now."

Michael hears some commotion at the entrance door. He looks over and sees the same scruffy woman trying to get back into the mall. No wonder. It's starting to rain heavily outside. A guard sees her and comes after her, grabs her by the arm, and pushes her back out the door into the rain. She screams at him, asking him how he could be so unfeeling. Watching her, Michael wonders if she, or some other unhoused person, in a state of anger, could have written that dreadful note.

He looks back at Wally. "Sad reflection on the news, don't you think Wally? Had the old man been powerful and well-connected, it would be a big story. But the death of a frail old man, not well known and without much money, gets little attention. Still, if what you say is true, it's not such a bad outcome for the mall. Anyway, let's keep it as quiet as we can."

"Mum's the word, dude. Oh yeah, I have something else to tell ya. I heard back from the corporation lawyer yesterday. You asked about our legal duty to report crime. Well, it's just like I thought. Under our state law, people don't have a legal duty to report a crime or a possible crime. There are exceptions, she said. If there's a police investigation, for example, and people are questioned about a crime, they do have a duty to say what they know. But they don't have to take the initiative. Bottom line: we don't have to report a crime."

"Thanks Wally. Good to know."

"One other thing, man. I found out that while threatening somebody with physical injury is a crime, it would have to be against a particular person, not people in general. So, from what I gather, the threat of an acid attack against people in the mall—against people wearing masks or pushing for a mask mandate—would not be a crime. It would just be speech—free speech. Stupid speech maybe, but free speech."

"Interesting. Thanks again, Wally. See you later."

Michael goes over to his office to see the Barkers. On the way, he thinks about what Wally said. It was almost as if Wally knew what happened—that some angry anti-masker got pissed off with the old man's sanctimonious attitude about masks, followed him into the washroom, and strangled him. Wally said it was a guess. But maybe it was more than a guess?

15

Michael waves the Barkers into his office. "Thanks again for showing me the note," he says. "Have a seat."

"Well, chief, we thought you'd know how to handle it," replies Mary.

"I've given the note some serious thought," says Michael, "and I've talked it over with security. At this point, we don't know for sure who the culprit is. We're checking the video from the surveillance cameras, but so far, nothing. We believe, though, it was an unhoused person, maybe drunk or on drugs, maybe with mental health problems, who did it on the spur of the moment. You just saw an example of what I'm talking about. We're getting more of these people in the mall all the time, some of them mean and angry. Many of them resist wearing masks. It wouldn't take much for one of them to write a nasty note against masks."

Michael pauses to scratch his head. "So, for the time being, our plan is to say nothing publicly. As I said to you before, we don't want to cause any unnecessary nervousness in the mall. But as a precaution, we've put our security staff on high alert. And we're still checking the cameras. I'll let you know if anything changes. In the meantime, I'd appreciate it if you'd keep it all quiet."

"But Michael," says Richard, "why not report it to the police? Why not have them investigate it? Maybe there are fingerprints, maybe there's DNA?"

"We've thought about it. And we may still do this, especially if we find out it wasn't an unhoused person. But the problem is that once the police are involved, word can easily get out about the threat, causing fear in the mall. Plus, the police are busy these days and there's not much for them to go on. How can they get fingerprints from a note with so many hands on it?"

"I see what you mean," replies Mary. "I'm willing to let it go for now. What do you think, Richard?"

"Yeah, well, okay. We can let it go. But I'm still puzzled by the whole thing. And I'm really disturbed by it. Really disturbed." The Barkers leave Michael's office and go back into the mall.

Michael wonders if the Barkers will say anything about the note. He worries they might. And he worries about a police investigation into the homicide. Wally could be right—they won't find anything and there won't be much publicity. But he also could be wrong. He's been wrong before. As Michael reaches into his fridge for a bottle of sparkling water, he hears a beep on his phone. It's an email from Cornelia.

Sweetie, I just got off the phone with Daddy. I told him about the note. He said it was a good idea not to report it to the police. It would be bad for business. But if you don't report it, just to be safe, he advised that you write it all down, explaining exactly what happened and your reasons for not reporting it. Then file it away. He said it's called memo to file. This way, Daddy said, if something bad happens later on and you are questioned about it, you are protected. It can't be said you are just making up reasons after the fact. Luv, C.

Michael thinks about it for a moment. Although Cornelia's father is a meddling old fart, he may have a point. Michael glugs down his water, goes to his computer, and does what his father-in-law suggests.

16

It is Monday morning. Si-Woo Lee is putting fresh bread and muffins on the shelves inside the Diplomat Bakery—the mall's only bakery. She gets a large paper sign, takes it outside, and tapes it to one of the store's windows. On the sign, in bright blue lettering, is today's bargain—sourdough bread $2.50. As she turns to go back into the bakery, she overhears two people talking. She looks around and recognizes the Barkers. They are focused on each other and don't see her.

"Mary, I still can't get it out of my head. I'm really upset about what Michael said the other day. I just don't get it. Why not take the note to the police? What is there to lose? Seems to me the chief might be more concerned about business in the mall than peoples' safety."

"I know what you mean, Richard. And I'm wondering about it too. How would we feel if there actually was an attack and we had done nothing? I think we'd feel guilty as hell! I wonder if we should go to the police ourselves. Or maybe to the media, maybe to *The Wolfville News*."

"Maybe, but I just don't know," says Richard.

"Don't know about what?" breaks in Si-Woo. "Is there anything wrong? What can I do to help?"

"Oh, hi Si-Woo," says Mary. "Didn't see you there. There is a problem. But sorry, we can't talk about it yet, to you or anybody else. Later on, we'll fill you in."

"That's okay. No big deal. But it sounds awfully serious."

"Si-Woo," says Richard, "would you like to join us for lunch today? We're going to have sushi, upstairs in the food court. Tables are harder to get these days, but I think we can find one."

"That'd be really nice, thanks. Sushi's not for me, but I'll get something else. My lunch break is at twelve-thirty. Can I catch up to you then?"

"You certainly can," replies Richard. "See you upstairs."

Si-Woo Lee is well liked in the mall. In her mid-fifties, she is cheerful, friendly, and usually has a warm smile. She's one of the regular mall walkers, getting her exercise before and after her shifts at the bakery, where she works part-time. She chats with people as she walks along and takes a genuine interest in what they have to say. Admired for her charity work, she frequently helps the unhoused people around the mall by giving them leftovers from the bakery. At Christmas time, although a Buddhist, she helps the Salvation Army by taking a turn ringing the bell and collecting donations. She also lends a hand in putting up decorations on the annual Christmas tree. Had she been able to, Si-Woo would have been a social worker or nurse. She loves helping people. But she didn't have the education.

People in the mall are unaware of the hardships she's faced in her life. Si-Woo grew up in dire poverty in a large urban center near Seoul, South Korea. She only had her dad, her mom having died of heart disease shortly after she was born. Her dad couldn't provide for her well, as he was disabled and surviving on an army pension. Then he died of lung cancer when she was six. She went to live with relatives, who were not much wealthier, and made it clear she was a burden.

To escape her poverty and her relatives, she happily married an older and upwardly mobile man when she was only sixteen. He had come from an affluent family, had a degree in computer science, and worked for a U.S. software company as a software designer. Then he got transferred to Seattle. She came with him, and it was arranged, through the company, that she would be sponsored for getting a green card, allowing her to live and work in the United States. She became a permanent resident and later a U.S. citizen.

A few years later, they had a son. But he was killed in a car accident, which put a terrible strain on the marriage. Her husband had blamed her for letting their son go out that night, and Si-Woo resented the accusations. The couple divorced. He moved back to Seoul, and Si-Woo was left to fend for herself. She worked at factory jobs and, through night school courses, became fluent in English. Eventually, she got a job as a bank teller in Wolfville, which she did for many years, until she was laid off thanks to the advent of banking machines. She now works at the bakery and lives alone in an apartment close to the mall. The mall walkers, and the other people she knows in the mall, are her family.

She walks with a noticeable limp, which she had acquired at one of her factory jobs. The driver of a forklift had carelessly slammed into her from behind, causing muscle and nerve damage in her left leg. The driver, thought to be drinking on the job, was promptly fired. But this was of no help to Si-Woo. Without the protection of a union and without compensation, she simply had to carry on.

After the lunch rush at the bakery, Si-Woo is hungry, and heads for the food court. She waves at the Barkers, sitting at a table close to the sushi bar. They already have their sushi. She decides she'll have what she often has—a burger and fries. She gets her food and joins the Barkers.

"Hi again," says Mary. "God, that burger looks good! Maybe I should've had that. Everything go okay at the bakery?"

"Yeah, but it was so busy. Everybody wanted to get some sourdough bread. I'm wiped out from it all. How about you? Things okay with you guys?"

"We're both doing okay," replies Richard. "We seem to be in reasonable health, except for some wheeziness I get from my asthma from time to time. We'd like to escape from it all ... do a trip, maybe to Hawaii. But with this horrible Covid situation, I'm afraid we're going to have to put it off for a little while."

"Probably for a long while," chips in Mary. "I think it's going to be years."

"That's too bad," says Si-Woo, taking a bite of her burger, "but it's understandable."

"Si-Woo, what are you going to do if you win the lottery?" asks Mary, eating a piece of her red dragon roll. "We sometimes see you at the lottery kiosk getting tickets. You always look so excited."

"Yeah, I'm hoping to win it big, just like everybody else. I often get tickets. I put a lot of my spare money into them. Maybe I'm addicted. But to answer your question, I don't know for sure what I'd do if I won. One thing I'd do, though, if I really won it big, is to help out the unhoused folks around here. They're in really bad shape."

"I know what I'd do," says Richard, laughing. "I'd go to Hawaii, soak up the sunshine, and drink Mai Tais by the pool every day. But I guess I'll have to wait for a few months." Richard fondly remembers their trip to Waikiki last December, just before Covid struck. Fantastic walks on the beach, beautiful sunsets. Not a care in the world.

"Get a grip, Richard." says Mary, looking annoyed. "As I told you before, it's going to be years, not months. Get it through your head. We're going to have to wait." She turns to Si-Woo. "What did you think of that march a couple weeks back? Quite the thing, wasn't it?"

"Yes, it was. But I don't agree with what the marchers are demanding. I certainly don't. I fully support a mask mandate. Requiring masks is a good thing for our community, it's based on science, it's the right thing to do. I say it to the mall manager all the time: 'Michael, you've got to bring in a mandate, you've got to do it as soon as possible'."

"We've been saying the same thing to Michael too," replies Richard.

"I'm also worried about racism in Marv's group," says Si-Woo. "I see in the news that Asian people are being attacked in downtown Wolfville. But it's not only in this city, it's also across the state and across America. These attackers blame Chinese people for the virus. But we're not all Chinese. I'm Korean. Even if I was Chinese, it's unfair. Why single out Chinese people or Asian people? This pandemic is a global problem. To blame Asian people is grossly unfair, and I think it's racist."

"Yes, it's incredibly unfair." says Mary, looking thoughtful and sad. "It shows an ugly side to our country, it shows we still have a deep undercurrent of hatred and racism. And it seems to not go away."

"There's one other thing I worry about," adds Si-Woo, dipping a fry into some ketchup. "I don't think you know but I have heart problems. It's in my family history, on my mother's side. Dr. Cortez says my test results show I'm at risk of a heart attack. He says it's important for me to keep active, take my cholesterol pills, keep my weight down, and avoid stress. I do try ... I do try to do all these things."

Si-Woo stops to take a bite of her burger. Some relish spills on the table. "Cripes," she says, mopping it up with a napkin. "But as you can see, I really like my burgers and fries. And I sometimes get stressed out. If I got attacked by a racist or one of those wacky marchers, I could get agitated and have a heart attack, maybe die from it."

"Oh my God, Si-Woo, what a terrible thought," says Richard, finishing his sushi. "We're living in difficult times, that's for sure. I wish things would settle down. You need to watch yourself, my dear."

"Thanks for your concern. And thanks to you both for the conversation. It was a good lunch, and it was great talking with you. I'm afraid I've got to get back to the bakery, sell some more sourdough. Stay safe."

As she leaves, the Barkers know what each other is thinking. If the note is serious, and if the writer is a racist as well as deranged, Si-Woo would be a perfect target for an acid attack. And, if this happened, it could have a fatal result.

17

As Si-Woo limps back to the bakery, Sofia Morellato slowly enters the mall and heads to the medical clinic. She has an appointment with Dr. Cortez. Looking anxious and haggard, she is wobbling and struggling with her walker, more so than usual. Power Walker zigzags around her, but she doesn't notice.

Michael, coming down the escalator with an espresso macchiato, notices her wobbling. Concerned, he catches up to her and asks how she's doing. She explains she's been having headaches and is going to see Dr. Cortez. He says he'll walk her down.

As they walk, Michael realizes Sofia would be such an easy target for an attack at the mall. He suggests to her that, in case of a fall, she might be wise to have her daughter or a friend with her when she comes into the mall. And if that's a problem, he volunteers that if he knows she's coming, he could arrange for a security guard to meet her at the door and do a couple rounds with her. She thanks him and says she'll consider it.

Sofia arrives at the clinic and sits down in the waiting room. Dr. Cortez comes out of his office and waves her in. "Hi Sofia, have a seat. Let's have a look at you." The doctor removes the bandage, inspects Sofia's face and head, and puts a clean bandage over the wound. He checks her blood pressure and makes some notes.

"How does it look, Doctor?" she asks.

"Looking good, Sofia. Your cut is healing fine, your bruise is looking as it should, and your blood pressure is okay. But how are you feeling otherwise? You don't look so good today."

"I don't feel so good. I've been feeling a bit woozy, and I've been having headaches. Started late yesterday. Maybe it's from the fall, maybe it's from hitting my head. My trembling is worse too. Could be that the medication for my Parkinson's isn't working so well. I just don't know." Sofia doesn't say anything about the dark thoughts she's been having recently, thoughts about suicide.

"Sofia, I'm going to increase the dosage of the L-dopa, so the Parkinson's is better under control. I'll give you a prescription to take to the pharmacy. We'll see how it works out. As for your headaches and wooziness, you'll probably be okay with more rest. But to be on the safe side, I'm going to get you an appointment at the hospital for an EEG. If you did have a head injury from your fall, this should tell us. And if your headaches continue, just take some pain killer."

"Thanks, Dr. Cortez."

"Sofia, I don't have another patient just now, so I'll walk with you over to the pharmacy. With your wooziness, you shouldn't be walking by yourself. Also, I don't feel comfortable with you walking home on your own. Is your daughter Tina at home?"

"Yeah, I'm pretty sure she's there."

"Okay, I'm going to have my assistant get in touch with her, have her come by and take you home. My assistant will also call the pharmacy and get your L-dopa ready."

A few minutes later, Sofia and Dr. Cortez put on their masks and slowly walk toward the pharmacy. Playing in the background is an old Elvis song, *Can't Help Falling in Love*. Sofia hums along, reminiscing about her teenage years in southern California where she grew up. She remembers walking along the beach with her first serious boyfriend. He had a convertible, and they'd often go to a movie and get a burger and milkshake afterward. It seemed they were always laughing, never taking things too seriously. But that was a long time ago.

"Sofia," asks the doctor, "how are your daughter and granddaughter doing these days?"

"I don't see them much, but I think they're both doing okay, at least physically. But I worry about Tina, about the influence Marv has on her. She won't wear a mask when she is around me, she's always spewing conspiracy theories, and she worships Marv like a god. I worry Marv is going to get her into trouble. And I worry that with her reckless behavior—never wearing a mask and never social distancing—she's going to get Covid."

"I can see why you're worried, Sofia. But perhaps in time Tina will realize what she's doing and change direction."

It's true, Dr. Cortez thinks, that Tina could easily get Covid. But the one who is more likely to get it, and possibly from her own daughter, is Sofia.

18

Into the mall comes Marv and his entourage. Marv is wearing dark sunglasses and his black cowboy hat. With him are Tina and the two black coats. In a rambunctious mood and walking with a swagger, they head for the medical clinic. Their plan is for Tina, who just got a phone call about Sofia, to find her mother and drive her home. After that, Tina would come back to the mall and join the others for drinks at a pub down the street.

The black coat with the pointed ears carries a portable Bluetooth speaker. As the gang struts along, he turns it on and plays a song from his phone by Hank Williams Jr., *Takin' Back the Country*. He knows Marv loves this song and country music in general. Which is why country music is played at all of Marv's rallies.

Marv and Tina hum along to the music. Approaching the group is a security guard who looks uneasy, knowing the playing of music in the mall is against the rules. But to avoid trouble, he turns a blind eye.

As the gang gets further into the mall, they spot a young family in front of them, all wearing masks. The father and mother have on blue surgical masks while their two daughters wear bright yellow ones, one decorated with balloons and the other with butterflies.

"What's wrong with you people!" yells Tina. "Why don't you take off those fuckin' masks? They look stupid and you're getting people worried over nothing. We need to get back to normal, you know." The family members all look horrified as the gang surrounds them. The youngest girl calls out "Mommy" and starts to whimper. The other one gets behind her father.

"You heard her," barks the handsome black coat, giving Tina a big smile. "Get rid of those bloody face diapers. They look disgusting!" Tina looks back at him appreciatively.

"This is America," Marv snarls. "You people shouldn't be caving into the elites, to the bloody know-it-alls who say we should all be wearing masks. Stand on your own feet and think for yourselves. And remember what it says on the New Hampshire car license plate—live free or die! And dad, you need to set a better example for your kids, teach them the value of freedom, not compliance."

The father looks agitated but says nothing. He gathers his family and they quickly walk away. As they do, Tina has a moment of feeling guilty. Maybe, she thinks, she was being a tad harsh in her language. After all, they were just a young family with two cute little girls. Maybe she overreacted. She has to watch her temper.

The group arrives at the clinic and ask for Sofia. They are told she has gone over to the pharmacy to get her medication. They head off to the pharmacy. Along the way, they meet Dr. Cortez, who is walking back to his office. The doctor tells them Sofia is at the pickup counter at the back of the pharmacy. Tina thanks him. But Marv scowls and gives the doctor the middle finger. The doctor looks back at him in disgust and shakes his head.

Dr. Cortez wrote a column in yesterday's *The Wolfville News*. Marv was ticked off that the doctor had the nerve to say they should all be wearing masks because of the scientific evidence. The doctor wrote—and Marv could hardly believe it—that it is conclusive from research that masks protect people from Covid. Yet just months before, as Marv recalled, the so-called experts, including the doctor, said the research was inconclusive. Which is it? For Marv, Dr. Cortez is a phony. He's a self-righteous fraud, and he's misleading the good people of Wolfville.

As they approach the pharmacy, the gang notices Si-Woo at a lottery kiosk buying tickets. They give her a dirty look.

"You Chinese," Marv growls, "you're always gambling. Think you're going to win it big, don't you?"

"Go back home," adds Tina, with a raised voice. "Go back to where you belong, go back to Wuhan or wherever it is you come from, and take the bloody virus with you." There I go again, she whispers to herself, letting my temper get the best of me. Why can't I learn to control myself better?

"Look," says Si-Woo, in a loud angry voice, "I belong here. This is my home. I've been living here since the nineteen-eighties. And I'm not Chinese, I was born in Korea. But I'm now American, just like you."

Hearing the raised voices, a group of shoppers gather around the kiosk to see what's going on.

"Gimme a break," yells Marv. "You Asians are all alike. Chinese, Koreans, what the hell's the difference?"

"You're making no sense," says Si-Woo. "Of course there's a difference, just like there's a difference between the English and the French. Let me say it to you again. I'm Korean, not Chinese. My father was a Korean soldier in the nineteen-fifties, and he fought against the Chinese invaders in the Korean War. He fought alongside Americans. He had one of his legs blown off! I'm proud of what he did. And I'm proud of my heritage."

Si-Woo remembers her father taking her out to watch the dragon dances in Seoul and to see the lantern festivals. She remembers his warmth, his laughter, and his affection and love for her. She is grateful she has these special memories.

"During the Korean War," she goes on, taking advantage of Marv's silence, "Americans and South Koreans were allies, and many were friends. I learned a lot about America when I was growing up. I learned it was the land of opportunity, a country that welcomed immigrants. I learned about the Statue of Liberty and its words: 'Give me your huddled masses yearning to breathe free'. I was deeply impressed. I was happy to move with my husband to the United States. We wanted a fresh start. I became an American. And as much as anybody else, I am an American. I *am* an American!"

Marv and the others ponder what Si-Woo has said. Marv finally has a response. "You might be American by some legal technicality, but you're not a *real* American. People like you come here, and you take jobs away from *real* Americans. You work for low wages, you weaken our unions, and you collect welfare. You take, but you don't give. You're not a real American at all."

"Yeah, you're not a real American," says the handsome black coat. "Go back to where you belong."

"Yeah, go home, you loser," says the one with the pointed ears.

"I belong here, right here," Si-Woo declares. "Why can't you get it through your heads!" Up to now, Si-Woo has been stoic and trying to hold back her tears. But the verbal attack is getting to her. She sits down on a bench by the kiosk and starts to cry.

19

Fuckin' crybaby. Are we supposed to feel sorry for her? No way. She's one of those people whining for a mask requirement. She deserves to get some acid thrown into her ugly face. Man, do I hate Asians. I wish they'd stick to being on their own continent. And the ones who are here, I wish to God they'd go back to where they came from. This land is not for them.

I didn't write the note. But I was glad to pin it up. I totally agreed with its contents, and I was eager to put it up. And I knew I wouldn't get caught. Nobody was around and the security camera above the bulletin board wasn't working. Hasn't been working for months.

Why do I hate masks so much? As Marv says, they're un-American. He's a great man—so smart, so inspiring. But even more than this, I find masks scary. They remind me of when I was a little kid. Whenever I cried, my father tied a cloth around my mouth to shut me up. He forced me to keep it on 'til I stopped crying. God, I could hardly breathe. I was terrified. Masks still give me the creeps.

When I put the note up, I thought the threat would be enough to scare people away from wearing masks. But the more I think about it, the more I like the idea of actually doing it, of actually attacking someone with sulfuric acid. What a rush that would be.

They say the main purpose of an acid attack is not to kill people but to humiliate them and make them see the results of their wrongdoing—ugly scars and burns. But the beauty of it is not just what it does to one person. It also affects others. Makes them think twice about doing the same thing. You might say it's a kind of deterrence.

I could threaten with a bomb or an AR-15. For sure, there'd be a lot more damage. But if I did that, I'd probably get dismissed as a typical shooter monster. A better bet is an acid attack. I'd get more sympathy. The victim wouldn't be some innocent bystander, but somebody who really deserved it, somebody who pushed for masks. And it would just maim them, not kill them. People would want to know why it happened. They'd find out that the reason was noble—that it was a protest against forcing people to wear masks.

I thought that by now, the mall would be buzzing about the note. I figured most

everybody would know about it. It would be
the center of conversation in the halls,
in the stores, in the food court, and on
social media. But word has not got out. I've
been ambushed. Somebody took the note down,
hidden it from view.

All the more reason I go ahead and actually
attack somebody with acid. That would get
their attention.

20

People around the lottery kiosk are troubled by Si-Woo's crying. More of them gather to see what's going on. Grumpy Bill comes out of his store to find out what the fuss is about. Michael, who happens to be walking by, comes over.

"What's wrong, Si-Woo?" asks Michael.

"They accuse me of not being a real American," she says, pointing to Marv's gang. "This is hurtful to me; it cuts me deep. I've been here a long time. I'm an American citizen, I raised a son, I worked hard in a bank, I've paid taxes, just like everybody else. And just like other people, I've struggled."

Si-Woo stops to clear some tears off her face. "I don't make much money—just my pension and working part-time in the bakery. But I pay taxes. I don't like them saying I'm not a real American, I resent it deeply."

At times like this, Si-Woo feels so alone. Her son would have turned thirty-six next week. She has no family in this country, or close relatives anywhere. There is no one close, to talk and share things with. *I wish I could share my life with somebody.*

"Who said you're not a real American, Si-Woo?" asks Grumpy Bill.

"Marv did," she replies.

"We were all just having a little chat," responds Marv. "Si-Woo, she just got a bit emotional, that's all."

"Why would you say she's not a real American, Marv?" asks Michael. "I know Si-Woo. She's worked here at the mall for years. She's an American citizen. As she said, she works, she pays taxes, she contributes to society."

"I stand by what I said," says Marv. "She's not a real American, she's a recent arrival to this country, an immigrant. My people have been here since the time of the Civil War. We're true-blue Americans. Hell, we're the backbone of this country. We helped build this country, made it into what it is today. Snowflake, over there, she's just a damn newcomer."

Grumpy Bill stares angrily at Marv. "Heavens to Betsy, Marv, we're all immigrants, except for our native peoples. Some of us have been here longer, that's for sure. But we're all immigrants. This is what America is about. There are no *real* Americans. My lordy, you've got to be more respectful. You're way out of line trying to downgrade Si-Woo that way. Heck, she doesn't deserve that."

Grumpy Bill keeps to himself, and barely knows Si-Woo. But from what he's seen of her in the mall, he admires her for her integrity and her work habits in the bakery, her positive attitude, and her friendliness, even to grouchy people like him. He knows from the manager of the bakery that even though she's had a difficult life, she works hard, keeps her nose to the grindstone, and seldom complains. And she's such a nice and warm-hearted person. He's glad to defend her.

Suddenly, Grumpy Bill jerks his head to his side forcefully and multiple times. Marv laughs. "What do we have here," he says, "a damn freak?" Grumpy Bill is red-faced. Si-Woo looks at Grumpy Bill in sympathy.

"Look Marv, there's no need for that," says Michael. "No need to be disrespectful of Grumpy Bill. And no need to call Si-Woo names like snowflake. You might not have meant it, but your language borders on being contemptuous or perhaps even hateful speech. We have anti-hate laws in our state, and we have rules against disruptive or disrespectful behavior in our mall."

Marv looks at Michael with disgust. "Look pal, the last time I checked, our country is a land of free speech. In America we're free to speak our minds. If snowflakes or politically correct people like you get offended, too damn bad. I know we have laws against fomenting hate. Hell, we're not Nazi Germany. But to say somebody is a snowflake or isn't a real American—that's part of free speech. So get real. Don't be an idiot. This is America, not Castro's Cuba or Communist China."

Tina, the black coats, and some in the gathered crowd applaud. Michael pauses to collect his thoughts. "Marv, I'm not saying you violated any laws. I'm just telling you that you're bordering on hateful speech. For common decency, you need to be more respectful to people, and you need to watch your language. And try to be compassionate to people like Si-Woo, people who have struggled to make it in a new country." A few onlookers applaud.

"Let me tell you something, dumbass. We've all had our struggles. It's not just wimpy Si-Woo who's faced adversity. I have too. I once applied for a job, my dream job of being the manager of a theme park. It was a lot of money, and if I got the job, I would have been on track for even bigger things. But they gave the job to some unqualified minority applicant, part of affirmative action. Now I work as a dispatcher for a taxi company. I don't hate minorities, but I resent the special treatment they get. Get it?"

"But listen Marv," says Michael, "you need to—"

"I don't have to listen to this crap, I've heard enough. Let's get the hell out of here." Marv waves to some people he recognizes at the back of the crowd and heads over to them. Tina and the handsome black coat exchange warm glances.

The crowd of onlookers disperses. Grumpy Bill walks over to Si-Woo and gives her a warm smile and a friendly pat on her shoulder.

He then returns to his store, and Si-Woo limps back to the bakery. Such a kind and considerate man, she says to herself. He might be grumpy on the outside, but I know he's got a heart of gold on the inside.

Marv yells back to Tina. "See you later in the pub."

"Yeah, I'll see you there," she responds, turning away. She wonders why they were so hard on Si-Woo. Go back home? What a way to talk. Why did she have to say that!

21

Tina walks over to the pharmacy and sees her mother coming into the mall. "There you are. I got a message from the doctor's office that I should take you home. Are you okay?"

"Yes, I'm okay," Sofia replies. "I was feeling a bit woozy earlier. But I'm better now. Dr. Cortez, he's been so thoughtful. He had my medication adjusted."

"Let's go then. My car is out in the south side parking lot."

"Tina," says Sofia, as they walk along, "I picked up some extra masks while I was in the pharmacy. Why don't you take one? I'd really appreciate it if you'd wear one when you're around me."

Tina looks at her mother in disgust. "Look, we've been through this a thousand times. Get it through your thick head, Mom, masks are for losers. I'm not going to wear a mask, and neither is Brianna. We don't like being told what to do. We're not going to give in to tyranny and the politically correct elites."

Sofia wonders how her daughter could think this way. Give in to tyranny? Where did all this come from? From Marv, of course. "Listen honey," she says, "I just don't want to get Covid. And I don't want you to get it either. Or little Brianna. That's why I'm on about it."

"Jesus Christ! Let's not go there anymore. Okay?"

"Please watch your language, Tina. I hope you don't talk that way in front of Brianna. You don't want to be a bad influence. Anyway, I just don't understand it. What's the big deal about wearing a mask? I know it's inconvenient. But it shouldn't be such a big deal."

Sofia listens to the music playing in the mall. It's *California Dreamin'* by the Mamas and the Papas. It reminds her of the time she moved to New York City, after getting a job as a social worker at a Manhattan hospital. It was winter and she was incredibly lonely. After only a few months, she moved back to sunny California. Back to her friends and family. She was so happy then.

"Mom, you need to wake up and smell the coffee. I was reading on the internet the other day just how dangerous masks are. I didn't know this before, but most masks—most of the paper ones, anyway—are made in China. I read they secretly put some kind of chemical—I forgot the name, but some chemical—into the masks, which affects the airways and then the brain. I read that the more people wear masks, the more muddled their thinking gets. This all comes from that chemical."

"You really believe this, honey?"

"Absolutely. But there's more to it than this. It hasn't yet been confirmed, but people suspect that it's a plot by the Chinese government to get our thinking distorted, get us to believe in communism. I told Marv about it, and he said he's not surprised. He said the Chinese and our own elites are in it together. It's all part of a global plan to bring tyranny and communism to America."

"This is craziness, Tina. Think about what you're saying. You shouldn't be on the internet so much. And you should be wearing a mask, especially when you are around me."

"That's it, damn it. I've had enough of you. I warned you if you kept on harping about masks, you wouldn't be able to see Brianna. Well, you've done it to yourself. From now on, I won't allow you to see Brianna. Hear me, I won't allow it."

Sofia looks shocked. "Tina, you can't mean that. You know how much I love Brianna. This would—"

"Stop right now. The subject is closed. You'll not get to see her. Now, I'm going to take you home."

Sofia stays silent. As they walk to the exit, she shakes her head in disbelief. She can't believe the extent of Tina's cruelty, cutting her off from her own granddaughter, how painful that's going to be. Why can't she get through to Tina?

She knows this problem is not unique to her. Many parents, when their children go astray, are limited in what they can do, no matter how hard they try. It's going to take something major, some serious event in Tina's life, to get her to change her way of thinking. Maybe Marv gets hit by a truck and dies, maybe he hooks up with somebody else and drops Tina, or maybe Tina gets sick from Covid and realizes the error of her ways. She knows she shouldn't think such things, but unless something big happens, Tina's going to continue on with all her craziness and her cruelty. Her thinking is distorted. She's obsessed with Marv and with the movement, just like an addict is hooked on heroin.

Sofia grasps at a positive thought. Tina did come to the mall to take her home. At least, at some level, she still cares about her mother, there's still a spark of inner goodness in Tina. So maybe, just maybe, there is hope she can bounce back and become her former self.

22

As Tina and Sofia head for the exit, Michael is joined by Wally Waller at the lottery kiosk.

"Get anything yet from the surveillance cameras?" Michael asks Wally.

"Nothing. My staff checked out the footage since the beginning of June. They said there was nothing unusual. Just the regular mall walkers, workers, cleaners, early morning shoppers, construction people. And some smelly street people. One of Marv's black coats came in for a coffee the morning the note was found, then left. That's about it. Nothing suspicious, it was all—"

A message comes over the PA system: "Shoppers, can I have your attention please. We have a lost child at the customer relations office. She says her name is Sarah. She has red hair and is dressed in green. Thanks for your attention."

Listening to the message, Michael has a terrible thought. With what's been going on in the mall—a homicide and a someone threatening to attack people with acid—the child could have met a bad end. *What am I thinking? A lost child is a common thing to happen in the mall and never a problem.*

"Wally, did you check the footage from the camera above the bulletin board? That's the really important one, it could be the key to the whole thing."

"Uh, well, we did have a problem with that one … and actually, with a few others too … including the one above the unisex washroom, which I think I told you about before."

"Yeah, I was wondering about that."

"These cameras haven't been working for months. When you look at the big monitor, at all the different screens, you'll see all the footage, except from these particular cameras. They're blank. Amazing. We've got over fifty cameras in this mall and … wouldn't ya know it … the video from the one you most want is blank. Isn't that fuckin' weird!"

"Yes, it is weird," Michael replies, raising an eyebrow. "Shouldn't they have been fixed, Wally? What's the problem? Why aren't these cameras working?"

Wally looks puzzled. He pulls at his hair. "Well, bro," he finally says, "I'm no expert. But my staff tell me it could be a problem in the cameras themselves, or with loose wires between the cameras and the monitor. Or there could be a glitch of some kind in the big monitor or the security software program. A while back, I phoned a technician to come and check it out. But nobody got back to me. I guess I'm gonna have to phone again."

"Wally, you really need to get on this. And you need to do it as fast as you can. Time's a passing. I'd feel a lot better if I knew the note came from some unhoused guy or harmless drunk who did it on the spur of the moment. If there's footage, this could give us the answer. Get on it, Wally."

"Okay, man. By the way, the police came in and asked me some more questions about the old man's death."

"Oh?"

"Yeah. I couldn't help them much. Seems they're at a dead end or close to it. They can't get any video footage from the camera above the washroom because it isn't working. And the footage they did look at from the other cameras showed nothing out of the ordinary. Plus, nothing showed up from the forensics investigation. So, they've got no leads. It's probably going to end up in their cold case files. A shame, isn't it?"

"Hmm. Those bad cameras. I'm sorry, I need to head back to my office. Catch you later."

Michael heads back to his office, reflecting on what Wally has said. A shame, isn't it? Why was he so sarcastic about the police being stymied in their investigation? He seemed to delight in it. And why is it that the security cameras we most need to be working, are the ones that aren't? Is this a coincidence? Why the delay in getting them fixed? It seems so strange.

Michael wonders if Wally himself is involved with the note, and perhaps also with the old man's death? After all, according to one of the guards, he was in the mall early in the morning at the time of both incidents. But ... no way. My imagination is getting the better of me. Wally has his problems but he's not evil.

23

THE WOLFVILLE NEWS

Thursday, June 25, 2020

MASKS TO BE MANDATORY ACROSS THE STATE

Governor Muriel Barley decided today, in consultation with the state department of health, to make masks mandatory in indoor settings, including stores, restaurants, bars, gyms, sporting venues, and shopping malls. Where masks had previously been recommended, they now will be required under a public health order.

This goes into effect June 30. Managers and those responsible for indoor venues will have the legal duty to display signs and enforce the public health order, subject to heavy fines and/or jail time. Violators will be subject to the possibility of smaller fines and/or jail time. The only exceptions to the masking requirement are children under age 2, people with certain medical conditions, and people who are eating or drinking in restaurants, cafes, and bars.

According to officials in Governor Barley's office, the reason for the public health order is the dramatic rise of Covid-19 cases, hospitalizations, ICU cases, and deaths. This, they say, is overwhelming the health care system and threatening the economy. Masks, together with other mitigation measures such as social distancing and regular handwashing, are our best defense against the virus until a vaccine or cure is found. The science is clear, declare the officials. Masks have been shown effective in limiting the spread of Covid.

Public health professionals are pleased with the decision. Dr. Juan Cortez, known for his advocacy of a mask mandate, says the requirement is a major step forward in controlling the virus until a vaccine is developed.

Store managers and business operators are worried they will lose customers, especially restaurants, bars, and night clubs. But most managers report they are willing to abide by the decision. Michael McQueen, manager of Wolfville Mall, says that although there may be initial problems and resistance, as the public becomes more familiar with the mandate and more supportive of it, businesses will fall into line.

Marv Hammar, head of a local anti-masking group, is outraged. He says the scientific research has produced mixed results on the effectiveness of masks. More than that, he says that a mask mandate is anti-American. "We are a land of freedom," he says. "People should be free to choose whether or not to wear masks, not be forced into it." According to Mr. Hammar, "a mask mandate is yet another step toward tyranny in America."

24

Michael and Cornelia are sipping white wine in the family room before dinner. Bobbie and Brandy are playing in the backyard.

"That's great wine, princess. What is it?"

"I picked it up yesterday at the wine store. It's a California Pinot Gris. It's from the Napa Valley. We haven't had it before. Supposed to be good, at least according to the Napa Vintage Reports." Cornelia takes another sip. "And yes, it's good, very good. No question about it. It's got a nice honeysuckle aroma and lemony flavor."

Honeysuckle? Really? Michael almost laughs out loud but then he contains himself. "Anything new with you, princess?"

"I sent Daddy a text telling him about today's big news story. He phoned me back later saying it was great news. It lets you off the hook. It's going to be Governor Barley who takes the blame if there's any backlash. Daddy said you can rest a lot easier now. It's great for your career and it's great for our family."

"Yes, it's good news. In fact, it's fantastic news. Before I left the office today, I got a call from a member of the board of directors. She said the word around Pacific Gold is very positive about me. The board members are really happy about how I handled the issue and about the outcome."

"That's great, Michael."

Michael looks out the back window and sees the girls playing some board game on the picnic table. He's glad to see them interacting this way. Better than them being on phones in social isolation. But it won't be long, I suppose, before they'll be pestering us for phones.

"Yeah, I'm happy too. It's odd how it all worked out. I really didn't decide anything. I didn't handle the issue at all. But I get the credit, which I gladly accept. And it's a good result for the mall. With the mask mandate, most of our shoppers will feel more comfortable in the mall, knowing they're better protected. Anti-maskers like Marv can't blame the mall, they'll have to direct their venom at the Governor."

"Let's have a toast," says Cornelia. "Here's to a great outcome."

They clink their wine glasses.

After taking a sip, Cornelia adds that the note problem is also solved. People will have to wear masks, whether they like it or not. So, she says, this nutbar has no reason to attack anybody in the mall and there's nothing to worry about. If anybody is going to be attacked, it'll have to be the Governor. Michael nods his head in agreement.

"Sweetie, one other thing before I call the girls in for dinner. I'd like to get some new furniture. What we have now is getting to look a bit dated, a bit tired. When my yoga group meets here, I'm embarrassed. So, on the weekend, can you come with me, and we'll check out some new furniture downtown?"

Michael grimaces as he thinks about the cost. "Well, I suppose I can, princess. But you know, I'm still earning the same money as before with Pacific Gold. It'll be some time before I get a higher salary. Wouldn't it be better if we did this later, after I get my promotion?"

Cornelia coolly stares at Michael. "Michael, surely to God we can afford a little new furniture! You know what I think? I think you should go to your corporate bosses—do it right away—and insist on a raise and promotion. The timing is right. They're happy with you right now. Daddy always says to strike while the iron is hot."

"I understand, princess. But there's a process to follow. I can't just go waltzing in and demand more pay. I have to prove myself over time."

"Michael, you need to be more aggressive. You need to *make* things happen."

"I hear you, Cornelia," Michael replies, exasperated.

"With a pay increase, we could have a decent vacation. We haven't had one in such a long time."

"But princess, we went to Florida just last year."

"You call that a vacation? We stayed at a barely 4-star hotel that didn't even have a spa. Remember? Didn't even have a great pool. No, I want to go to Maui and stay at a 5-star resort on the south coast. I read about one that just opened. It got fantastic reviews in Condé Nast Traveler. Michael, you've got to get your act together and get that promotion. And you've got to do it right away."

Michael's face reddens and he furrows his brows. "Cornelia, have you ever stopped to think about the costs of a vacation like that? Look, you're not the one working, I'm carrying all the load. You've got to understand that I'm giving it my best shot, I'm trying my hardest to get that promotion."

"Listen up, Michael, you've got to do more than just try hard, you've got to step on the gas, and actually get that promotion. We've been waiting forever, while you make excuses. If you can't get your act together and make enough money for us to have a decent life … I'm thinking of leaving you. Taking the girls and moving back to Georgia."

"What! You can't mean that, Cornelia. You can't be serious."

"You bet I'm serious, mister. Daddy said I'd be welcome anytime. If you don't want this to happen, get your act together and do it fast. Understand?"

Cornelia abruptly stands, gulps down her Pinot Gris, and goes out into the backyard to collect the girls for dinner.

25

It's a quiet dinner. Cornelia hardly speaks. Michael asks Bobbie and Brandy what board game they were playing outside. They explain it's a game called Dinosaur Escape. The goal is to get dinosaurs safely onto an island before a volcano erupts. Michael listens but he finds it hard to concentrate.

After dinner, as Cornelia loads the dishwasher, he says he needs to go out and get some fresh air. He's going to have a short walk. He won't be long. She doesn't reply.

It is getting dark as he walks down the street toward the park. He wonders if Cornelia was being serious. Would she really leave him? Or did she just say this in a moment of anger, without meaning it. But she spoke with such conviction. She could have meant it. Then again, would she actually take the girls and move down to Georgia, thousands of miles away?

Michael looks up and sees a bright object in the southern sky. Venus? No, this time of the night, and this time of the year, it's probably Jupiter.

If Cornelia really did leave him, it would be devastating. They've been together a long time, and he loves her, and he really loves Bobbie and Brandy. He can't imagine being separated from his girls—they mean the world to him. Being apart from them would be painful. What would it be like, he wonders, to talk with them only through Zoom or Skype. How could he possibly endure this kind of arrangement?

Michael hears dogs barking in the distance. Maybe they're trying to scare off some racoons. Maybe a bear. One was reported in the area last week.

It may not come to that, he reassures himself. Cornelia did not categorically say she would leave him. She only said she was thinking about it. She wouldn't do it if he gets his promotion and gets it soon. So, there's hope. He still has time to make it happen, keep her happy, keep his family together.

Michael again hears dogs barking. It's got to be a bear. Dogs around here wouldn't get that worked up over racoons.

It's going to be difficult to get that promotion. Pacific Gold is happy with him now, but business in the mall has been slipping, sales are down at most of the stores, and it's getting harder to rent vacant spaces. The problem is not just Covid. There has been more and more online shopping, and the manager of Sunrise Mall—Brenda somebody—has been stealing away customers. So, it's going to be an uphill battle. He's got to figure out something to turn Wolfville Mall around. If he can do it, he'll get his promotion and Cornelia will be happier.

Why is Cornelia so bloody difficult? Why is she so determined to get her own way in everything? He reflects on the advice his counselor gave him a couple years earlier—be more assertive with Cornelia, don't back down so much, be honest about your feelings. The counselor said if he would be more assertive and honest, this would be healthier for their marriage.

Michael also remembers what his mother had told him, shortly before she died a decade earlier. After meeting Cornelia and getting to know her, his mother advised him to be wary of Cornelia's pushiness, to stand his ground, and not be overly compromising. "Michael," she said, "you need to stick up for yourself more, and not let Cornelia walk all over you. It would be much better for you and for your marriage."

Michael recalls trying to follow all this advice. It made perfect sense. But it was so hard to follow through. It wasn't in his nature to be forceful and aggressive. He wasn't that kind of person. Besides, he thought, was it really such a bad thing for him, or for anyone, to be patient, compromising, and accommodating?

Michael returns home. In the kitchen, he notices a note pinned on a cork board beside the refrigerator. It's a message from a teacher, congratulating Bobbie for her good work on a science project. Michael smiles, proud of his daughter. A note. He's reminded of the terrifying note in the mall. Though the Governor's mask mandate could mean the end of the threat, it's also possible the person who wrote the note will still attack. Maybe, just maybe, this person is the same person who killed the old man in the washroom.

If it is, we've got a psychopath on our hands. And even if it isn't, if it's a different person, we've still got someone with incredible anger and hate. I've got a gut feeling we're not finished with this twisted piece of work. Something could set off the note writer again. We still could have an attack in the mall, maybe a fatal attack. If this happens, never mind a promotion. I could lose everything. I could lose my career, my marriage, even my children.

Pressure Rising

December 2020

26

THE WOLFVILLE NEWS

Tuesday, December 8, 2020

VACCINES COMING TO STATE BUT ROLLOUT UNCLEAR

Governor Muriel Barley announced today that vaccines for Covid-19 will start coming to the state, including to Wolfville, next week. The first shipment arrives December 14, followed by another one in three weeks. Both are messenger RNA vaccines and administered in two doses.

The vaccines are over 90 percent effective. The first groups to receive them will be frontline healthcare workers, followed by people with underlying medical conditions and people over age 70. After that, people will receive them in stages based on age.

Vaccines will be distributed through designated pharmacies that have formed partnerships with the state and large facilities such as conference centers and sports venues. Pharmacy distribution for locations inside shopping malls, department stores, and big box stores will need to get the approval of the mall or store before the distribution can begin, pending a decision by the Governor's Office.

Anti-government and "anti-vaxxer" groups are critical of the announcement. Many of the critics are the same ones who were angry about masks last summer and have similar objections. Much of the acrimony about masks had subsided after Governor Barley's declaration of a statewide mask mandate and public support for the mandate. But anger is building again over vaccines, directed against both the vaccines and the rollout plan.

Marv Hammar, leader of a local anti-vaxxer and anti-masking group, tells reporters he is infuriated about the plan. The vaccine, he says, has been developed much too quickly, making it potentially dangerous. In his view it is also an unnecessary encroachment on personal liberty by Big Pharma and intrusive government officials. According to Mr. Hammar, the campaign to get Americans vaccinated is yet another step toward tyranny in America. "Requiring us to wear masks," he says, "was one step. Injecting us with vaccines, unknown in their effects, is another."

Mr. Hammar is organizing a rally against the vaccine rollout this Thursday at Wolfville Mall. There will be a march around the outside of the mall, ending with Mr. Hammar giving a speech at the entrance to the pharmacy.

Michael McQueen, manager of the mall, tells reporters that the rally and the march are permitted under mall policy. The mall, he says, supports free speech. However, he adds, because the mall is private property, there is no legal right to assemble and protest. The organizers need to be peaceful and respectful or permission will be withdrawn.

27

It is noon on Thursday and people are gathering for the rally in front of the mall. Despite the cold December weather, Marv's been successful in mobilizing lots of people. The crowd is getting bigger and noisier. Country music is playing and some in the crowd are singing along.

Michael comes outside to observe the scene. He scans the crowd and is surprised at its size, much bigger than the one last June. There must be well over five hundred people, he estimates. He's amazed at all the flags and banners, the hoopla, the excitement, and the TV cameras. He notices the Wolfville Police at the back. He also notices the many onlookers on the sidelines, among them Grumpy Bill, Dr. Cortez, the Barkers, and Power Walker. Although he's not sure, he also thinks he sees Wally Waller standing at the back, looking on eagerly. Isn't it supposed to be Wally's day off? Remembering the rumors of Wally being a white nationalist, Michael wonders again if his head of security is a quiet supporter of Marv.

Wearing his black cowboy hat, Marv jumps onto the platform and grabs a bullhorn. Merle Haggard's song *Okie from Muskogee* is just ending. "Friends," he roars, with his eyes flashing with anger, "these new vaccines are an abomination. They've been rushed through too fast, and we really don't know what's in them. Yet our dear government leaders, along with Big Pharma, expect us to meekly accept them. They expect us to allow the medical people to inject us with who knows what. Some say these vaccines could cause asthma or even cancer. Others say they might lead to sterility or infertility. We don't really know. But why, why in the hell, should we take a chance? Why should we—we the people—be expected to take a chance? I say we need to resist. We need to resist. We need to resist in the name of liberty. Just as our ancestors fought the British, we need to fight the tyrants of today. We need to fight against the elites who are coercing us into getting injected. We deserve respect! Our choices deserve to be respected! Down with tyranny! Down with the vaccines!"

There is thunderous applause. The crowd starts to chant "down with tyranny, down with the vaccine." American flags get waved, a 1776 banner pops up, and a Confederate flag is raised high in the air. Marv asks for some water. Tina tosses him a bottle and he takes a couple of swigs.

"Patriots," he continues, "here at the mall, here in our community, the vaccines should not—absolutely should not—be given out. The mall management has been given the power to approve or not approve the pharmacy in doing this. I say to hell with the pharmacy. I say the mall should do the right thing. The mall management and the owners should not, repeat, should not allow this to happen. This is our community. The mall is at the center of our community. I say these vaccines should not—and I can't say it strongly enough—should not be allowed here. Down with vaccines! Down with tyranny!"

Again, there is thunderous applause. Led by Tina and the black coats, the crowd chants "No vaccines here, no vaccines here." Tina then yells out "We love Marv, we love Marv." The crowd follows her lead. Marv waves to the crowd in appreciation, jumps off the platform, and joins his girlfriend and the black coats. They start assembling people for the march.

Michael is disappointed and frustrated with what he sees. He thought the controversy over Covid was long over. Following the Governor's announcement of a mask mandate last June, and with the rising death count from Covid, there had been growing public acceptance of the need for action against the deadly virus. And with this acceptance there had been relative calm and unity. But now, Michael thinks, the divisiveness is returning. Marv is stirring the pot, and it's going to affect the mall. *Things were going so well.*

Business in the mall has improved thanks to an expensive new advertising campaign; a major upgrade to the mall, made possible by generous funding from the corporation; and the re-opening of the gym, restaurants, and movie theaters, though with some restrictions on seating. It also has helped that Christmas crowds and Christmas sales have been better than usual. Senior management at Pacific Gold let it be known to Michael that his request for a promotion was looking positive, though no final decision had been made.

And on the home front, Cornelia has been supportive. Happy about his prospects for higher earnings, she has been out scouting for new houses in Blue Mountain Heights. Only once did she mention leaving him. That was on her birthday when he failed to take her—because he forgot to make a reservation—to a new expensive French restaurant for dinner, one with a 3-star Michelin rating. Other than that, she's been good. Even her father has been supportive. Cornelia reported Daddy saying, and Michael could hardly believe it, that he was proud of Michael for his skillful handling of the masking issue.

So, thinks Michael, all has been good. But now things are getting screwed up because of Marv and his nasty band of anti-vaxxers. If there's an escalation of conflict, if people around the mall feel more angry or afraid, and if they influence others, business again could suffer. If this happens, Michael's chance of a promotion could go up in flames and he could even lose his job. And Cornelia could leave him as she threatened before.

Marv's followers are assembled, and the march is about to begin. Michael comes over to speak with Marv.

"Marv, looks like you've got a good-sized crowd here. Listen, we went through this last June, but let me repeat. We're allowing you to have your march around the outside of the mall. But you have to keep it peaceful. Otherwise, according to our policy, you may be prohibited for an indefinite period of time from having another rally and march. Understand?"

"Sieg Heil!" shouts the black coat with the pointed ears.

"Sieg Heil!" repeats the handsome one.

"We get it," says Marv. "But understand this, pal. You need to tell the pharmacy it can't go ahead with the vaccines. We know you have the power to do this. Make sure you use it wisely, amigo. Understand?"

"The mall does have the authority. But we're not going to make a decision quickly or arbitrarily. We're going to consult widely with people—with everyone around the mall who has a stake in the issue. And we're going to consider your views as well."

"Make sure you do, you weasel."

"Remember now, keep it peaceful, Marv."

"Well, well, the tyrant has spoken. Glory hallelujah!" Marv shouts to the crowd.

"Sieg Heil!" shrieks Tina.

There is a loud clang on the pavement. Tina has dropped her smart phone. Looking concerned, the handsome black coat rushes over, picks it up, and quickly gives it to her. Seeing it's not damaged, she gives him a big warm appreciative smile. He smiles back. Marv ignores this exchange, keeping his eyes on the crowd.

"Okay then, let's go," yells Marv. The crowd begins its march. Marv's plan is to go along the sidewalk on the south side of the mall, and then along the east side to the pharmacy on the northeast corner. As the marchers get moving, as he did before, Marv worries about the possibility of violence or a racist incident. He instructs his black coats to drop back into the crowd and make sure everything is kept peaceful. He tells them to warn his followers that if there are any taunts or provocations by onlookers, to keep calm and not to respond unless absolutely necessary.

The march proceeds with hardly any trouble. The only incident is an old scruffy man who staggers in front of the march clutching a bottle of red wine. After taking a couple of gulps, he starts to shout "Sieg Heil." Slurring his words, he does it several more times. On Marv's instruction, the black coat with the pointed ears comes forward, grabs hold of the old man, and forcefully shoves him out of the way. The man spins around and stumbles through a side door into the mall. He drops the bottle, and it breaks on the floor. The wine spills out, leaving a foul smell. Shoppers nearby are revolted.

The march continues, stopping in front of the outside door to the pharmacy. Marv gets up on a bench to say a few words. Tina hands him a bullhorn.

"Friends, Big Pharma is making humongous profits from Covid. The drug companies get big bucks in public investment, they pay hardly any taxes, and they're going to reap billions of dollars from an unproven vaccine we know little about. And it's not just the corporate executives and investors who profit. It's the lawyers, accountants, scientists, and politicians ... it's everybody connected to these damn companies. Plus, it's pharmacies like the one you see in front of you. They profit, or want to profit, from a vaccine that could be more dangerous than the virus itself. They tell us it's safe. Bull! They're just trying to gaslight us. I say no to Big Pharma, and I say no ... no, no, no ... to the pharmacy in front of you. Just say no!"

Tina starts to chant "Just say no, just say no." The crowd joins in and the chant gets louder, and is repeated for several minutes. Marv takes a couple swigs of water and continues. "Patriots, in America, we the people matter. We the people must consent to the decisions that affect us. Do we consent to this pharmacy injecting us with these god-awful vaccines? I say, Hell no!"

Led again by Tina, the crowd chants "Hell no, hell no." This goes on for several minutes.

"We don't consent," yells Marv, "we don't consent. This is our community. We have a right to a say in what goes on. We don't want the mall to allow this, we don't want the mall to give permission to this bloody pharmacy. We won't stand for it. Just say no! Just say no!"

Tina claps her hands wildly and the crowd gives an ear-splitting cheer. Tina then restarts the chant, "Just say no, just say no," and the crowd joins in. After some time has passed, Marv thanks his supporters for coming and tells them they should hold their heads high, they should be proud of fighting against the injustice of these dreadful vaccines. He suggests they head home, waves, and the crowd disperses. Marv is pleased with how things have turned out.

The mall returns to normal. A booming female voice is heard through the PA system. "Shoppers, there's been a spill by the entrance door on the east side of the mall. We apologize for the odor and we assure you that the spill will be cleaned up shortly. But watch your step. It's slippery. You have yourself a great day and God bless America."

28

Mary and Richard Barker are doing their usual early morning rounds in the mall. Christmas music is playing, and holiday decorations are in the stores. At one end of the mall, a Christmas tree has been set up. At the other end, a table has been assembled with a menorah on it to recognize Hanukkah. Power Walker speeds by the Barkers, giving them a big smile.

"Richard," asks Mary, "what did you think of the march yesterday?"

"With the way Marv was talking, I thought there'd be trouble. He really gets them riled up, doesn't he? But it turned out to be a fairly tame event, except for the old-timer dropping the wine. Oh, did it ever smell bad!"

"What's going to happen now," says Mary. "Can Marv really get enough people on board to influence the mall, to get the mall to block the pharmacy from giving out the vaccines?"

"I doubt it."

"But you're often wrong, aren't you?" she replies, with a sly smile. "My guess is he'll do it. He's a determined guy. I think he and his band of morons are going to ramp up the pressure, and they're going to get their way. And worse, I think they're going to get people scared of the vaccines, so scared they won't get vaccinated. And if enough people don't get vaccinated, this virus is going to be around for a long time—for years. We're going to be in this mess for years. I'll bet that before this is all over, we're going to have over a million people dead in this country, dead from Covid. Just because of these idiotic people!"

"Mary, get yourself together. You're being far too pessimistic. For sure, Marv's going to have some success. But most people are sensible. Look at what happened with the masks. In the end, Marv didn't get his way, we got a mask mandate. I think most people are going to realize that vaccines are the key to getting us out of this hellish situation. We don't want to be walking around with masks on forever. We want to get back to normal. Most people understand this, they understand that getting back to normal means getting vaccinated."

"I'm not so sure. A lot of people think differently from you and me. They agree with Marv. They're going to resist vaccines, just as they still resist masks. Look at what's going on in our mall. You see most people wearing masks, yes, but you also see some dimwits who don't. And what do the security guards do! They either turn a blind eye, or they politely ask the delinquents to *please* wear a mask. They appease these morons. How pathetic is that!"

Sofia Morellato comes around the corner, struggling as usual with her walker. The Barkers greet her and ask how she's doing. Sofia sighs and tells them she has to go to the hospital later in the day. She's been getting severe headaches and Dr. Cortez is concerned. He had her do an EEG last summer to rule out a head injury from the fall she had in the mall. The results showed no evidence of an injury. But with these recent headaches, she says, the doctor had wanted her to get an MRI and arranged an appointment at the hospital. It's supposed to get a fuller picture of her brain activity and, hopefully, will rule out a head injury. Tina, she adds, is going to drive her.

"Sorry to hear about this," replies Richard, "it must be worrying. How's Tina doing these days? We saw her with Marv at the march yesterday. She's a real disciple of his, isn't she?"

Sofia pauses before answering. She has a pained expression on her face. "I worry about Tina. I've been worrying about her for a long time now. She's been so mesmerized by Marv—thinks he's some kind of savior. She'll do almost anything for him. It seems she's lost herself as a separate person. She's become a part of Marv. An appendage. I think it's so sad, and so dangerous."

"She certainly was helping him out big time yesterday," says Mary.

Sofia nods. "I also worry about her addiction to conspiracy theories. She told me a couple days ago she read on the internet that these Covid vaccines are dangerous. Said they contain toxic substances that hurt people, that could actually kill people. I couldn't believe it. I told her to get off the internet, it's addling her brain. But she won't listen."

"Wow, that's amazing, Sofia," says Richard.

"But worse for me, Tina still won't let me see my little Brianna. I think I told you about this before. Tina has forbidden me, actually forbidden me, from seeing my own granddaughter. It's really killing me. I haven't seen my little girl since last summer."

Mary is taken aback. "You haven't? Why, that's unbelievable, it's almost unforgiveable. How can a mother—or any parent—do that kind of thing, use her daughter as a kind of weapon against her own mother?"

"Yeah, it's unbelievable, and it hurts me every day ... every single day. Sorry, I've got to get home. Got some things to do before going to the hospital. See you people later. Goodbye. Ciao."

The Barkers watch her leave and then continue their walk. As they approach the bulletin board, they suddenly see another note. To have a better look, Richard takes it down and reads it aloud to Mary.

This is another warning. Don't you dare call for vaccines. Don't you dare say there should be vaccines in our pharmacy. If you do, I'll for sure throw sulfuric acid into your face. You'll be deformed for life. My patience is running out. Last time you were warned about wearing those fuckin' masks. You didn't

listen, but I let it go. This time I won't let it go. SAY NO TO VACCINES!

Once again, the Barkers are stunned. Richard's mouth is wide open, as if he had a spear thrown into his back. "I can't believe it," he says. "Not in my wildest dreams did I think there'd be another note. This is absolutely absurd."

"Yeah, it's absurd. More than absurd!" Mary replies, with a bewildered expression. "It's so hard to process. We've now got ourselves not just one but two horrible notes. Plus, from last summer, that unsolved murder—the killing of the poor old man in the washroom—with a mask stuffed into his mouth."

"They never did find out who did it, did they? The police didn't get any leads."

"Yeah, that was wild. But what about this note, Richard? What should we do?"

"Well, let's think it through. We'll go get some coffee and figure out something. But we should keep the note with us, don't you think?"

"Yeah, we should do that."

As the stores open, the Barkers go up the escalator and search for a table in the food court. Tables are easier to find now, with the easing of the seating restrictions. Mary finds a table while Richard gets them each a cappuccino. The old Elvis song *Blue Christmas* is playing in the background.

They analyze the note. Mary points out that this note is different than the previous one. The handwriting is different. The strokes are slanted to the left rather than to the right. Maybe it means they are two different people or one person pretending to be another in order to create confusion. Richard points out another difference. This time the writer says I *will* throw, rather than I *may* throw, sulfuric acid. Could this mean the person is more serious this time? That he or she is actually going to do it?

Mary wonders who the writer, or writers, could be. Richard speculates that the leading suspects are the same as before. Could be an unhoused person, or Marv, or Tina, or one of Marv's black coats, or one of Marv's other idiot followers. Marv could have paid somebody to do it, or somebody could have been inspired to do it on Marv's behalf. Mary agrees and suggests that they go see Michael.

The Barkers finish their cappuccinos and head for Michael's office. Along the way, they come across Si-Woo, who has a worried expression on her face. She seems to have been crying.

"What's the matter, Si-Woo?" asks Richard.

Si-Woo's bottom lip quivers. "You … you probably think I'm being overly dramatic, but I feel I'm being followed." She stops and takes a deep breath. "About an hour ago, I got some weird looks from this guy in a hoodie—a young guy, I think, maybe in his late twenties. He was standing outside the bakery, peering in through the window. Then I saw him again later, walking behind me. I sped up a bit, but I can't walk very fast because of my limp. I was really getting scared. Maybe it's my imagination, but it seemed to me, based on the way he looked at me, he had feelings of hatred toward me. With all the anti-Asian incidents we've been hearing about, I was thinking he could attack me. It's really upsetting."

"I don't like to say this," Mary replies, "but you're probably right. You could get attacked. You're well known in the mall, and you speak out all the time about the need for vaccines, and before that, for masks. So, it's not surprising that people who are racist, who blame China for the virus, might want to attack you. You really need to watch your back."

"Did you see what the guy looked like?" asks Richard.

"Not really, the person was wearing a dark hoodie and a mask. Average height, average weight, that's about it."

"Well, anyway," says Richard, "you should report it to Michael or security. And you need to be really careful."

"Yeah, you're right, I'm going to have to watch it, especially with my heart condition. When I saw the guy coming up behind me, I could feel palpitations in my heart. It's probably nothing but I'll have to see Dr. Cortez about it. I wish things could be more normal."

"We do too," says Mary.

As Si-Woo limps back to the bakery, the Barkers continue toward Michael's office. As they walk, they are both thinking the same thing. Si-Woo has good reason to be scared. It's an admirable thing to speak out about the need for vaccines. But there is also danger in doing it. Mary then asks a question that neither of them know the answer to: "Would the person who followed Si-Woo be the same person who wrote the note?"

29

The Barkers knock on Michael's door. Michael gets up from his desk and welcomes them in.

"Coffee?"

"No thanks, chief, we just had our quota for the day," says Richard.

"How about a piece of carrot cake? Brought it from home this morning. Nice and fresh."

"Not for me," says Richard, grinning. "I've got to watch my figure."

"Well," says Mary, "I wouldn't mind trying ...." Then she looks at Richard. "Uh, well, I guess I better not."

"So, what's up?" asks Michael.

"A couple of things," replies Mary, as she sits down. "One is about Si-Woo. We just ran into her. She thinks somebody might be following her in the mall. She's really afraid of being attacked. And Michael, with all the anti-Asian feeling around here, we think it could happen. Remember that terrible incident a few days ago downtown. Somebody punched a Chinese woman in the face and kicked her while she was down. She was bruised and cut badly. There was even blood on the sidewalk. They caught the whole thing on a security camera."

"Yeah, I remember it, I saw it on the TV news." Michael looks up in the air with a pained expression. "I'm really sorry to hear about Si-Woo. She's such a terrific person. It's possible Si-Woo was imagining things that don't exist. She could just be hyper-sensitive. Still, on the other hand, I agree that she could be attacked. There's lots of angry people out there, lots of disturbed people blaming Chinese folks for the pandemic."

Michael thinks about the recent attacks on Asians. Why is this happening? It seems we've made so much progress in America against the forces of racism and intolerance. We've got laws against discrimination, we've got anti-hate laws, we've got civil rights laws, we've got anti-racism education in our schools. And it's frowned upon socially to use racist language or target people because of their race or religion. So, what's going on? Could it simply be frustration because of Covid, frustration that brings out the worst in people? Or could it be something deeper, an undercurrent of racism in American society that has not really gone away?

"Well, what can be done about it?" says Mary, breaking into Michael's thoughts. "We don't want to see Si-Woo so upset. She doesn't deserve this. She shouldn't have to feel afraid in the mall. No one should. And besides this, Si-Woo has a heart condition. An assault could set off a heart attack."

"Tell you what," says Michael. "I think you'd agree, we don't want to cause undue alarm in the mall. Nothing has actually happened. But I'll talk to security and put the word out. We'll have the guards pay Si-Woo special attention and watch her movements in the mall. We obviously can't do anything when she goes home at night, but in the mall, we'll keep an eye on her, at least for a certain period of time."

"Good idea, chief," says Richard, looking relieved.

"I think you said you have another issue?"

"Yes," says Mary, "it's troubling and I don't think you'll be happy about it."

"What is it?"

"There's been a second note. We saw it earlier this morning on the bulletin board, just like before. Couldn't believe it. We took it down and decided to bring it to you. Have a look yourself. And again, please don't mention who gave it to you."

Michael reads the note. His jaw drops and his face turns white. "I can't believe this," he says to himself. *I thought we were past all this. Nothing has happened since last summer, since the first note was put up. So, what's going on? Why is this happening again? And why the repetition? A march, then a note, then the Barkers coming to see me about the note. Groundhog Day or what!* Michael's recalls seeing the old man with the mask jammed into his mouth. Why did he look so horrified? Who did this to him?

"Michael," says Richard, breaking into his train of thought, "you'll notice the handwriting is different—so it might be a different person. Plus, the threat is more forceful. It says I *will* throw—not I may throw—acid into your face, as it did last time. What do you make of this?"

Michael takes a deep breath and thinks about it for a moment. "Uh, yeah, I see what you mean. I'm not sure what to make of it. And I'm not sure how to respond to the note. I'm going to have to give it some thought."

"Michael," says Mary, "you can't pussyfoot around on this. You ignored the first note and maybe you were just lucky. Nothing happened. But this time, as Richard says, the threat is more menacing, more powerful, more serious."

"I get what you're saying, Mary. But there's no need to rush a decision. The guy who wrote the first note ultimately didn't follow through. Maybe it was just a bluff. It's possible, it's possible," he emphasizes, "it'll be the same thing this time. Don't get me wrong, this is serious business, I'm obviously concerned. But I want some time to think about it. I'm first going to check with my head of security. Just hold on a second."

Michael sends Wally Waller a text, asking if he's got time to drop by. Almost immediately, Wally texts back, saying he just got back from his medical appointment downtown. He'd come by in twenty minutes or so.

"Okay," says Michael, looking down at his phone, "I just got word from Wally, my security chief. He's going to come by shortly. So, I'll get back to you on this in a couple days. And oh, while you're here, can I ask you a quick question?"

"Yeah, okay," Mary responds. "What's on your mind, chief?"

"I'm asking people around the mall what they think about the vaccine rollout plan. What do you think? Should our pharmacy in the mall be given permission to distribute the vaccines?"

"I say yes, definitely yes," Mary replies quickly. "I trust the health professionals. They say vaccines are necessary to fight the virus. Who am I to quarrel? The faster we get the vaccines out the better, and the more people we get vaccinated the better. Marv and his looney followers obviously disagree, but they're anti-science cretins. Wolfville Mall is the center of our community. It doesn't take a genius to know that vaccines should be given out to where the people are, not somewhere else. The logical spot to do this, at least in our community, is the mall pharmacy. I think most folks around here would agree."

"Well, I certainly agree," adds Richard. "We need to get to herd immunity as fast as we can. To do this, we need vaccines, and we need as many access points to vaccines as possible. As Mary says, the mall is where people around here come. There's plenty of parking and buses."

"Okay, thanks for your thoughts."

The Barkers leave Michael's office. As they walk back into the mall, they talk about Michael's response to the note. They are puzzled by his comments and about his hesitation to take quick action. They both wonder if he realizes just how serious the threat really is. Danger is looming but Michael seems to be waffling on what to do. Why can't he be more decisive? Does he know something we don't? Then, Richard asks a question that startles Mary. "Does Michael know who wrote the note and is he trying to protect this person?"

30

Wally arrives at Michael's office door soon after the Barkers leave.

"Come in Wally, have a seat."

"What's goin' on, man?"

"Wally, I've got two things to talk to you about. But do you mind if I have my sandwich while we're talking? Want anything? I have another sandwich. Cheddar cheese and pickles."

"Naw, I'm okay, bro, I had something earlier."

"First is about Si-Woo, the Korean woman who works at the bakery. She thinks she is being followed and could be attacked. With all the anti-Asian feelings around here, I don't doubt it could happen. So can you alert the staff to watch out for her? Give her special attention for a few weeks. When she's doing her walks in the mall, check her on the monitors. Apart from anything else, if something were to happen to her, it would be bad publicity for the mall."

"Okay, boss, no worries, I'll tell the staff."

Michael wonders how sincere Wally is. If he really is a member of a white power group, he won't be that eager to protect Si-Woo. He won't make much of an effort. *I'll have to check up on him later, make sure he's following through.*

"The second thing, Wally—and you're not going to believe it—there's been a second note. Just like the first one, it was pinned up on the bulletin board. Have a look."

Wally reads it and grimaces. "My God, dude, this guy is really a weird piece of work. He keeps at it. And he seems more determined this time. I *will* throw sulfuric acid, not I *may* do it."

"The writer could be a female. We just don't know. But take a look at the handwriting, it's different."

"Yeah, you're right, it's slanted to the left. Wonder why that is. But the paper, if you look at the paper, it's the same, it's dirty and stained, and the handwriting, it's still sloppy. My guess is whether it's one or two people, guy or gal, we've got a sick homeless idiot, or idiots, on our hands, either playing games or going off the deep end. My advice, like before, is that we simply ignore this sicko. It worked last time. Nothing happened. It'll work again this time."

"I'm not so sure, Wally."

"Well, boss, if you decide to respond, if you alert the public and the police, there'll be the same risk as with the first note. It'll be bad for the mall, bad for business. You know as well as me, over the last few months, business in the mall has been improving. Why risk going backward?"

"You make a good point. Tell you what. Let's sleep on it. Can you drop by my office tomorrow, say around lunch? We'll talk through it some more."

"Sure thing, man. See ya tomorrow."

As Wally leaves, Michael is puzzled about why his security chief is so adamant about ignoring the note. He did this with the first note as well. If he really is on the side of the anti-vaxxers and anti-maskers, wouldn't he want the message in the notes to be widely known to the public? Wouldn't he want shoppers to be scared of getting vaccines and wearing masks? Why should he care if the business in the mall suffers from the publicity? His own job is secure. It just doesn't add up.

But if Wally's responsible, maybe he didn't anticipate the Barkers would take the notes down and keep them out of public view. Then, once he was confronted with the notes, once he saw them, fearing an investigation, he figured it was best to urge they be ignored.

Michael's office phone rings. He picks it up.

"Why didn't you make more of an effort?" A woman is on the line.

"I'm sorry, I don't understand. Who is this?"

"I'm Lisa Sommers. I'm calling from Astoria." Michael assumes she means the small city at the north-west tip of Oregon, not in New York. "My brother, Jason Sommers, was strangled in your washroom last June."

"My condolences, Lisa. I'm deeply sorry about what happened to your brother."

"Look, you're the manager of the mall. Why didn't you make more of an effort to find out what happened to my brother? I've been phoning around, checking with people, with the police, your security guards, the manager of your bookstore, workers in the mall. You did nothing. There was no publicity about it, just a little story in the back pages of your local newspaper. You could have done more. You could have talked to the media, you could have put up notices in the mall, you could have made people more aware, you could have tried to help the police more. But you didn't. You kept it all quiet. Now, the police have stopped their investigation. It's a cold case. My poor brother, there's no justice for my poor brother!"

"But I tried—" says Michael.

"Tried? You did nothing. How can you live with yourself!" Lisa ends the call.

Michael shakes his head. "No, no, no," he says to himself. *She's upset, and it's understandable. She needs somebody to blame. But how can she blame me? It's totally unfair. What more could I have possibly done?*

31

That evening, Michael and Cornelia are having their usual pre-dinner wine in the family room. The girls are upstairs on the computer, playing a new game.

"Good wine," says Michael. "What are we drinking this time, princess?" His mind isn't on the wine. He keeps thinking about the phone call. *I'm sorry about what happened to her brother, I really am. But I'm not to be blamed. I did what I could, I did what any reasonable mall manager would do.*

"It's Pino Grigio from Italy. The Lombardy region. I picked up a couple bottles after my yoga session today. I agree, sweetie, it's good. We haven't had it for quite a while. It's got that nice spritzy sensation and the flavors of lime and white nectarine. It's acidy and it's alive."

"It's wonderful, princess." How can it be alive, Michael wonders. "Anything new with you? Your yoga session go okay?"

"Yes, it went well. We were over at Alexandra's place again. Afterward, and after I went to the wine store, I checked out a new house that maybe we could move to. It's in Blue Mountain Heights. Lovely house, great view. I know we can't get too serious about a new house yet, until your promotion gets finalized, but I'm just checking things out, getting a sense of what's on the market."

Michael wonders about the cost. But then again, he tells himself, it's probably harmless. Cornelia needs a distraction. "Okay, I suppose it makes sense."

"So, what's new with you, sweetie? Any progress on the vaccines front?"

"I met with a member of the board of directors early this morning. I wanted to know the board's view on whether or not the mall should let our pharmacy distribute the vaccines. She told me—just like with the masks—the decision is mine to make. The board trusts me to make the right call."

"Is this good or not?" asks Cornelia, sipping some more of the white.

"Nice to be trusted, that's for sure. But it does put a lot of weight on my shoulders. It makes a lot of sense to give our pharmacy the green light. But it could be divisive. You saw the support Marv has. If there's a lot of controversy, if Marv is able to grow his support, the mall could lose some business, at least in the short term. And I could get blamed."

"You don't want to get blamed. You've been making a lot of progress recently. Business has picked up, and the mall will get busier as we get closer to the holidays, but, Michael, you can't take your eye off the ball. You can't take a chance on losing business. That would be horrible for us."

Michael looks upward. He hears laughter and the girls giggling up in their room. Must be a great game, he thinks. I wish I were their age. But again he thinks of the phone call. It keeps coming back.

"Yeah, it would be horrible," he says, drinking some more wine. "That's why I feel this weight on my shoulders. I've got to figure out the right thing to do."

"You do, Michael, you absolutely do. I've already told my yoga friends that you are a rising star in the corporation, that you're going to get a huge promotion, that we're going to be moving into a big new house in Blue Mountain Heights. They were impressed, even

Alexandra. If it falls apart, I'm going to be crushed. And Daddy's going to be so disappointed."

Michael cringes. Why can't she just cool it? Why can't she be more moderate in her expectations? But he remembers what Cornelia told him if he wasn't successful—that she'd leave him and take the girls to Georgia. He's got to be cautious in what he says. "It's not going to fall apart, Cornelia. I just have to be careful, that's all. I'm going to consult with people first, as I did with the masking issue. I'll talk to some shoppers, then Grumpy Bill and Dr. Cortez. Hopefully, there'll be a consensus on what to do. If there is, it'll make my job a lot easier."

Cornelia pouts. "Well, let's hope so, Michael, let's hope so. We obviously need the money, you need to get your promotion, and you need to be popular in the corporation, seen as a winner. As I told you before, it won't be long before we'll need to look for new furniture and for a private school for the girls."

"I have another problem."

"Another problem! Well, what is it?" Cornelia snaps. "You always seem to have problems. Problems, problems."

"A second note appeared on the bulletin board this morning. I haven't shown it to anybody, only Wally, my security guy."

Cornelia throws her arms in the air. "So, what did it say?"

"About the same as in the first note. It's a threat of an acid attack. Except this time, it's about vaccines, and the writer says he or she *will*—not just *may*, but *will*—throw sulfuric acid into somebody's face if the mall okays the pharmacy giving out the vaccines."

"So, what are you going to do?"

Michael lists his three options. First, he could alert the public, through notices in the mall, posts on the mall's website, and announcements over the PA system. Second, he could notify the police, which probably would mean the public would find out. Or third, he could ignore the threat, assuming it'll come to nothing. He adds that Wally supports the third option since the writer is probably someone playing games, and if word leaks out to the public, business in the mall will suffer.

"Wally makes a lot of sense," says Cornelia. "You need to do what's best for the mall—keeping the shoppers happy, keeping them buying at your stores. You obviously don't want this pattern to be disturbed in any way. After all, you want your promotion, and you want your bosses to be happy with you. Isn't this a no-brainer?"

"But one question I keep asking myself, Cornelia. What if an acid attack actually happens and I have done nothing? What would I say to the police? What would I say to the public?"

Cornelia raises her arms and pulls at her hair in frustration. "It's ridiculous, Michael, to even ask this question. You've got nothing to worry about. Think about it for a second. You've got all these strange people in your mall—the demented street people, the weird anti-vaxxers and anti-maskers, who say bizarre things all the time. So, it makes perfect sense, it seems to me, that you, as the mall manager, would think the note was written by one of these loonies. And it makes perfect sense for you to ignore the note. Who could possibly blame you?"

"I suppose you're right, Cornelia."

"Of course I'm right! I'll run it by Daddy. See what he thinks."

"Yeah, okay," says Michael, finishing his wine. "Makes sense. I'm hungry—I'll get the girls."

Heading upstairs, Michael hears the voice of his dad in his ear. "Do what is right even if it's not what's best for your career." But what does it mean, Michael wonders, to do what is right. Does it mean to err on the side of caution and alert the public? Jeopardize his career and risk his relationship with Cornelia? Should he really take a chance of having his family broken apart and his daughters living thousands of miles away? Would his dad really want him to do that?

That night, Michael has another dream about gorillas. Two of them are chasing him around with bullhorns. It is happening inside a hospital, full of Covid patients. One gorilla shouts, *Do what is prudent, do what's best for yourself and your family.* The other one yells back, *Follow your better angels, do what's right for your community.* His daughters are on hospital beds. Dr. Cortez is looking inside their mouths. He pulls a blue surgical mask from each girl's mouth.

32

The next morning, Michael decides to get a sample of opinions about the vaccines issue. He arranges for a kiosk to be set up in front of the customer relations office, and for a banner on it with the words, "Give Your Opinion About Vaccines in the Mall." He gets himself some coffee and stands in front of the kiosk with a clipboard.

As he sips his espresso macchiato, he sees two older women coming toward him, indicating they want to talk. He introduces himself and asks them what they think: should the mall give the pharmacy permission to distribute the Covid vaccines?

"I think my sister will agree with me," says one. "We don't approve of the vaccines at all. So, we don't approve of the pharmacy having anything to do with the devilish things."

Michael looks puzzled. "Why's that?"

"We agree with the leader of the protest, the one with the black cowboy hat. The vaccine, as he said, was created too fast and we don't really know the side effects. But more important for us as Christians, God does not approve of the vaccines. God is the one who knows best. He created us, He gave us natural immunities. If you end up getting Covid, it's because you don't have enough faith in God, you don't live a holy life. You need to trust in God, not in unholy medical interventions."

"I also heard, from our pastor," adds the other sister, "that the vaccine is a sign of the beast. It signifies an alliance with Satan and a rebellion against God."

"Really?" says Michael, sipping some more of his coffee.

"Yes. It's all in the Book of Revelation. And one other thing our pastor told us. The vaccines come from the cells of aborted children. How evil is this! This is the work of Satan. No way can we support this wickedness."

"Appreciate your comments on this, ladies. Have yourself a great day." Michael rolls his eyes as they walk away. But he reminds himself he's here not to judge, only to record people's views. He has to keep an open mind.

A young couple and a little girl, presumably their daughter, come over to him. He poses the same question.

"My wife and I have talked it over and we're both in agreement," says the man. "We're glad the vaccines are coming. We realize because we're younger, we'll have to wait a few months to get our shots. But we're happy to know they're coming. We really don't know what the fuss is about. The vaccine's been tested, it's based on science, everybody should be happy it's going to be available. How else are we going to get past this virus?"

"And for us," adds his wife, "the pharmacy is the perfect place to get the vaccine. We live fairly close to here, we go to this pharmacy all the time. It's convenient for us and I think it's convenient for a lot of people."

"Okay," says Michael, "many thanks for your thoughts."

Next are two middle-aged men. "I'm opposed to the vaccines," says one, "which means I'm opposed to them being in the pharmacy. I've done research about them online. I found out there's all kinds of problems and side effects. They can cause asthma, allergies, and even cancer. They can make women infertile, they can make men sterile, and they can cause children to have autism. So, why in the hell should we allow them at all? That doesn't make sense. For God's sake, man, you need to keep them out of our pharmacy and out of Wolfville!"

"To make matters worse," says the other one, "I've heard that the companies have put some kind of chip—I think it's called a magnetic tracking chip, something like that—anyway, they've put this damn thing into each vaccine, to keep track of people, to have control over them. It's all part of mind control, part of a government plot to make America into a police state. At least that's what I've been told."

"Uh, I see," replies Michael, his jaw dropping. "I thank both of you for your comments. Very interesting. Well now, you have yourself a nice day."

Michael looks at his watch. Lunch time. Time to go back to his office and meet with Wally. After he gets a staff member from customer relations to take over his post, he goes up to the food court, picks up some sushi rolls, and rushes back to his office. Along the way, he almost gets hit by Power Walker, who—not surprisingly—is dashing through a group of shoppers and giving them a scare.

"Come in, Wally, have a chair. I'm having some sushi for lunch. Want a roll?"

"No thanks, I hate that shit. I'll grab some chicken wings and fries later on."

"So, did you do any more thinking about the note?"

"Ya, I did. The more I think about it, bro, the more convinced I am it's from a drunk street guy, or maybe two of them in cahoots. I'd say it's either gibberish or the words of a wackadoodle. Nothing's gonna come out of it. Best to ignore it."

"I've also been thinking about it some more," replies Michael, finishing off a piece of a spicy tuna roll. "I agree it could be an unhoused person. But it could also be an anti-vaxxer, maybe one of Marv's followers. It's quite possible Marv hired or motivated someone to write the note, in order to influence people, turn them against the vaccines."

"C'mon, man, no way. Definitely not. Marv wouldn't do that. I'm sure it's a bluff or a scare tactic coming from some looney. Nothing will actually happen. Best to forget about it."

Michael remembers his earlier speculation that Wally is behind the notes. "Wally," he says, "I'm not entirely convinced, but it's possible you're right. So, at least for now, I'm not going to do anything. But to be on the safe side, I want you to alert the security staff, tell them to monitor the mall for any strange people or strange behavior, and also remind them to watch out for Si-Woo. And I want you to call your company and get some extra security guards hired for this month and maybe beyond. Enough to have another guard for each shift. We really need to be on top of this."

"Gotcha." Wally looks pleased. That's not a surprise. Not only has Michael agreed with him but he has also asked for more guards. More guards mean a higher profile role for him in the mall and pay increase too.

Michael coughs, then thinks of something else. "And make sure there are always staff in the monitoring room to check the cameras in real time. We want to be able to deal with some threat or problem immediately, not just look at video after the fact."

"Will do."

"Oh, and one other thing, Wally. Get the staff to check the video on the morning the note was posted, December 11. See who was around. And give special attention to the footage from the camera above the bulletin board. It's fixed now, right?"

"Ah, well, no, I'm afraid it's not," says Wally, looking embarrassed and turning red. "A technician was supposed to come in last summer and check out that camera, plus a few other ones, but he just didn't show up. I phoned again and the same thing happened—he didn't show up. Then, after the mask mandate was announced and things quietened down, I forgot all about it. But I'll get on it now. And I'll get the staff to check out the video from the other cameras."

Michael's about to lambaste Wally, but he remembers Wally's connections at Pacific Gold and restrains himself. "Jeez, Wally, this should have been done a long time ago. Make sure you get it all checked out as fast as possible. And if there's any problem or any delay with the company you're dealing with, get a technician in from a different company. Let me know if that's a contract problem."

"Got it. See ya later, bro."

Wally leaves, and Michael finishes his last California roll. He wonders why that camera has not been checked. Months have gone by, many months, and still that camera, plus the other ones, have not been looked at. It doesn't make sense that months would go by and multiple cameras aren't repaired, that a technician just didn't show up, and that Wally just forgot.

33

Early the next morning, Wally leaves his office and heads for an entrance to the mall on the east side. A security guard in the monitoring room had reported to him earlier that a camera showed a homeless man sleeping near the door. Wally wants to check this out for himself.

He wishes Michael would listen to him. If the mall had a tougher policy on street people, there'd be fewer of them and there'd be more shoppers in the mall. This would help the mall, it would help with security, and it would benefit Michael. Why doesn't Michael get it? In any case, he appreciates that Michael is beefing up security. We need more staff. Hopefully, we can keep the extra staff after the end of the year.

Wally passes by the bakery, noticing an amazing aroma in the air. Cinnamon, maybe? Si-Woo is busy putting fresh bakery items out on the shelves. Wally wonders if she still feels she's being followed. He doesn't bother stopping to chat with her. Surely to God she feels safer now. As Michael requested, he had alerted the security staff about her situation. She's been getting the special treatment Michael had asked for. She shouldn't be whining anymore.

Wally approaches the door and sees an elderly black man napping on a bench, probably homeless, snoring loudly. The man is scruffy and wearing ragged clothes. He has no face covering on and is reeking of alcohol. The smell permeates the air.

Wally looks around and sees there's nobody in the area. But soon there'll be workers and shoppers coming in through the door. He has to act quickly and get the old man out of the mall.

"Hey man," says Wally, "it's time for you to wake up and leave the mall. This is no place for the likes of you. You shouldn't be sleeping here." The man doesn't budge. Wally taps on the man's shoulder. He still doesn't move.

"Hey, wake up, you moron," says Wally. Wally shakes him on his shoulders. "Wake up, dummy," he shouts.

The man slowly sits up. "Where am I?" he says.

"You're in Wolfville Mall, dingleberry. People like you aren't supposed to be sleeping here. Respectable people are gonna be coming in. Time for you to hit the road."

The man gets defensive. "Are you saying I'm not respectable?"

"That's exactly what I'm saying. Now get the hell out and never come back." Wally grabs the old man by the arm.

"Who do you think you are," the man says, resisting. "You're a wannabe pig. You're not a real pig, you're just a wannabe pig."

Wally is fuming. He asks the man to please stand up. As the man gets up, Wally punches him hard in the stomach. The man doubles over, screaming in pain and peeing in his pants.

Si-Woo comes around the corner in time to see Wally hit the man. She'd seen the old man earlier and was bringing muffins for him.

"What are you doing?" she yells at Wally. "Who do you think you are? You can't treat people this way. Didn't anybody tell you, didn't your parents tell you, you need to treat people—*all* people—with respect, even people who are down on their luck."

"Look," Wally says, "you didn't see it, but this moron pushed me, spit on me, called me names. I was only trying to defend myself. He wasn't—and isn't—even wearing a bloody mask."

"You don't need to be so violent and harsh. Why didn't you get backup from the other security staff and ask the man—politely—to leave? If necessary, you could have escorted him out, but have done it gently and respectfully. You didn't need to be so cruel."

"We're done here," says Wally. "I don't have to listen to any more of your bleeding-heart shit. I need to get back to work."

Wally grabs hold of the man, takes him to the door, and pushes him out. Si-Woo walks the other way. This Wally, she thinks, is a dangerous man.

34

Si-Woo wonders if she should report Wally's behavior to Michael. It certainly is not something she wants to do. No way she wants to get anybody into trouble, even Wally. It could get him fired. But she did see Wally punch the man and she knows the rumors about Wally being a goon and a racist. He might do it again. She decides she should report it to Michael and get it on the record. Michael can decide what to do.

As she limps around a corner on her way to Michael's office, there's an intense pain on her side. She yells out. Power Walker has just slammed his sharp elbow into her. He swings around, comes back, and apologizes profusely, saying he was trying to pick up speed because he was so behind in his exercise schedule.

"Thanks, but can I make a suggestion to you?"

Power Walker nods.

"When you're rushing around and slamming into people, hurting people, and doing it over and over, you're creating bad karma for yourself. Bad things are more likely to happen to you. But if you can slow it down, be more considerate of people, be helpful to people, you'll get rewarded. You'll create good karma for yourself, and good things are more likely to happen to you. Can you think about this?"

Power Walker gives Si-Woo a big warm smile. "Thanks for caring. I'll do my best." He walks away, perhaps a fraction slower.

Si-Woo continues on to Michael's office.

"Come on in, Si-Woo," says Michael. "Have a seat."

"Thanks," she replies. She sits, still feeling the sting from Power Walker's elbow.

"Nice to see you. I heard from the Barkers about you being stalked and also your fear of having a heart attack. Sorry to hear about this. I hope you're doing okay now."

"Yeah, I'm doing okay, I guess. I did see Dr. Cortez yesterday about my heart condition. He checked me out and said things looked fine. But to be on the safe side, he'd make an appointment for me to see a cardiologist at the hospital."

"Good to get things checked out. Listen, Si-Woo, I want to let you know that we've beefed up security. We're getting in more security guards for the mall and we're doing more monitoring of the halls and entrances. You should feel safer. I know there's a lot of dangerous people out there. We want you—and everybody in the mall—to feel protected from any danger."

Si-Woo thanks Michael, then tells of her reason for seeing Michael. Michael says he'll need to talk to Wally and get his side of the story.

"He can't dispute what happened," says Si-Woo. "It's on video. There's a security camera above the entrance door."

Michael promises to investigate. As Si-Woo gets up to leave, Michael remembers something he was wondering about. "Si-Woo, can I ask you something?"

"Sure."

"I see you at the lottery kiosk quite a bit. You buy a lot of tickets. So, what are you going to do with the money if you win it big? It's obviously none of my business, but I was just curious."

Si-Woo sits back down and collects her thoughts. "I don't mind telling you, chief, I've been thinking about it myself. The Barkers asked me the same question a few months back. Well, first, I'd keep something for myself. I'm no Mother Teresa, I wouldn't give it all to the poor. I'd get a new TV set, maybe some new clothes, maybe some new furniture. But after that, I wouldn't get into any big spending on myself. I don't fancy a new car or a trip around the world. I don't have any family here, so there are no relatives to give the money to. The one thing I'd like to do, though, is to help the unhoused people around here. They really need help."

"How would you help them?"

"Well, there's no shelter around here for them to go to at night. That's why some of them come into the mall, to get warm and dry. I know a shelter's not the full answer to their problems. Some of them wouldn't use it anyway. But some of them would. And if there is a shelter, they could get warm and they could get some food and support. So that's what I would do with the money. Help to build a new homeless shelter."

"It would be useful, that's for sure. And it would help me out a lot. Fewer of them would be coming into the mall, scaring away our shoppers." Michael and Si-Woo both smile at Michael's attempt at humor. Michael is impressed with Si-Woo's way of thinking. Cornelia certainly wouldn't think this way. Neither would most people.

"I've got to go now," says Si-Woo. "Got to get back to the bakery. Bye for now."

Si-Woo is right, Michael thinks. Wally does seem to be on a short fuse, and he could do it again. He'll talk to Wally and get his side of the story, but then what? Should he just give Wally a stern warning? Or should he also put the incident on Wally's record? But if he does this, it could be bad for his own career. Wally has connections to the board of directors. A board member could retaliate against him and try to block his promotion. And if this happened, how would Cornelia react? She wouldn't be happy.

Michael's thoughts are interrupted by a beep on his phone. He looks and sees it's an email from Cornelia.

Hi Sweetie. I just got off the phone with Daddy. I told him about the second note. He was really surprised. He says you should do the same thing as before. Ignore it. Nothing is going to happen. But to protect yourself, write it all down, date it, and sign it. Memo to file. Explain why you chose not to respond. Emphasize the fact there are so many odd and weird people in the mall. Luv, Cornelia.

How incredibly patronizing! How did his father-in-law ever get to be so arrogant and presumptuous? To keep peace in the family, Michael reminds himself he has to be patient and respectful of the pompous old ass. But he's tempted to tell Cornelia and her father that he's one step ahead of them. He's already done what his father-in-law advised.

35

Joe Talkback: Good morning Wolfville! Welcome to Talkback, the most popular morning radio chat in the city. I'm your host, Joe Talkback. For today's first call, we are talking about the Covid vaccine. Safe? Or harmful? I'm here with Dr. Juan Cortez. He's a very highly regarded doctor in the city and has a practice at Wolfville Mall. He's also a prominent champion of public health. We all know what the message is from the public health types, so I'm going to put him on the spot, and then it's your turn. But let's keep it respectful. Welcome, Doctor.

Dr. Cortez: Good morning. Glad to be here.

Joe Talkback: Doctor, are you planning to get the Covid vaccine yourself?

Dr. Cortez: Absolutely. As soon as it's available and it's my turn, I will go and get it. In fact, I look forward to getting it. As a health care worker, I deal with people who are ill or at risk all the time. With the vaccine, I can better protect myself and I can better protect others.

Joe Talkback: But from what we hear about the vaccine, you must feel anxious about it. Give us your honest opinion: do you feel hesitant about getting the vaccine, even just a little tiny bit?

Dr. Cortez: Not in the least. I have no hesitation whatsoever. I've been vaccinated as a child for measles, mumps, chickenpox, and so forth. Since becoming a doctor, I get vaccinated for the flu every year. I'm used to it. I don't think twice about it. It's part of life, it's part of keeping healthy.

Joe Talkback: But Doctor, with this particular vaccine, with this Covid vaccine, don't you think it's been developed too quickly, much too quickly, therefore, making it suspect? From what I hear, the politicians were desperate to get it out and Big Pharma fast-tracked it. What do you say to that?

Dr. Cortez: You raise an interesting question. It may appear this vaccine has been developed quickly. But we need to keep in mind that research into how to respond to a modern pandemic has been going on long before Covid-19. Researchers have been looking at data from previous coronaviruses for a long time now, since MERS in 2012 and SARS in 2002. So, the creation of the Covid vaccine has not been all of a sudden. Researchers have been building on past developments for many years.

Joe Talkback: Okay, that sounds complicated. Let's keep it simple. These vaccines can make you really sick, can't they? Isn't it true they can kill you?

Dr. Cortez: Let me make two points. Number one, the vast majority of people have no problems. Some people may experience mild side effects such as soreness in the arm or low-grade fever. But these effects dissipate quickly. Number two, the gelatin and egg proteins in the vaccines can cause allergic reactions, but only in very rare cases. If you have this kind of allergy, just tell your doctor and precautions will be taken.

Joe Talkback: So, let's talk about the rollout. The plan is to get the vaccines out through a combination of pharmacies and places like conference centers and sports arenas. But the government hasn't decided if this applies to pharmacies inside malls and larger stores. You're at Wolfville Mall. Should the mall allow the pharmacy there to distribute the vaccines?

Dr. Cortez: Yes. We have to get the vaccines out quickly, to a lot of people. That will save lives. Pharmacies are ideal for getting vaccines out, and the more, the better, including ones in malls. People go to pharmacies for their medications and other medical needs, and usually the closest one. They trust the people there. So yes, all pharmacies should have the vaccine, including the one that serves a lot of my patients at Wolfville Mall.

Joe Talkback: One final question from me, Doctor. You are very passionate about this issue. How come? Why not be content just to make the big bucks? Why not sit back and relax? Take life easy.

Dr. Cortez: You are quite right, I am passionate about prevention, which is what vaccines are all about. Many years ago, my wife died from pneumonia. She could have done more, and I could have done more, to prevent this from happening. Had she had a vaccination early on, a pneumococcal vaccination, it wouldn't have happened. I learned the importance of prevention the hard way. It's true, I'm very passionate about prevention, and I'm very passionate about vaccines.

Joe Talkback: Okay, let's open up the lines. Caller number one, what's your question?

Caller 1: Doctor, I did some research myself on these vaccines. I read on the internet that they inject microchips into them and they use these microchips, through cell phone towers, to track people, control them, and turn them into robots. It's part of a government plot. Do you think there's any truth to this?

Dr. Cortez: There's no truth to it at all. Not only is this false, but it is also technically impossible. If you've ever seen the tracking chip that veterinarians put in pets, you'd know those things are easily big enough to see. And even those only work with a scanner close to them.

This story about chips in the vaccine is a conspiracy theory that unfortunately—very unfortunately—is widely available on the internet. It's rejected by virtually all scientists and medical researchers. I suggest it's wise to be suspicious of anything you read on the internet.

Joe Talkback: Thanks for your interesting question, caller. Caller number 2, what's your question?

Caller 2: Doctor, how did you get your medical license anyway? I think you are a moron. I think you are a complete—

Joe Talkback: Stop. No need to be rude, dude. We've got to be civil here. Now what's your question, caller?

Caller 2: Damn it, I don't think we need these blasted vaccines at all. Best to leave it to nature. When people get infected with something, they develop natural immunity to fight the infection. Why shouldn't we just allow natural immunity to deal with the problem?

Dr. Cortez: Your question is a good one, sir. It is true, when we get infected with a virus like Covid-19, we develop natural immunity or antibodies to counteract the virus. These antibodies are helpful, up to a point. But they weaken in their effectiveness over time, and they are less helpful in people with underlying conditions. The vaccine helps strengthen natural immunity, so even if people get sick, they don't get as sick, or for as long, and that means they won't spread Covid to others as much. The vaccine helps people who take it, and others too. Also, based on past experience, natural immunity is not great at dealing with new variants of the virus, which are sure to come. This is why we also need a broad vaccine-induced immunity. Research has shown that the new Covid vaccines provide us with much better protection than we would have if we relied only on natural immunity. But thank you for your question, it is an important one.

Joe Talkback: Yes, it's an important question. I'm afraid that's all the time we have for this segment. After the break, we're talking Christmas trees—artificial or real? Thank you, Dr. Cortez, for dropping by, we appreciate your time and your thoughts about vaccines.

36

Michael closes the radio app on his phone. He'd come in early to ensure he'd have some quiet time in his office to catch the interview, and thinks it went well. It won't convince the hard-core anti-vaxxers, but it might persuade some of the undecided. The doctor's calm and authoritative voice, and his handling of those questions at the end, were nicely done.

He sends a text, letting the doctor know he is dropping by in an hour. That should give Dr. Cortez enough time to get back to his clinic. He looks forward to congratulating the doctor on the interview. The doctor would probably appreciate positive feedback. Dr. Cortez sends back a happy face emoji. Michael turns his attention to some work orders and salary approvals needing signatures.

When Michael heads to the clinic, he sees Si-Woo at the Salvation Army stand, ringing the bell and collecting donations. He gives her a big smile and drops a ten-dollar bill into her box. Playing in the background is *Jingle Bell Rock*. It's nearing lunch time and the mall is getting busier.

Michael is sitting in the clinic's waiting room for nearly fifteen minutes when Dr. Cortez arrives, out of breath and looking troubled. The doctor motions Michael into his office.

"What's wrong?" asks Michael.

"I'm not sure, but I think somebody was following me. Just after I came into the mall, I could feel someone behind me. I looked around and I saw a person in a hoodie, maybe black or dark blue. With really mean eyes. Don't know who it was. The lighting wasn't good, and the person was wearing a mask. Anyway, after a few seconds, he or she just disappeared into the crowd."

"Must have been scary."

"It was, Michael, it really was. But I suppose it's not surprising. As you know, I've made some enemies around here, from what I say about vaccines."

Michael nods his head in sympathy. "Well, we can check out the cameras, see if we can identify the person, report it to the police."

"You know, chief, as I think about it, don't bother. I'm just letting you know, for the record. There're so many people in hoodies, and nothing actually happened. It might have been something innocent. Maybe I'm just being paranoid. But if it happens again, I'll get in touch, maybe we can take further action."

"Okay, Dr. Cortez. We can leave it at that for now. I'll make a note of the incident and put it in a file. I just came by to congratulate you on the interview. I thought you did a terrific job, and I'm sure you convinced a lot of people. And you were very diplomatic, especially with those callers at the end. I couldn't believe their questions."

"Thanks for saying so, Michael. Sorry, but I got back late and I've got a patient coming by shortly, so maybe we can talk later?"

"Okay. Bye for now."

Michael heads back to his office, feeling uneasy. The note, the strangling of the old man last summer and the call from his sister, Si-Woo being followed, and now somebody could be after the doctor. Maybe he should let Dr. Cortez know about the note. That way, the doctor would be more on guard, and in a better position to defend himself. But on the other hand, maybe he shouldn't say anything. The more that people are told about the note, the more likely word's going to get out, spelling bad publicity for the mall and a loss of business. Besides, the doctor said he wasn't sure he was being followed. So, it's probably best to let it go.

37

The next morning, Michael is sitting in his office drinking coffee and waiting for Wally. He shuffles papers on his desk and flips through notes. He's not looking forward to the discussion, knowing he has to be very careful in what he says to Wally.

He hears a familiar knock. "Come on in, Wally. Want some coffee?"

"Yeah, man, I really need it. I'm still groggy from last night's party. It was a wild one." Wally takes a seat.

Michael clears his throat as he hands his security chief a cup of coffee. "Wally, I've got a couple things to discuss."

"I'm listening, bro."

"First, I understand you punched an elderly black man the other day. The day before yesterday, first thing that morning."

"Who said that?"

"Sorry, I can't tell you."

"C'mon, man, I've got a right to know my accuser. And, don't worry, I won't retaliate. I promise."

Michael wants to protect Si-Woo, but there'll be footage of the incident. A security guard may have already seen it. He might as well tell Wally now.

"Okay. It was Si-Woo."

"Asian bitch! She's really got it in for me."

Michael is taken aback. "Jeez, Wally, watch your language. We need to be professional around here. Si-Woo reported it to me because she thought it should be on the record. She didn't want to do it, but she thought she should."

Wally is wild. He jumps up, paces, and looks like he wants to punch somebody. "I'll bet! No way she didn't want to do it. No bloody way. She probably couldn't wait."

"Look Wally, you can't deny it happened, or at least that something happened. It'll be on video. There's a camera above the entrance."

Wally calms down, realizing he can't deny it. "Okay, but listen to me, Michael. The old-timer was being an ass. He resisted me asking him to leave the mall, he swore at me, spit at me, called me names. Maybe I overreacted a bit, but he deserved it."

Michael stares at Wally in disbelief. "Come on, Wally, you shouldn't have done this. You went against our rules about how to handle unhoused people. Maybe you were provoked, but you're supposed to show restraint. Plus, we have the fact you hit an African American man. There could be legal repercussions. We don't want to have the NAACP coming in to see us."

"Look, man, if I get rough, or rather, if I overreact a bit, I do it with everybody, equally. You know what the problem is? Street people coming into our mall with their dirty smelly clothes, scaring away the shoppers. These people could be black or white or brown, Catholic or Muslim, it's all the same to me. I kick the assholes out."

Michael pauses for a moment. "Wally, I'm going to give you a break. I'm not going to put this on your employment record. But I'm going to make some notes about what you said and what Si-Woo said, and I'll put it in a file, just in case the matter comes up later. I have to give you a warning though. Next time there's an incident like this, take a deep breath and show restraint. You are the head of security, other security guards follow your lead. It's important the rules get observed."

"Gotcha."

"Good. There's one other thing—"

There's screaming coming from the mall. Michael and Wally run out of the office. Michael wonders if it's the threatened acid attack.

In the mall, near the offices, a woman in a blue ski jacket is shrieking at another woman. The other woman had brought a long-haired orange cat into the mall, in a stroller. The woman in the blue jacket screams about having an allergy to cats. The cat owner swears at her, tells her not to be such a baby.

As they are about to come to blows, Wally rushes between them. Two other guards appear. They lead the blue jacket woman a few feet back and talk to her, while Wally talks to the cat owner. He explains to her, firmly but with a sympathetic smile, that a cat in the mall is against mall rules and has to be taken outside. One guard escorts her out of the mall while the other stays with the blue jacket lady and ensures she is calm.

Michael and Wally return to the mall office. Michael is impressed by how well Wally handled the situation. The guy has serious problems, but he is not all bad. No one is all bad.

"You handled that well."

"Thanks. You were saying there's one other thing."

"I want to get an update on the security situation. I assume you've alerted the staff to be on guard for any strange people or anything out of the ordinary in the mall."

"Yup. I talked to all the staff. I didn't, of course, say anything about the note, but I mentioned the possibility of some odd things happening this time of the year. They are aware."

"And did you ask them to watch over Si-Woo?"

"Yeah, she's getting the special treatment you wanted. No worries there. She should be grateful I tossed the old guy out the other day, even if she didn't like how I did it."

Michael decides it is wisest to not respond. "Can you add Dr. Cortez on the list of people to watch? I saw him yesterday and he told me he thought he was being followed. He wasn't positive about this, but to be on the safe side, it might be a good idea to give the guards a heads up."

"Yeah, I can do that, man. But it's not surprising somebody has it in for the doctor."

Michael wonders again about Wally being sympathetic to the anti-vaxxers. "Hmm. And oh, how's the hiring going?"

Wally pauses to scratch his neck. "Two extra guards are already here. The other three will be here in a couple days. They all have experience. We're gonna be in good shape."

"Good. Now, what about the video from the cameras? Was the staff able to check the footage for the morning of December 11, when the note was found?"

Wally nods his head. "Yeah, they did it yesterday. They told me there wasn't anything out of the ordinary. Just the usual people in the mall—cleaners, workers, staff, some early morning shoppers coming in for breakfast, and the regular mall walkers—the Barkers, Power Walker, Sofia Morellato, plus some others, I forget their names. Oh, there was also one of Marv's black coats coming in for a coffee, the one with the mustache. But nothing at all suspicious. It was all normal."

Michael ponders the words 'all normal'. His mind goes back to the hate-filled notes, to the strangling of the old man, and to the angry phone call from the old man's sister. If only it was 'all normal'. If only ... if only.

"One final thing, Wally. What about the camera above the bulletin board? Did you get it working? Do we have video from it yet?"

"Nothing yet, Michael. I wasn't having any luck with the security company we normally use. So, I phoned a different company yesterday. They said they'd send out a technician in a couple days. I'll keep on it and make sure it happens. But don't forget we don't know yet where the problem is. Whether it's in the camera or somewhere else."

Michael is about to complain about the delay, but then thinks of something else. "I'm curious about something. Do you know how far back the video recordings go? If we get the system working and get footage from that particular camera on December 11, can we also go back to early June and get footage from the time the first note was pinned up? Because if we could, we'd get a better picture of who is responsible for the notes, whether it's one or two people, whether it is an unhoused person or somebody else."

"I'm no expert on this," says Wally. "But from what's been told to me, if a technician can get the system up and running, get all the cameras working, it's possible we could go back. They tell me the video files gets archived once a week and then stored for a while. A couple of months. So, unless the camera itself is damaged, we could go back. But I'm pretty sure we couldn't go back to June."

"Okay, Wally, keep on it. Thanks for your time. I'll see you later."

As Wally leaves the office, Michael wonders again about his head of security. Wally has a temper, or something, but he's cooperative. He's not being evasive. But why the big delay in getting the security system repaired? Why aren't all the cameras operating? Is Wally hiding something?

38

That afternoon, Michael leaves his office and heads for the sporting goods store. He has a meeting with Grumpy Bill at two.

"Howdy chief," says Grumpy Bill. "Let's go to my office at the back. Sorry for the mess. We just got in a big shipment of hockey equipment. Find yourself a seat."

"No problem, GB," says Michael, clearing off some hockey sticks from a chair.

"You'd probably like to whack Marv with one of those, wouldn't you?"

"I guess I would, in one of my darker moments."

"Understandable. I'd like to slam that knucklehead, myself. Can I get you some water, maybe a pop?"

Michael declines. He explains he's here to get the business point of view on whether the mall's pharmacy should distribute the vaccines. Grumpy Bill tells him the business association is divided. Some managers say yes, it would bring more customers into the mall. Others say no, it would be controversial and scare away business.

"And your own thinking, GB?"

Grumpy Bill's head jolts to the side a few times. He collects himself. "Sorry about that. I'd say people in our area are becoming more supportive of the vaccines, just as they were, earlier, of masks. Most people trust science and the medical profession, not quacks and conspiracy theories. And most people are coming to realize that vaccines are an important way of getting us out of this doggone Covid mess. Most will want to get their shots as soon as possible, and as conveniently as possible. Around here, this means going to our local pharmacy, where they get their medications. So yes, our pharmacy should be allowed to do it. For sure, there'll be some controversy—Marv and his gang of nincompoops will be screaming about it. But overall, it's the best thing to do. Mind you, I'm not in favor of the vaccines myself. I have doubts about their effectiveness. But the public is becoming more supportive of them."

"So, this is your recommendation, GB, for me to give the pharmacy the go-ahead?"

"No, I didn't say that, chief. Maybe you weren't listening. I said public opinion is shifting in that direction. But it's not there yet. There's still a fair bit of division. Remember what the Governor said. Until a final decision is made, a mall or box store has to approve a pharmacy giving out the vaccines. The safest thing to do, I'd say, is simply to wait it out, don't decide anything yet. Wait 'til Governor Barley makes a final decision on the rollout. My guess is it won't be very long. In all probability, pharmacies will be given permission. Once this happens, if there's a backlash down the road, which I doubt, the Governor will take the heat, not you."

"Prudent thinking, GB."

"Golly, I do try to be prudent."

"Well, you could be right. Maybe this is the smartest thing to do."

"Yer darn tootin', chief, it is the smartest thing to do."

Michael fills in Grumpy Bill about Si-Woo's concern about being followed in the mall, and the extra security steps taken. He knows Grumpy Bill has become fond of Si-Woo.

"Gee willikers, Michael, this is a horrible situation. Thanks for telling me. I'll also look out for Si-Woo. She doesn't deserve any of this. Terrible, we have all this anti-Asian feeling. I wonder what gets into these people. Why do they have to go looking for scapegoats?"

"I wonder about it too, GB. Here's something else you might find interesting. You know how Si-Woo is always buying lottery tickets? Well, I asked her what she'd do with the money if she won it big. She told me she'd use a good chunk of it for a new homeless shelter in the area, a place our unhoused population could get something to eat and some support to deal with their issues. Quite something, isn't it? And I don't doubt she'd do it. You know how she likes to help these people. How many folks do you know would even think about doing this?"

"Gosh, not many. Mind you, I don't agree with her thinking about these hobos. They shouldn't be given handouts. This only encourages them to stay in the gutter. But I've got to admit, Si-Woo deserves a lot of credit for what she tries to do. Her heart's in the right place. She's the real deal."

"Couldn't agree more," Michael replies. After a little more chat, Michael heads back to his office. Along the way, he notices how busy the mall is. People must be going to a late afternoon performance of the new *Spider-Man* movie at the multiplex. It's good to see the movie theaters open again. Even though there is restricted seating, more people are now coming out to see movies, which means more people are coming into the mall, spelling more business for the mall. Maybe things will work out for him after all.

39

As Michael comes into his office, he notices there is a message on his office phone. It's a soft woman's voice.

"Mr. Manager, I've got an important message for you. You better listen, and you better listen good. I know you've got two beautiful daughters. I know where they live. Lovely house you've got. And I know where they go to school. Valley View School, isn't it? My, they look so pretty out in the schoolyard. Be a shame if one of them was to get hurt. If you know what's good for you, and if you don't want to see Bobbie or Brandy get hurt, don't allow the vaccines in the mall. Understand? You'll be sorry if you do. Really sorry. You have yourself a nice day."

The call abruptly ends. Michael is shaking. If anything were to happen to my girls, anything at all, he thinks, he could never forgive himself. He doesn't have a choice—he can't go along with Dr. Cortez. He has to do as Grumpy Bill recommends, and simply do nothing. Play it safe. Be prudent.

Michael wonders who the caller was. A rabid anti-vaxxer? A friend of Marv? Was she the one who wrote the notes? Was she calling on her own behalf, or on behalf of Marv, or somebody else?

Should I contact the police? No, it was from an unknown number, probably by somebody on a payphone or with a burner phone. These people hardly ever get caught. Besides, I don't want the publicity.

He calls Cornelia and explains what's happened. She shrieks into the phone. After she calms down, he suggests to her that since it's now the holiday period and the girls are just out of school, she should arrange for them to visit their grandfather in Georgia, until things settle down at the mall. It'll be nice for them to see him anyway. She quickly agrees. She says she'll arrange for the flights tonight and have them fly out tomorrow. Michael also suggests that she, herself, stay out of sight, keep a low profile, until the threat has gone. Again, she quickly agrees.

40

It is close to noon. Grumpy Bill leaves his store and heads for the bakery. Mariah Carey's song *All I Want for Christmas is You* is playing. He's decided that since he is going to keep an eye on Si-Woo, he'll try to get to know her a bit better.

"Howdy, Si-Woo, how goes it?"

"Not bad, GB," replies Si-Woo. "I'm just packing up a few leftover Danish pastries to take over to a couple unhoused women. I noticed them earlier by the main entrance."

"Well, I just came by to see if you want to go upstairs for lunch. My treat."

"Is this a date?" says Si-Woo, jokingly.

"Not really," replies Grumpy Bill, not knowing quite how to respond. "But I just thought you might be hungry, might want some company."

"Sounds good. Thanks for the invite. Can you watch over the bakery for a few minutes? I'll deliver these to the women and be back as quick as I can. My co-worker Marcie is going to come in—she should be here by now—and take over my shift."

"Okay, see you later alligator."

"GB, you've got to get with it. Get past the 1950s. You need to upgrade your language a bit, don't you think?"

Grumpy Bill smiles, knowing she's teasing. She limps away into the mall, and he waits patiently in the bakery. No one comes in. A few minutes later, her mission accomplished, Si-Woo arrives back at the same time as her co-worker. Si-Woo gets her cash drawer and takes it to the back while Marcie takes over the register and puts her drawer in.

"I'm ready to go," says Si-Woo. "What are we having for lunch?"

"Well, how about Korean?" Grumpy Bill replies with a sly grin.

"Hmm ... sounds good. I need to get away from the burgers and fries."

"Okay, let's go upstairs. I think I'll have the barbeque beef. Love the way they do it. What about you, Si-Woo? What are you going to have?"

"For me, it's going to be the chicken bibimbap."

"What the dickens is that?"

"It's basically mixed rice with savory chicken and some crunchy veggies. It's popular."

As they go up the escalator to the food court, they see an excited group of children below them rush by an older woman, knocking a shopping bag out of her hand. Oranges and grapefruits land on the floor and roll down the hall, scattering in every direction. Power Walker comes to the rescue, gathering up the fruits and putting them back into her bag. The woman gives him a big smile. He smiles back.

"Gee, that's unusual," says Grumpy Bill. "Power Walker is being helpful rather than crashing into people."

"I had a little talk with him the other day, after he banged into me. I explained to him the meaning of karma. I said being careless and disrespectful, by banging into people, creates bad karma, leading to bad outcomes. I said you should work on creating good karma for yourself, being kind and helpful. You'll be rewarded. Maybe he got the message."

"Gosh, I hope so."

They get their food, find a table, and remove their masks. As they start to eat, Grumpy Bill tells Si-Woo he had heard about her being followed and asks how she's doing. She explains she's feeling okay, but she feels she has to watch her step these days, given all the anti-Asian racism that's around.

Grumpy Bill sympathizes. His head twitches. He grimaces in embarrassment. Si-Woo turns away, pretending not to notice.

"This bibimbap is really good," she says. "And how are you doing these days? I see you're doing a booming business at your store."

"I'm doing just dandy, thanks. And business is great. Despite the virus, sales are up, especially in skis and hockey gear. Obviously not as high as before Covid, but higher than I expected. In fact, I've had good sales in all three of my stores."

"So, what are you going to do with all your money? They say you can't take it with you, you can't ...." Si-Woo stops, thinking she's being too bold. "I'm terribly sorry, GB, I'm way out of line. You don't need to answer that. It's none of my business."

"No, no, I don't mind telling you, Si-Woo. I don't have a wife or children to leave my money to. I'll leave my money to relief organizations I trust, ones like the International Red Cross, ones that deal with emergency situations like earthquakes, floods, and so on. And also help with rare medical conditions. Do you know that there are still people in the world who suffer from leprosy?"

"I remember hearing about that."

"But I have a question for you, Si-Woo. Why do you care so much about those dang street people around here? Michael tells me you said if you had the money, you'd build a homeless shelter for them. But it seems to me these people would be better off if they were left to fend for themselves. It would give them the incentive to get a job or get some education, so they can turn their lives around. What you may be doing—and correct me if I'm wrong—is to take away any incentive, discourage them from doing better."

Si-Woo chews thoughtfully for a few moments. "When you think about it, GB, my desire to help them isn't that different from your wish to help people in emergency situations. It's all about helping people who can't help themselves, isn't it? And keep in mind, I'm only doing the bare minimum, enough to give people who are down on their luck food, warmth, and counseling, and a sense that somebody cares. This provides them with hope, until they can develop the strength to move forward in life."

"But by golly, aren't they more likely to develop that inner strength, as you put it, if they have to do it themselves, if they are not being propped up by do-gooders? No offense, I'm just trying to be honest."

Si-Woo is about to reply but is stopped by some squealing children—a boy and two girls—at the table next to them. The children are yelling at their parents to get them more fries. When their parents say no, they start to throw food, some of it landing on a nearby table and some of it in the white beard of an old man walking by. The parents scream at their children, then collect them and angrily leave the food court.

"What was that about?" asks Si-Woo. Grumpy Bill shakes his head.

Si-Woo provides her interrupted answer. "I've looked into the characteristics of unhoused people in America. It's not a random thing, you know, when people become homeless. It's usually triggered by something major in their lives, like losing their jobs or maybe their family, and along with it, losing their self-esteem and confidence. It can also happen because of addiction or mental illness. And for younger people, because of abuse in their family and involvement in the child welfare system, especially multiple foster homes. On top of this, it can be connected to discrimination. I don't know if you know this, GB, but the unhoused disproportionately come from Indigenous, black, and minority communities."

"I've heard that, but there's still individual responsibility. Si-Woo, you can't blame everything on society or on peoples' childhood."

Si-Woo finishes her bibimbap. "I'm just saying that people sometimes have problems and I try to help them, just like you help people who suffer because of earthquakes. I just try to help people who are down on their luck."

Grumpy Bill pauses and thinks about what Si-Woo has said. "You said yourself you are only doing the bare minimum. That's not a criticism—you, uh, have your own concerns. What's in it, anyway, for you to help these dang hobos?

"I was raised a Buddhist in South Korea. And what I learned must have stuck. I was taught in my family, and at the temple, to believe in karma and to try to attain good karma. The concept gets complicated, but karma essentially means that our thoughts and deeds shape our future. You reap what you sow. So, good karma means that when we do good deeds, this leads to good outcomes. Don't get me wrong—I don't believe, as some Buddhists do, that good karma gets rewarded in the next life, that we get to come back as more enlightened people, not as bats or toads. In my view, we receive good outcomes in this life, whether it's happiness, love, friendship, peace of mind, or all of the above."

Grumpy Bill looks doubtful. "I've seen people in the world of business cheat and lie, deceive others, routinely. They're really bad people. Yet they also have long, healthy, and prosperous lives. If I remember my Bible correctly, I think it's in the book of Psalms, it's not unusual to see the wicked prosper while the righteous suffer. How does this square with good and bad karma?"

Si-Woo folds her napkin and places it on her plate. "I don't know all the answers, GB. Maybe the wicked don't really prosper? Perhaps they don't have inner peace, perhaps they suffer from a guilty conscience. All that I know is that karma is real, and that good karma is a strong and positive force in the world."

"Sounds too dreamy for me." Grumpy Bill shakes his head. "But I enjoy talking about this with you. It makes me think."

"I enjoyed it too," says Si-Woo, thinking how much she likes Grumpy Bill, despite his contrariness. His folksy talking might be over the top, but he has a certain charm and honesty that she's drawn to. And if he did ask her to go out on a date, she'd accept.

41

"**S**ofia, what can I do for you this morning?"

Sofia has an early appointment with Dr. Cortez.

"Doctor, I still have this problem with headaches. I thought I should let you know, see what you think, see if there's anything that can be done. Mind you, they're not migraine headaches—there's no throbbing pain—but they're nasty and they happen fairly often."

"Yes, we spoke about this before. Let me check your blood pressure first."

Dr. Cortez then checks Sofia's blood pressure, records the numbers, and reviews her medical record. Her blood pressure is fine, and he asks how the medication is working for her Parkinson's. She replies that she seems to be okay, at least on that front.

The doctor looks again at her medical records. "The results of the EEG you had last summer showed no evidence of a head injury from the fall you had in the mall. And I just checked the results of the MRI you just had. Same thing. Negative. No evidence of a head injury. So, your headaches can't be explained from this, which of course is a good thing."

"But what else could explain them?" she asks.

He gives Sofia a list of the possibilities: heavy drinking, a change in diet, a change in sleeping patterns, poor quality lighting, too much screen time. Sofia shakes her head and says no to all of it.

"There's something else that can trigger headaches," says the doctor. "Anxiety or stress or depression can do it too. I know you've been concerned about your daughter Tina. Do you feel a lot of stress or anxiety about it?"

Sofia fidgets.

"Sofia, are we onto something here?"

"Yeah, I guess we are. I'm deeply worried about Tina and also my granddaughter Brianna. I wake up in the middle of the night, worrying. I worry about Tina getting deeper into the anti-vaxxer movement, about her getting influenced by wild conspiracy theories, and getting more and more connected to that horrible Marv. He says jump and she says how high. And he swears so much. It rubs off on Tina. She uses bad language more and more. Tina won't even wear a mask when she's around me. Imagine that! Putting her own mother in jeopardy! And she says she won't be getting a vaccine."

"You mentioned your granddaughter. Why are you worried about her?"

"Tina refuses to let me see her anymore. My little Brianna, my own granddaughter. It's been really, really, horrible. I haven't seen her since last June—that's almost seven months now."

Dr. Cortez shakes his head. He is astounded. "Why did Tina do that? It seems so drastic."

"Tina said if I kept on asking her to wear a mask, she'd stop me from seeing Brianna. Well, I did ask. And so, she cut me off, as a kind of punishment. I desperately miss my Brianna. I love her so much. And I'm sure she misses me too. You know, Doctor, I looked after Brianna almost every day the first year of her life, when Tina went to work. We were, and we are, very close. I worry about the influence Tina is having with Brianna. Children need stability, love, and good role models, don't they? I don't think Brianna is getting it."

Sofia starts to tear up. Dr. Cortez hands her a box of tissues.

"And I lost my husband a year ago. He was the love of my life. Now, I feel I'm losing my little Brianna, as well as my daughter. It's eating me up."

Dr. Cortez gets up, goes over to Sofia, and pats her on her arm. "So sorry to hear about this, Sofia. To be cut off from your granddaughter, that's tough. And it sounds like you are suffering from major anxiety, which isn't surprising. You might consider some counseling. Do you want me to refer you to a professional counselor? There are some pretty good ones in the area."

"Maybe. I'd have to think about that."

"It can be helpful. People sometimes don't want to go because they think there's a stigma. But I assure you it can help."

"Appreciate that, Doctor. I'll think about it."

"Anything else on your mind, Sofia? The stress probably explains the headaches, but I sense something else is going on."

"Well, Doctor, because of all this stress, and my Parkinson's, I sometimes get into some pretty dark places ... dark places in my thoughts. To tell you the truth, I'm thinking about ending it all. I'm thinking about suicide. Not tomorrow or next week. But if things don't get better, if my Parkinson's gets worse, if I feel I can't hold it together anymore, I'm thinking I'll do it. Would you be willing to help me? I know the law in our state allows it."

"Sofia, I'm so sorry, so sorry you feel this way."

"But Doctor, would you be willing to help me?"

Dr. Cortez pauses for a few minutes. He then explains to Sofia his views on the issue. He doesn't have any religious or moral objections to assisted suicide. If one of his patients was suffering from an illness and asked for assisted suicide, and if it was a rational and informed decision, he would help. "I wouldn't be happy about it, I certainly wouldn't, but I would help. It's consistent with my duty as a doctor to do no harm, and supports a person's choice and dignity."

"I'm so happy to hear you say this, Doctor. Thank you."

Dr. Cortez clarifies for Sofia the current law in their state on assisted suicide. While the law allows for assisted suicide, there are conditions. A person must be terminally ill with less than six months to live, verified by two doctors. Another is that a person must be mentally competent, also verified by two doctors. And another is that a person must wait two days between a written request and getting the lethal medication, allowing time for a change of mind. If there is no change of mind, the person must administer the medication herself or himself.

"Seems reasonable to me," says Sofia.

"To me too," replies the doctor. "We do need to have safeguards in the process. But Sofia, we're not there yet. We're far from being there. There's no denying that you've hit some major bumps on the road. But you know, you're doing reasonably well, given the circumstances. There is hope your Parkinson's won't get any worse, at least for some time, and there is hope your daughter will get back to having a normal relationship with you. I can see this happening. Maybe not next week, but down the road."

"If only … if only it were true."

The doctor smiles at Sofia. "I know it's difficult, but you've got good reason to think things will get better."

"Thanks, Doctor." Sofia is about to get up and leave but Dr. Cortez motions for her to hold on a minute.

"Just one other thing, Sofia. Would it be okay with you if I spoke to Tina about your anxiety? I would certainly protect your right to privacy. And I wouldn't mention anything about your request. I would just let her know I'm concerned about you. That might wake her up, get her back on track."

Sofia looks puzzled. "Well, I guess that'd be okay. Thanks again, Doctor. Arrivederci."

Sofia gets up. Dr. Cortez helps her with her walker. He escorts her into the hall, gives her a hug, and waves goodbye. Playing in the background, as it so often is this month, is *Jingle Bell Rock*.

42

How pathetic is that? The old lady gets a hug from our good doctor, the same doctor who preaches about the importance of social distancing. I read his columns. I know what he says. And I know hypocrisy when I see it.

Hell, I wish they'd stop playing that damn song. If I hear Jingle Bell Rock one more time, I think I'll scream. Why do they have to play that fuckin' Christmas music anyway?

When I pinned up the second note, I thought it was really smart the way it was written. Different handwriting to confuse any wannabe Sherlocks.

Why am I so much against the vaccines? Marv's got it right. This is America. Elites shouldn't be pushing them down our throats. They should be respecting our freedom and choices. I hate needles and I hate vaccines, I refuse to be forced to get any. Fuck 'em.

And threatening people makes me feel good. It always has. When I was a kid. I remember the buzz I got from being a bully in school. I just loved picking on the younger kids. There was one day, I think it was in middle school, maybe grade 8, when a new kid in school said something I didn't like. I put the kid in a headlock and took him downstairs to a washroom. I stuck his head in the toilet and flushed it. He was really mad, but he never told on me. Too scared. I got such a kick out of it.

I'm disappointed there's still not talk about the note. Word just didn't get out. People should be talking about it, they should be worried about it. That was the whole point. But some horrible person took it down, sabotaged me. So, I'm going to have to actually do it—carry out an attack. Then there'll have to be publicity. Nobody'll be able to keep a lid on that!

I've been practicing. I bought some sulfuric acid at a hardware store, and I got a big water gun. Man, it can hold a lot of acid. I filled it up and took it to a park. I tested it out on some plants and a couple ducks. Then I shot at a squirrel going up a tree. Hit its tail. It made a loud crying noise and jumped down on the ground, chasing around its rear end. It was so funny. Now I know I can do it, and I can do it in the mall.

But who should I go after? The crippled old lady with the walker is deserving. I've heard her pushing for vaccines. She's got some nerve. And the doctor's also deserving. I know many people think he's a good doctor. But he's a really bad influence. He's gotta be stopped.

I don't know for sure who I'll attack. Maybe I'll attack a bunch of them, go on a spree. But whoever I attack, it'll give me such a thrill—a thrill from planning to do it, from doing it, and from the memory of doing it. A kind of trifecta.

43

Michael and Dr. Cortez happen to arrive together at the mall the next morning. At the front entrance, they see a couple of unkempt men sleeping against one of the walls. One is snoring and the other is thrashing his feet, perhaps from a bad dream. Si-Woo comes around the corner, carrying a tray with muffins and coffee.

"Always at it, aren't you Si-Woo?" says Michael.

"It doesn't stop," she replies, "especially this time of the year. It's getting colder out there and more of them are coming in. They need some food and a bit of hope."

"Great you're doing this," says the doctor. "I'm sure it's appreciated."

"And more good karma for you, Si-Woo," adds Michael, with a warm smile.

Michael and Dr. Cortez walk further into the mall. The sound system is playing John Lennon's *So This is Christmas.* Michael and the doctor hum along. There are early morning shoppers and construction workers getting their coffees, and cleaners are wiping the floors. In the distance they see the Barkers walking, and Power Walker flying by.

Around a corner, they notice a tall ladder with someone at the top, inspecting a surveillance camera. A panel in the ceiling has been removed, just above the community bulletin board. A man comes down the ladder and says something to the security chief.

"Hi Wally," says Michael, "what's going on?"

"Say what?"

"What's happening?"

"Uh, well, we're doing an inspection. I'm having Sanjay here, our security technician, check out the surveillance camera, along with a few other ones down the way. We had thought this one wasn't operating. We weren't getting any video from it. But Sanjay tells me the camera is working fine. So, the problem's gotta be somewhere else, with the software probably. Anyway, after we're finished here, we're gonna check out the other cameras, see what's up with them."

"Good luck with it, Wally," says Michael. "Let me know how it turns out."

Michael and Dr. Cortez continue on to the clinic. As they get to the door, Michael looks at his watch, realizing it is later than he thinks.

"I've got to get over to my office now, Doctor. But one quick question. I've been wondering about your stalking incident. That person in the hoodie—have you seen them again?"

"No, I haven't, chief. And I don't think I've been followed again. But I did get a death threat last night at my home. Scary stuff. I reported it to the police. I guess I'm going to have to change my number, and get some security at my house."

Michael is horrified. "What! That's terrible, just terrible! We've got some deranged people around here. I'll get in touch with our security people. Have them keep an eye on you, and monitor the cameras around your clinic."

"Thanks, chief."

"I probably don't need to tell you this, but you should be extra careful, supremely careful. You need to keep a low profile, stay off the radio talk shows, that sort of thing. At least until the vaccine controversy dies down. I don't want to hear about you getting attacked."

"Are you worried that if I was attacked, it would mean negative publicity for the mall?"

"Ah, well, no, not at all. Just thinking about your safety."

"I'm kidding, chief. Look, I appreciate your concern, I certainly do. You've got a good heart. But I won't be intimidated. I won't back down from my principles, public health is just too important. I'll tell you what, though. I'll watch what I do more closely and avoid risky situations."

"That's good to hear. Okay, I've got to go now. See you later." As Michael walks away, he wishes he could be as principled as the doctor. But he's got a family to think about. He's got two daughters. He's got to be prudent. Doesn't he?

44

Dr. Cortez goes into the medical clinic, checks his mail, and enters his office. He's nervous. First task of the day is phoning Tina about her mother.

He wonders how he should phrase his message. On the one hand, he needs to make Tina realize that Sofia is in bad shape, needs her daughter's help, and needs the support of her family. Tina needs to be convinced of the importance of spending time with her mother, and trying to get her into counseling. At the same time, he needs to be diplomatic and not get Tina's back up. He also has to respect Sofia's privacy and rules about doctor-patient confidentiality. And he can't mention suicide.

"Tina, this is Dr. Cortez calling, hope I'm not interrupting anything. If I am, I can easily call back.

"Hey, Doctor. No, I'm just sitting here at the kitchen table having coffee with Marv. What's up?"

"I'm calling to let you know I am concerned about your mother."

Tina asks him to wait a moment while she puts the call on speaker phone, so Marv can hear too.

"As I was saying, Tina, I want to let you know that I am worried ... and I can't emphasize this too much ... I am worried about your mother. She is not in any immediate danger, but she doesn't look well. She worries a lot and she continues to be upset about the loss of her husband, your father. This can be hard on anyone, but it's especially hard on a surviving spouse where there's been a long and close loving relationship."

Tina interrupts. "Yeah, they were close. But my mom is a worrywart. She's always been a worrywart. She gets upset by almost everything. She even gets upset when I don't wear a mask around her."

Dr. Cortez presses on. "Tina, I rarely phone the family of my patients, but family is part of a person's environment. Your mother is fragile and could benefit from the support of her family. It would be good for her if she could spend more time with you, and Brianna. You know how she loves her granddaughter. Tina, I know you are supportive of your mother, but at this point—more than ever—she really needs your love and understanding, and she needs strong family support. She could also benefit from some professional counseling. This would—"

Marv speaks up, and his voice gets clearer as he moves closer to the phone. "Now hold on Doc. Counseling is for crybabies. It's for weak people. Tina's mother is as strong as an ox and she's tougher than you think. And if she needs help, Tina is here to help her. Look, you've got a lot of nerve phoning here and bothering Tina. You're a phony. With all of your talk about masks and vaccines, you're a damn—"

"Please Marv, be nice, the doctor is just trying to help."

"Trying to help, my ass!"

Dr. Cortez tries to calm things. "Tina, I don't want to cause any trouble. I know you are a supportive daughter. I'm phoning just to let you know that your mother loves her family, and at this point in her life, she can really benefit from the strong support of her family. I'll leave it at that. Thanks for listening. And have a good day."

Dr. Cortez ends the call, hoping he got his message through to Tina. He knows it would have been counterproductive to press her too much, but he thought it important to at least try to alert her to the problem. He wonders if his message will sink in.

45

THE WOLFVILLE NEWS

Tuesday, December 22, 2020

FINAL DECISION MADE ON VACCINE ROLLOUT

Governor Muriel Barley has made a final decision on the vaccine rollout. In consultation with the department of health, the Governor has announced that the vaccines for Covid-19 will be distributed through all pharmacies, conference centers, sporting venues, and other designated places.

This is the similar to the preliminary plan announced two weeks ago, but pharmacies inside shopping malls, department stores, box stores, and large grocery stores do not need approval by their landlord. All pharmacies that have agreed to partner with the state are now authorized to administer the vaccines.

Officials in the Governor's Office say this is necessary to get vaccines out as quickly and widely as possible. Unnecessary restrictions or delays are to be avoided.

The reason for haste, the officials add, is that the Covid situation in the state is worsening. There has been a steady and alarming increase in the case numbers, hospitalizations, ICU cases, and deaths. Vaccines, they say, have been shown to be effective and the state is going to move quickly to get them out.

The decision was applauded in the public health
community. Dr. Juan Cortez, Wolfville doctor and
well-known advocate of the vaccines, says that not
only are the vaccines effective but there is growing
public confidence in their value. He points out
that as shown in polls, most people now intend
to get vaccinated. Only a minority are opposed or
hesitant.

Malls and big box stores also approve of
the decision. Michael McQueen, manager
of Wolfville Mall, says that before the
Governor's announcement, he was giving serious
consideration to approving the pharmacy inside
his mall for distributing the vaccines. People in
the community around the mall, he reports, were
increasingly supportive of this.

Not everyone supports the plan. Marv Hammar,
leader of a local anti-vaxxer group, says he is
deeply disturbed. He says Covid is not that serious,
no more serious than the flu. He argues the
problem of the virus has been vastly overblown by
the media and the medical establishment.

Also, Mr. Hammar say the vaccines have been developed too quickly. "Big Pharma wants to make huge profits and the industry does not care a whit about the effects of the vaccine on people. It is too dangerous to proceed," he says. "The madness has to stop."

Mr. Hammar claims parallels between his resistance and the one during the American Revolution. Back then, it was a struggle by American patriots against the tyranny of the British. Now, he says, it is a struggle by the patriots of today against the tyranny of arrogant elites telling the people what to do.

The fight for liberty, he says, is as important today as it was during America's founding. In his words, "forcing people to wear masks, ordering lockdowns, and badgering folks into getting dangerous vaccines is un-American. We'll not stand for it. We're going to resist."

46

It is early afternoon and Michael has just finished reading the news. His phone beeps with an email from Grumpy Bill.

Chief, I just saw the news. The Governor sent us an early Christmas present. Well done, Michael. Didn't I tell you a non-decision is sometimes better than a decision. By golly, we dodged a bullet again, didn't we? If there's a problem now, it's on our gov. GB.

Michael puts down his phone and smiles. Yeah, Grumpy Bill did get it right. It worked out nicely. But he still wonders if he really handled it the right way. It's understandable that he'd want to protect his girls and his wife. Who can quarrel with that? But shouldn't he have shown more courage? Shouldn't he have been more like the doctor or his dad?

There is a loud knock on his office door. Michael sees that it's Wally and waves him in.

"How's it going, Wally? Everything okay on the security front?"

"Yeah, pretty much," says Wally, sitting down. "All our extra security people are in place. Big brother is in full swing."

"Anything at all suspicious?"

"Nothing suspicious, nothing unusual. Usual last-minute Christmas crowd. There's more of those dumbass street people coming in, but they're not causing any problems, at least for now. And nothing to report about Si-Woo or the doctor. We're keeping a close eye on them and everything's okey-dokey."

"What about the surveillance cameras? Are they all working?"

"Well, bro, there is some news on that front. Remember the other day I had the security technician, Sanjay, check out the camera above the bulletin board and some other ones too. He tells me they're all working fine. And he couldn't find any loose wires. So, the problem's gotta be with the big monitor or, more exactly, the software in it."

Michael looks irritated. "So, can he fix it?"

"Sanjay said it's too complicated for him to deal with. We're gonna have to get in a specialist who knows the software. Might take some time, especially this time of the year."

"Damn! Look, Wally, we've got to get it all working and we've got to do it fast. You need to get somebody in here right away."

"I hear you, boss, I'm working on it."

Shortly after Wally leaves, there is another knock on the door. Michael is surprised to see it's Cornelia. "Hi there, princess, come on in." He greets her with a kiss and they both sit down.

She skips saying hello. "Michael, you've got some weird customers in your mall today. I saw some woman running by, covered in tattoos, with drawings of really hideous skulls. She just about knocked me flying. Didn't even apologize. She was in a mad rush and talking with some tall guy in a black coat, looked like Hitler."

"Oh, that'd be Tina. She's Marv's girlfriend. Yeah, she's a bit strange. Hmm, I wonder what she'd be doing in the mall with the black coat?"

Cornelia doesn't respond, and instead updates him on how the girls are doing with her father in Georgia. As she talks, Michael recalls the nasty phone call and threat that led to their trip away from home. What kind of a woman, he wonders, would threaten my girls, just to get at me, bully me into doing what she wants? Cornelia stops talking about the girls, and is waiting for him to say something.

"So, princess, what brings you in here today?"

"Just doing some last-minute Christmas shopping for the girls. I want to send them a few things. But I'm afraid there's not very much here."

"Ouch! You can't mean that. This is a big mall. There must be something here!"

"No, not really. I was looking for some designer clothes, tops and jeans. But the ones I saw, even at your so-called higher end stores, were pretty common. I'm going to have to go downtown for nicer things."

Michael wonders about Cornelia's snootiness. Has it gone up a notch? Is she going to become like her arrogant father? But he is getting distracted. He has great news that she should be really happy about. He tells Cornelia that the Governor has finalized the vaccine rollout plan, leaving it up to the pharmacies whether to give out the vaccines. "It puts me in the clear," he says. "If there's a backlash, it's on the Governor, not me."

"Wow, that's great," says Cornelia, looking relieved. "Thank God, thank God for that. And our girls ... we won't have to worry about them anymore. It's over."

"Yes, the issue's been settled. I suppose our girls can come home in a few days, maybe a bit after Christmas. You can hold back on sending them any gifts."

"Yes, I'll do that. I'm so glad to hear this, Michael. This is wonderful. I'll arrange a flight for the girls as soon as I can. Listen, let's have a celebratory dinner tonight."

"Okay, let's do it."

"I'll make some seafood risotto, and to go with it, I'll get out a nice cold bottle of Sauvignon Blanc. I have one in mind, a premium Marlborough from New Zealand—top of the line—with that intense taste of pink grapefruit, and a hint of ginger and lemon pith."

Lemon pith? Am I hearing that right, Michael wonders. "Uh, yeah," he says with a grin, "that's really great wine, really great. But you know, princess, there's still one thing that worries me."

"What's that, sweetie?"

"The note. Whoever wrote the note is still out there. It still could happen. The acid attack. This monster could do it, even now. Could actually throw acid into somebody's face, right here in the mall!"

Cornelia stares coldly at her husband. "We've talked about this before, Michael. It's just not going to happen. You don't need to worry so much. Listen to me. If some weirdo has a problem with the vaccines, or with the pharmacy, it's on the Governor. The creep will have to go to the Governor's mansion and throw some acid at her. You said it yourself, you are in the clear, the mall is in the clear."

"I agree it's not likely to happen. But it still *could* happen."

"Okay, okay, *anything* is possible. But in the off-chance it happens, and we talked about this before, you're not responsible. You've got all kinds of kooks and loonies in the mall: raving street people, raving anti-maskers, raving anti-vaxxers. Who could blame you for ignoring an off-the-wall note? There are so many freaks and losers in the mall."

"You're probably right, Cornelia."

"Get hold of yourself, Michael, stop thinking about it."

If I only could, Michael tells himself. But my brain won't shut off. The images keep coming back. Somebody in a dark hoodie, holding a bottle of sulfuric acid, chasing around innocent people in the mall, catching up to them, terrifying them, throwing acid into their faces.

Cornelia breaks into Michael's thoughts. "Daddy wants to know if we were checking out any private schools for the twins. I told him we plan to do it, but we have to wait for your promotion."

"That's right, we have to wait." Michael is annoyed at her father's intrusion. Why does the old shit have to keep badgering us, telling us what we need to do?

"But he said it's really important we get on it," says Cornelia. "We need to speed it up. If we want to give the girls a good chance in life, and he really emphasized this, it's critical we get them into a good private school so they can get into the Ivy Leagues or one of the top-notch universities. The public schools just don't cut it."

Michael glares at Cornelia. "I went to public schools. I did alright."

"Yeah, you did okay, I guess. But we want our daughters to really excel, to do better than okay, don't we? If we can get them an Ivy League education, they'll be on track for a high-powered job, maybe a lawyer or a surgeon. Maybe even a judge like Daddy. And to get this education, they obviously need good preparation, the kind you can get in a private school."

"But I never heard Brandy or Bobbie say they want to be a surgeon or lawyer. In fact, Bobbie told me the other day she wants to be a pop singer like Taylor Swift."

"Cut the sarcasm, Michael. You know what I'm talking about."

Michael looks up at the ceiling and sighs. "Well, I appreciate what you're saying, Cornelia. And I agree a good private school can boost their chances. Now, if this is what they really want, that's great, I'm all for it. We'll support them and we'll help them as best we can."

"You bet we will," says Cornelia, sternly. "We definitely will. Over the last few days, I've been checking out private schools. I've been comparing them in terms of class size, test scores, that sort of thing. Plus, I've been looking at their track records in getting their graduates into the top universities."

"So, what did you find?"

"I found a really great one in Blue Mountain Heights, where we'll be living next year, or so I assume. It's called Mountain View School. It's at the top of the ratings and I love their motto: 'With us, no mountain is too high'."

"That's impressive," replies Michael, smiling. "I suppose they'd also say, with us, no cost is too high."

"Michael, I'm getting sick and tired of your sarcasm. Cut it out. For your information, the tuition is forty thousand per student each year, which isn't bad, considering their reputation and track record. Daddy said he can help us out with the costs."

"Even so, that's eighty thousand. It's a ton of money ... a *ton* of money. Even if I get my promotion next year, it'll be a huge chunk out of my earnings. We'll have to go into major debt. And I don't want any charity from your father."

"Michael, you can do this. You *need* to do this. If you really love Bobbie and Brandy, if you truly love them and if you truly love me, you'll do it. You'll find a way."

"I'll try."

"You need to do *more* than just try, Michael, you need to *actually* do it. You need to get some steel into your spine." Cornelia looks at her watch. "Listen, I've got to get going. See you back at the ranch."

As soon as Cornelia leaves his office, Michael worries about her financial demands. He fidgets with his pencil. If they're really going to send their girls to an expensive private school, and move into a fancy house, he's desperately going to need that promotion, and a big salary increase. He'll have to improve the mall and bargain hard with Pacific Gold.

He steps into the crowded mall. The sight of many shoppers is pleasing but triggers a dark thought. If the twisted person who wrote the note does attack, he or she will probably do it when the mall is crowded, just like it is now. There'll be more victims to attack and a better chance of getting away. And if this happens, an innocent person could get disfigured or even die. How would he feel about that, if he had done nothing? He tells himself to cool it, to stop being paranoid. He should put his worries aside until after Christmas, and enjoy the holiday period with his family.

He remembers earlier Christmases he had with his dad. One of his best Christmas memories was when his dad took him to a nature reserve up in the mountains. They saw all kinds of wildlife, including reindeer, moose, gray wolves, and lynx. His dad talked about the need to respect nature—the woods, the weather, the wildlife—and people too. All different animals were part of the forest, and all different people were part of humanity. Michael wonders why he isn't more like his dad. His dad encouraged him to be principled when making decisions, and not worry about being pragmatic or strategic? Why can't he listen to what his dad told him so many years ago?

Clearing

August 2021

47

Tuesday, August 10, 2021

VACCINE PASSPORTS CONSIDERED

Controversy is brewing in Wolfville over reports that vaccine passports are being considered. If implemented, people would need to show proof of COVID vaccination through paper cards or QR codes on phones in order to enter indoor establishments such as restaurants, bars, gyms, sports arenas, movie theaters, and shopping malls.

They could also be required, at state and federal levels, for air and train travel and for certain jobs.

Vaccine passports, sometimes called certificates or passes, are being implemented or considered in places such as Israel, Singapore, the European Union, British Columbia (Canada), New York, and San Francisco. In the Pacific Northwest, there are plans to introduce them in Seattle and in surrounding King County. They are now under discussion in Wolfville.

Public health officials and advocates say they are a necessary step in the fight against Covid-19. Though most people in the state are fully vaccinated (two doses), officials warn of serious problems. They point to the continuing surge of Covid cases and deaths, the arrival of the deadly Delta variant, and major pressures on the health care system.

They emphasize that vaccines have been shown to be effective in combating the virus. Since vaccines are effective, the officials argue, passports make people more likely to get them.

Dr. Juan Cortez, local doctor and public health advocate, says that people who get vaccinated are much less likely to get the virus and, if they do, much less likely to die from it. So, it is logical, he says, that people be encouraged to get the vaccine. A key means of encouragement is to require people to have passports for entry into indoor venues. This is especially important, he adds, because with the lifting of seating restrictions and other limitations, more people are going to restaurants, movie theaters, and other indoor places.

The passports could come to Wolfville in several ways. They could be implemented as part of a public health order by the city or surrounding county. They could be required, as in other parts of the state, through a public health order by Governor Barley. Or they could be required by a private company or organization. There are reports, for example, that passports are being contemplated by Wolfville Mall.

The initiative is facing strong opposition from civil liberties and anti-vaxxer groups. Marv Hammar, leader of a local anti-vaxxer group, has scathing words for the initiative. He calls it "un-American, communist-inspired, and yet another step toward tyranny in America."

Mr. Hammar says the passports are a kind of measure you'd expect in "Nazi Germany, Stalinist Russia, or Communist Cuba, not in freedom-loving America." According to him, "they invade people's privacy, they are discriminatory, and they violate the sacred principle of liberty."

Mr. Hammar says he will mobilize his supporters and organize rallies in front of city hall and the county executive office. He will also lead a group to the Governor's mansion, joining others from across the state in a major protest in front of the mansion. But first, he will speak tomorrow at a rally at Wolfville Mall. In no way, he says, "will the would-be tyrants in charge of the mall be allowed to require passports."

The manager of the mall, Michael McQueen, says the passports are merely being considered. No final decision has been made. He also says that because the mall tries to accommodate political speech, permission for the protest has been given. But it has to be kept orderly and peaceful.

48

It is noon, and Brianna is crying uncontrollably. Tina has taken her to the rally, and Brianna has been frightened by a QAnon supporter who is wearing a grotesque white mask and screaming obscenities at a nearby security guard.

"Don't be scared, sweetheart," says Tina, chewing gum as usual. "It's just one of our supporters sticking up for our country. I know him. He's a really nice dude, kind and super friendly."

"Can you shut the kid up?" Marv snaps at Tina.

"Marv, for God's sake, she just turned four. You were four once, didn't you ever cry? Brianna just got scared by Glenn over there with the mask, that's all. She'll stop in a minute."

"You're right. Mom told me I did cry a few times when I was a little kid. It's just we don't want her growing up to be a weakling."

Brianna settles as the rally gets louder. Even though it is a sweltering day in August, Marv has assembled a huge crowd in front of the mall. He figures it's close to a thousand people. Country music is playing, and people are starting to chant "down with tyranny," "fuck passports," and "we support Marv." American and Confederate flags are waved, and signs displayed include "no to vaccines," "refuse passports," and "no to mandates."

Near the mall doors, watching it all, are Michael, Richard and Mary Barker, Grumpy Bill, Si- Woo, and Sofia Morellato. Sofia looks longingly at Brianna at the front. She hasn't seen her for well over a year. She also looks intently at Tina, disturbed that she'd bring her daughter to this kind of event. Wouldn't this be considered a form of child abuse, she wonders?

The Hank Williams Jr. song *We Don't Apologize for America* ends, and that's Tina's cue to get up on the platform and introduce Marv. She asks the handsome black coat if he'll watch Brianna. He smiles at her and Brianna, says he's happy to do it, and takes Brianna's hand. Tina gets a bullhorn and jumps up on the platform. Sofia fears for Brianna's safety.

"Patriots," Tina yells, and the crowd quiets. "We have here one of the greatest heroes Wolfville has ever produced. He's never let us down. He's always been fighting for us. Like the great heroes of the American Revolution—Washington, Henry, Paine—he's been leading us in our fight for freedom, in our fight against tyranny. Let's give it up for the one and only Marv Hammar."

There is thunderous applause. Led by Tina, the crowd starts to chant "we love Marv," "we love Marv." Marv leaps up onto the platform and takes the bullhorn from Tina.

"Friends," he roars, "our patriotic forefathers fought against the tyranny of the British. They fought for liberty, won the war, and created the United States of America, the land of the free. Today, we continue that fight. It's not against the British this time. It's now against our establishment, our establishment elites. It's against the dastardly tyrants right here in our own backyard, who are trying to turn us into God damn serfs."

Marv stops and glugs down some water. "First, these people insisted we had to wear those disgusting masks. Then, they declared we had to get vaccinated, Big Pharma laughing all the way to the bank. Now, they say we've got to get vaccine passports. Can you believe it? We'll need to show passports if we want to go into a restaurant or a bar, if we want to go to a football game, if we want to go to a movie. They're also talking about proof of vaccination for travel and being able to work at certain jobs. It's unbelievable, simply unbelievable!"

Marv stops again for water. As he looks out over the crowd, he senses that people are angrier than before, and more on edge. He decides that he should tone it down a bit, keep the crowd under control. He doesn't want any violence or confrontations with onlookers that would create bad publicity for the cause.

"Patriots," he says, "there's no way we'll allow vaccine passports at this mall, or anywhere in the city of Wolfville, or in the county, or in the state. We won't stand for it. There's many reasons, but I'll give you just three. First, and you know this as well as I do, it's an invasion of our privacy. These passports will be out there for all to see, and who knows, who knows who'll be looking at our private health information. One day, it'll be some restaurant worker, the next day, some snooping government agent. Second, it's discrimination. People who choose not to get injected will get barred, actually get barred, from public services, travel, and jobs. How sick is that! Third, it's an infringement of our precious liberty. We should be able to go to a movie or a pub without having to show a bloody passport. This isn't Mussolini's Italy, damn it. This is America, land of the free."

There is deafening applause. "Friends," Marv continues, "Thomas Paine, one of the great heroes of the American Revolution, once said, 'These are the times that try men's souls'. What he said back in 1776 applies to us today. We're in for a deadly fight and it's going to be tough. Our arrogant elites are dug in deep, and they're determined to control us. Well, we won't let them. We're not going to let them control us. Freedom is so sacred, so incredibly important, and so worth the struggle. We're gonna oppose them hard, and ... we're gonna win, we're gonna show them we won't be controlled."

Again, there is loud applause. Marv gets down from the platform and, with Tina and his black coats, begins to organize people for the march around the mall.

Michael comes over to talk to him. "Marv, you know the drill. Keep it peaceful. Our agreement was for only three hundred marchers. Three hundred, no more. And it's probably a good thing for you because they seem to be in a rambunctious mood today. I'm sure you don't want trouble."

"Not lookin' for trouble," replies Marv. "My people love peace. But be aware, my friend, vaccine passports are not a direction, repeat, not a direction, you want to go in. Get it?"

"We don't make quick or arbitrary decisions, Marv. Before we make a final decision, we'll get input from all sides, including from you."

Michael then goes over to talk to a group of police officers who are monitoring the crowd. He thanks them for being there and reminds them that their visibility should help to keep the crowd orderly. He also speaks to the mall security guards who are looking on. Michael wonders where Wally is, and then remembers he took the day off. Not ideal, but Michael couldn't refuse a day Wally was entitled too.

"Okay troops," Marv yells, "let's march. Tina, can you keep track of the number who are joining the march? Once it gets to three hundred, tell them sorry, but the tyrants who run the mall won't allow any more people."

"Got it, Marv." Tina turns to face the crowd but slips on the edge of the sidewalk and falls. The handsome black coat rushes to her side and gently helps her up. She thanks him and tells him she's okay. He looks relieved. Marv, talking to some people in the crowd, doesn't notice any of this.

The march begins, with Marv and his black coats leading the way. Going to the back is Tina, doing a head count. All is orderly, until halfway around the mall.

Marv hears voices at the back that are getting more animated. There are chants of "you will not replace us, you will not replace us." Marv directs his black coats to go back and urge people to keep it peaceful. "If there's trouble, we might get shut down. And tell them we might get denied any future rallies or marches. This doesn't help the cause."

But it's to no avail. As the marchers pass the pharmacy, which has an outside entrance, some of them yell obscenities, a dozen rush inside. They knock over displays, push aside the pharmacy workers. One marcher smacks an older worker in the face, another smashes a window, and another spray-paints a swastika on one of the walls. The police quickly move in, and many of the marchers run off. Additional police arrive, restore order, arrest a few marchers, and start talking to witnesses. They order the remaining crowd to disperse. The march is over.

Marv has been asked to wait at the site, and he cooperates. Eventually a senior officer informs Marv there is no evidence to show he was responsible for what happened. The witnesses have said Marv tried to prevent the rampage. Still, the officer says that he'll have to send in a report to city and county authorities, and to the mall, which will be taken into account when and if Marv requests permission for another rally or march. The officer also says that, once they've reviewed all the witness statements and surveillance footage, there will likely be charges—vandalism, assault, and the expression of hate—but for now Marv is free to go.

Marv knows that even if no charges are laid, the march is going to be reported in the media, which will hurt his image. He's going to have a hard time countering the claims that he and his followers are a bunch of violent goons and racists. How will he ever be able to have another rally or march? It's a major setback for his cause.

49

S ofia Morellato is walking in the mall. The stores have opened, but it's still early. Sofia is struggling with her walker as usual, and has a strained look on her face, but she's enjoying the music, Buddy Holly's *That'll Be The Day*. Walking up behind her are Mary and Richard Barker. All of them are wearing masks.

The Barkers slow their pace to chat with Sofia as they walk. Complaints about the hot August weather are the first topic of conversation. Then Sofia shares that she had a terrible quarrel with Tina yesterday. She had asked Tina if she could visit her granddaughter. But Tina refused. "It's been over a year," Sofia explains, "and I still can't see my little Brianna. It's killing me." The Barkers empathize.

"Sofia," says Richard, "what did you think about the march the other day? Quite the ending, wasn't it?"

"It was dramatic, that's for sure. But it troubles me, it really does, that we've now got violence and open racism. And my daughter's part of it all." Sofia sighs. "One good thing though, it's a big step backward for Marv. His reputation is going to take a hit. And it's going to be hard for him to have any more marches."

The trio pass Si-Woo talking with Grumpy Bill outside the pharmacy. They are having what appears to be an intimate conversation. Further along the mall are two older men, with shabby backpacks, quietly sitting on a bench. They look really beaten down. Power Walker races by them, waving and then greeting somebody in the bookstore.

Mary asks Sofia what she thinks about the idea of vaccine passports. Sofia says she'd feel a whole lot safer if she knew people around her were also vaccinated. She hopes the Governor will go ahead and make the passports mandatory across the state. And she hopes Michael will do the same for the mall.

"We feel the same," says Mary. "We're fully vaccinated, but it would be nice if everybody had their shots. I'm afraid we've got quite a few delinquents, people like Marv and his followers. I think the passports are in everybody's self-interest. They'll encourage more people to get vaccinated and, with that, more herd immunity, and less chance for the virus to spread. Richard also supports them, but as you might expect, for highfalutin philosophical reasons. He tells me they're justified because they're based on universal ethical principles, which we come to realize through our reasoning and judgment. Isn't that right, Richard?"

Richard looks indignant. "It is, Mary. You support them out of selfishness, and I do for ethical reasons."

"Well, now, aren't we high and mighty!"

"One of us has to be," says Richard, coughing into his arm. "Sorry about that. I'm afraid this cough of mine is getting worse. And so's my sore throat. Asthma, I guess. The humidity and the ragweed."

As they pass the bulletin board, Sofia stops and points to a typewritten note there. "I don't have my glasses on. What's it say?"

The Barkers look at each other in horror. Richard takes the note down and reads it aloud.

This is my third and final warning. I've put up with the masks and the vaccines. But I'll not stand for vaccine passports. I'm putting you on notice. If you push for the fuckin' passports, and if the mall doesn't say no, I'm gonna act.

I'M GONNA ACT! I'm gonna douse you with sulfuric acid. Hear me, you assholes. You have a week. That's it. Then watch out.

Sofia's jaw drops. She starts shaking like a leaf. "What on earth? What on earth is this about? I can't believe it. What language! Who would write such disgusting filthy words?"

"Sofia," says Mary, "this is actually the third note. Richard and I took down the first two notes—one was in June last year, the other in December—and gave them to Michael. The chief decided it was best to put a lid on it. He thought it was an idle threat, that nothing would come of it. He said it was probably some deranged nutbar, maybe one of those unhoused people, who was just sounding off."

"Yeah, that's right," adds Richard. "All three notes warn of an acid attack. The first was against masks, the second against vaccines, and the third, as you can see, against passports. The notes are basically the same. Except that this third one, it seems, is more serious and ominous."

"So, you're saying the notes are basically the same?" asks Sofia, looking puzzled.

Mary examines the paper and feels it. "Mostly the same," she says. "But there are a few differences. The first two were written on dirty stained paper, but this one is on clean fancy heavy weight paper. And the first two were sloppily handwritten; this one is printed in a fancy font."

Sofia takes the note from Mary and looks at it closely. She recognizes the paper and the typeface. She gasps but says nothing.

"There's one other difference," adds Richard. "In the first two notes, the time of attack was left vague. In this one, there is a definite timeline. The person says an attack could come after a week, meaning it could happen next Friday."

"I'm not clear about something," says Sofia. "You said one person was responsible. But from what you said before, about the paper and the presentation, there could be two or three different people involved."

Mary and Richard look at each other with confused expressions on their faces. "Sofia, we don't know," says Richard. "It could be separate people, probably buddies of some kind. Or, it could be one person pretending to be more, trying to mess us up, confuse us, for whatever reason. My bet is it's just one person."

"Any idea who it is?" asks Sofia, with a quivering voice.

"We've talked about it before," replies Mary. "Could be one of Marv's followers or admirers, maybe a security guard or somebody working in the mall. Or maybe one of our unhoused people, somebody who has gone off the deep end. We don't know."

Sofia recognizes the premium quality white paper. Tina uses it for her work printing invitations to weddings and special events. And the fancy typeface is a calligraphy one that Tina often uses, candlescript. Is it possible that Tina printed the note and pinned it up, or had somebody else pin it up? *No way my daughter could do such a thing.*

Sofia thinks of another question. "Who do you think could be attacked?"

"Well, we've talked about this before too," replies Richard, coughing again. "Most likely somebody who has openly advocated for things this guy doesn't like—masks, vaccines, passports. High-profile people like Dr. Cortez."

"I've said I support the passports," says Sofia. "So, it could be me."

"I guess it could," says Richard, trying to clear his throat. "And it could be one of us. But if I were the attacker, I'd go after Michael. The note said if the mall doesn't reject the idea of passports, there'll be an attack. Who does this point to? It points to Michael, assuming he doesn't reject the passports."

"Speaking of Michael," says Mary, "we better get over to his office and show him this note. He'll have to decide what to do."

50

Michael is in his office, checking the mail. The due dates on invoices remind him September is approaching. He wonders what's ahead for him in the fall.

The summer has been good. No decision has been made about his promotion, but his contacts at Pacific Gold tell him he shouldn't worry. Senior management is pleased with his performance. And why shouldn't they be? Despite Covid, the mall is doing well. Sales are good and shoppers are happy—happy with the renovations, the promotions and advertising, and the competitive prices. New leases have filled empty spaces and the new stores have brought in more shoppers.

Not everything's been positive. The manager at Sunrise Mall is aggressive and determined to outperform his mall, and she's had some success. Her sales and customer visits have been going up too, and at a faster rate than at Michael's mall. Another concern for Michael is the fallout from Marv's march. Will the violence mean fewer shoppers? Will more shoppers now go to Sunrise? If this occurs, will Pacific Gold sour on him? And what if Covid gets worse again?

At home, things are also going well. Cornelia has been less pushy, and her father has been less intrusive. And, of great help to Michael, the girls insisted they stay at their same school for another year. Cornelia has reluctantly agreed to delay plans for an expensive private school, and agreed to postpone her pursuit of a house in Blue Mountain Heights until Michael's promotion goes through.

Michael's thoughts are interrupted by a sharp knock on the door. He welcomes Sofia Morellato and the Barkers.

"Coffee?" he asks.

"No thanks, I'm past my quota," says Sofia, taking a chair.

"Same with us," says Richard.

"Well then, what's up?"

"I'm afraid we've got some bad news, chief," says Mary. "We found another note this morning on the bulletin board. Have a look. And again, please don't say who gave it to you."

As he reads the note, Michael pales. He jumps up from his chair and paces the office. He wonders why things always seem to be going around in circles: a march, a note, then the Barkers coming to see him about it. Why is it always the Barkers that discover the notes? He forces himself to focus, get back to reality.

"So," he says, "we've got ourselves another disturbing message. But I see it's printed this time and on clean paper. Might mean it's a different person, or maybe the same person pretending to be somebody different. I suppose it doesn't matter, a threat is a threat."

"But Michael," says Richard, "it's not just another threat ... it's much more disturbing, and more serious. And there's a definite time of attack mentioned. Could happen after a week, which means it could be next Friday."

"Yeah, I can see that."

"One other thing you need to bear in mind," adds Mary. "You yourself could be a target. The note says if the mall, meaning you, doesn't say no to the passports, there'll be an attack. Think about it yourself: who would be in the crosshairs of this psycho? Well, it could be Dr. Cortez or somebody else pushing for the passports. But it certainly could be you. You're the guy in charge."

"Well, I haven't thought about that," says Michael. "But I suppose you're right."

"What do you intend to do, chief?" asks Mary. "You can't just ignore this. Something's got to be done."

"I realize that, Mary. But just give me a few minutes, give me a chance to think it through."

Rubbing his hands together, Michael continues to pace across the room, collecting his thoughts. He then tells them that one thing he can do is increase security, bring in some extra security guards. And arrange for more signage to be put up, telling people they're being watched. He returns to his chair.

"That should deter them," he says, to both himself and the others. "Not sure what else we can do." The image of the old man with the mask jammed into his throat comes into his mind, and the phone call from the old man's sister—Lisa—berating him for not taking any action.

"You should alert the public and bring in the police," says Richard. "This is serious stuff. Don't you get it?"

"I agree with Richard," adds Mary. "You must admit, chief, this threat is a big step up from the previous ones. You can't just ignore it and hope it'll go away. You need to act."

"Okay, I think you're right, I need to do more. But give me a couple days to figure out exactly what to do. Can you do that?"

They look at one another and reluctantly agree. Michael thanks them and assures them he'll take action. He then asks, since they are there, what they think about vaccine passports, and whether the mall should require them. They reply that they all support passports, and that he should require them in the mall, regardless of the threats.

Struggling for breath, Richard starts to cough.

"That doesn't sound good, Richard," says Michael. "You should get that checked."

"Just my asthma. If it gets any worse, I'll see Dr. Cortez."

After they exit, Michael agonizes over what to do. Should he alert the public about the threat? Bring in the police? And now another person knows about the notes. Even if he wants to keep it quiet, isn't word going to leak out to the public? And if it does, how will it affect business in the mall? If business slips off, his chance for a promotion could go up in smoke. He could even lose his job. And Cornelia might leave him, as she's threatened before.

And what if I am the target? He wonders what would it feel like? Would he be scarred for life? How would Cornelia react? If he were disabled, or perhaps if he died from the attack, how would Cornelia carry on? His life insurance is not that generous. Then he has a cynical thought. If he died, how would Cornelia get her big fancy house in Blue Mountain Heights?

51

After lunch, Michael heads over to Wally Waller's office. It's busy in the mall and the Bee Gees' *Stayin' Alive* is playing. That's an oldie, he thinks, but probably appropriate for the afternoon shoppers.

He knocks on Wally's office door and waits for a response. He hears a heated conversation behind him, though he can't make out the words. He glances around and sees Tina talking with one of Marv's black coats, the handsome one with the mustache. What are they plotting, he wonders. Or arguing about.

Wally opens the door. "Come on in, bro. Have a seat. What's goin' on?"

"A couple things. First off, Wally, I'd like to get your take on having vaccine passports in the mall. Good or bad idea?"

"Bottom line, it's an awful idea. Can't think of any positives. Except I've heard some people say they'd feel safer coming into the mall, knowing others have got vaccinated. But that's about it."

"So, what's the downside?"

Wally scratches his head, gathers his thoughts, and launches into a long list of all the extra security work involved in checking passports. Shoppers wouldn't like the hassle or delay, and they'd probably take that resentment out on security guards, as they already do with the masking requirements. He takes a gulp of his pop. "Just leave it to the city or the Governor. Let them take the flak."

"Thanks for your suggestion, Wally. I'll think about it. There's something else. I'm afraid I got some bad news."

Michael hands Wally the note. As Wally reads it, his eyes widen and his jaw drops. He looks absolutely stunned. Michael wonders if he is genuinely stunned or just pretending to be. If he is pretending, he's an awfully good actor.

"So, what do you think?" asks Michael. "This is the third note and the most serious. It was found this morning on the bulletin board, same as before. What do you think?"

Wally mulls it over for a few minutes. "Well, Michael, I have to admit, this is more serious. It definitely is. This creep gives us a clear timeline—it's gonna happen in a week. I really don't know what to say. I thought we were past all this crap. But this looney keeps coming at us. He just doesn't stop. He keeps threatening and threatening!"

"How do you know it's a male, Wally?"

"Well, I can't imagine any woman coming up with this shit. It's not lady-like."

"We just can't rule it out, Wally. We can't rule out anybody. Could be male or female, an unhoused person, a disgruntled worker, maybe even a disgruntled security guard."

Wally glares at Michael. "C'mon, man, one of my security guards? No way! You've gotta be kiddin'. I know these people, they've all been screened. No way, Michael, you can *definitely* rule them out."

"All I'm saying, Wally, is that we just don't know."

Wally puts his hand under his chin and considers the matter. "Well, bro, I think it's best to ignore the note. I agree it's more disturbing. But ya know, at the end of the day, we ignored the other two notes, and nothing happened. I'm thinking now it's all a bluff. Even this last note, it's a bluff. All these notes are an attempt to scare people in the mall. Scare them into doing what this creep wants—no masks, no vaccines, no passports. The guy doesn't have the courage to actually do anything. All the creep can do is pin up notes."

"Maybe you're right. But Wally, we can't do nothing. At the very least, we need to beef up security, like we did last December. You can start by calling your company and getting some extra guards in here. I think five would be good. Better get them in here right away. You can also put up some more signs at the entrances warning people they're under surveillance. Again, you need to do this pronto. Got to get it done within a week."

"Don't worry, bro, I'll get it done. I'll start right away."

"Good."

"And what about the cameras and the surveillance system? Everything okay? Please tell me everything is working."

"The system is mostly working, but … I'm afraid, not entirely," says Wally, with a look of embarrassment. "I can explain."

"Go ahead. This better be good."

Wally explains that he finally got a technician to come in last March, a specialist from Seattle who knows the security software well. There are not many of these people around, which is why it took so long. She confirmed the issue was software, and fixed it. For a while, we could see video in the monitoring room from all the cameras in the mall, all fifty of them.

"For a while?" asks Michael. "What's the problem?"

"A few weeks after she left, the video from a bunch of cameras on the west side went blank, including, I kid you not, the ones above the bulletin board and the unisex washroom. She said something like this could happen, and if it did, call her back. I did call her back, but she was off sick for a few weeks, and their office was short-staffed, and she's been delayed. But she's coming. I got a text from her last week, and she could be here any day now."

Michael is fuming. "What a piss off. But I guess it's better late than never. Wally, let me know when she gets here and fixes the problem. We need to get everything working. And if she doesn't get here in a couple days, call her back and tell her it's an extreme emergency. Try another company. We need the cameras working."

"Gotcha. See ya later."

Michael leaves the security office and wonders again about the long delays. Is Wally trying to throw up roadblocks? Could he be worrying about what the video might reveal? Could it show his involvement with the notes or with the old man's death?

Maybe there's an innocent explanation? Maybe Wally simply goofed up at the start by forgetting to get the system fixed. Maybe, after the late start, as Wally said, it took a long time to get a specialist to come in. This kind of thing has happened before. And maybe, after that, once the system did get fixed, there was another glitch and further delay. All of this is believable. It could be a series of mishaps. Wally might be a ruffian and a racist, but that doesn't prove he had anything to do with the notes or with the death of the bookstore clerk.

52

When the note was handed to me, I was so excited to pin it up. The message was dead on and it was brilliantly presented. Instead of being handwritten, it was typed on clean high-grade paper. Anybody trying to figure out who did it would be confused.

I'm really mad now. I was mad about the masks. I was mad about the vaccines. But this plan to bring in vaccine passports is over the top. Imagine forcing people to show proof of vaccination if they wanna get a burger or go shopping. Marv is absolutely right. It's an attack on our freedom. I'll do everything I can to stop it.

The note's been taken down. Love to know who it was. But no matter. I'm gonna go ahead in a week. I'm gonna strike after the week is up. A good time to do it, I figure, will be late afternoon, when there'll be a lotta shopping and people getting ready to go to a movie. They've taken off the seating restrictions in the theaters so there should be tons of people around. Man, I'm raring to go. I've been practicing with my water gun almost every day for the last week.

I've got a good plan. Just before I strike, I'll go into the washroom in the big restaurant—where there's no security camera—and put on a hoodie. It's got a big inside pocket which'll be perfect for the water gun. I'll find my target, rip off its mask, squirt lots of acid into its face, and escape into the crowd. It'll be perfect.

I love this kind of thing. One of my happiest memories was the day our neighbor got a new car. He was so happy and proud. Late that night, I went out with a sharp knife and slashed it up—the doors, tires, hood, top, everything. When the guy saw it the next morning, he went ballistic. But I was on cloud nine. I got away with it! Nobody ever found out.

I got away with a lot of stuff later too. I did get charged for beating up a few kids and sending two of them to the hospital. But that was only probation and community service. Nothing more than that. I never killed nobody … except for that one guy.

So, my mind is made up. I'll strike next Friday. The only thing that could change my mind is the mall saying no to passports.

53

Joe Talkback: Good morning Wolfville! Welcome to Talkback, the most popular morning chat in the city. I'm your host, Joe Talkback. For today's first call, we are talking about the vaccine passports. Dr. Juan Cortez, local public health champion, and with a practice at Wolfville Mall, is back, and today he's going to defend vaccine passports. Welcome back.

Dr. Cortez: Good to be with you again.

Joe Talkback: Well doctor, this is really a radical idea, isn't it? Critics say it's something you'd expect in Communist China or Cuba, not America. Don't you think it's too extreme for America?

Dr. Cortez: No, it's not extreme at all. It's not a radical idea. Vaccine passports have been around a long time, going back to when vaccines were developed. To fight smallpox, back in the 1800s, American border officials required people who wanted to enter our country to show proof of vaccination, either in the form of a vaccination certificate or a unique scar on their arm indicating inoculation. For people traveling overseas, or in some jobs, proof of vaccination has been required for diseases like typhoid, cholera, and polio. So, the idea of vaccine passports is nothing new.

Joe Talkback: Good point. But how do you justify this for Covid? Isn't it like hitting a finishing nail with a sledgehammer? Over the top?

Dr. Cortez: No, it's appropriate to the seriousness of Covid-19. The virus is getting more deadly. Cases are climbing, hospitalizations are going up, and deaths are increasing. We know from the research that people who are not vaccinated are significantly more likely to get Covid and to die from it. So we need as many people as possible to get vaccinated. How do we encourage them to get vaccinated? Well, since many people like to go to movies, restaurants, pubs, music concerts, and so forth, we make it a requirement for them to show proof of vaccination to get into these venues.

Joe Talkback: Isn't this bribery?

Dr. Cortez: Encouragement is a better word. People are not being forced to get the passport. They can watch a movie at home. They can get takeout from a restaurant. They can watch basketball on TV. I know it's not the same thing. But we have a public health emergency on our hands. Covid is deadly. We've got to get people vaccinated and we've got to encourage them to get vaccinated.

Joe Talkback: But you must admit, Doctor, it's undemocratic. Many people don't want this pushed down their throats. They don't want so-called experts telling them what to do.

Dr. Cortez: In Wolfville, in the whole state, vaccine passports are just being considered. They are not policy. I agree some people are hesitant. It was the same with masks. But public opinion is increasing for support of passports. When authorities announce they will be putting the passports into effect, and I'm sure this will happen soon, the measure will reflect the will of the people. Most people want to feel safe when they go into restaurants or movie theaters. They want to know others are vaccinated. So, they will support the measure. This is the will of the people, this is democracy.

Joe Talkback: Doctor, I think I heard you cough a bit earlier. You don't have Covid, do you?

Dr. Cortez: Sorry, I didn't mean to scare you. No, I've got my two doses, I'm fully vaccinated. The cough is from allergies I get this time of the year. It's ragweed season and I'm afraid I get affected.

Joe Talkback: Now, Doctor, even if vaccine passports are the will of the people, this doesn't make them legitimate. In America, people in authority can't violate our basic rights in the Constitution. Don't the passports violate our basic rights? Don't they violate our privacy rights, for example?

Dr. Cortez: Sorry, but could you just explain how they could possibly violate our right to privacy.

Joe Talkback: Be happy to. My personal health information—and I'm sure you'd agree—should be kept private and confidential. It's for me alone, or for me and my doctor. My vaccination status is part of my personal health information. I want it kept as a private matter, whether I'm vaccinated or not. It's my business, nobody else's. Now if I'm forced to disclose my vaccination status on a paper card or QR code to a restaurant employee or a theater worker, I'm losing my privacy. This person could easily pass along the information to somebody else.

Dr. Cortez: While privacy is important, it's not an absolute value. We have a huge public health emergency on our hands. Some loss of privacy is justified to fight this deadly virus. And keep in mind, you are not being forced to go inside a restaurant or a theater. You can simply choose to get takeout food or watch a movie at home. And it's highly unlikely the worker cares very much about your vaccination status.

Joe Talkback: I'm not sure many people would agree with you on that. But let's talk about the violation of another right. In our country, we have a right to equality before the law. We have a right not to be discriminated against on grounds such as race, religion, sex, and disability. But with vaccine passports, people are being discriminated against. If the passports go into effect, people who are not vaccinated will be discriminated against in services, travel, and even jobs. It will be a new version of Jim Crow. How can you possibly defend this?

Dr. Cortez: Most Americans believe in equality, and they rightly reject all forms of unfair and arbitrary discrimination. But discrimination based on vaccination status is not the same thing as discrimination based on grounds such as race and religion. To exclude a Muslim from working in a grocery store is arbitrary and unfair discrimination. Their religion has no effect on other people. But to exclude an unvaccinated person from coming into a restaurant is not discrimination. Their health affects other people. The exclusion is not arbitrary. Protecting the health of customers in a restaurant is a responsibility of the restaurant. That covers everything from food safety to making sure diners are not spreading a highly contagious and sometimes fatal disease.

Joe Talkback: But people wanting to eat at the restaurant would be plain out of luck if they aren't vaccinated, or just want to keep their vaccination status private. They get no choice, no freedom, to eat where they want.

Dr. Cortez: I agree their choice would be more limited, and necessarily so, given the importance of public health. But they should, and I think, would be accommodated as much as possible. They could order takeout food at a restaurant, for example. And the proof of vaccination would be in place only as long as there was a public health threat. After the threat has passed, the policy would end.

Joe Talkback: Yeah, like income tax was temporary. I've done enough talking. Let's open up the lines. Caller number one, what's your question?

Caller 1: Doctor, I don't know what country you're from, but this is America, land of the free. Our most prized value is freedom. It's a basic right under our constitution. Vaccine passports are an obvious and disgusting violation of our freedom. I think you're un-American. And I think you are a complete idiot!

Dr. Cortez: Freedom is a prized value. I couldn't agree more, and thank you for mentioning that. We all agree people should be free to do what they want as long as they don't harm others. But if I go into a crowded restaurant or theater without being vaccinated, I pose a risk of harm to others. If I spread Covid to you and you get sick, I take away your freedom to live a healthy and happy life. Freedom is for everyone. If I do something that diminishes the freedom of others or harms others, society has the responsibility to step in and limit my freedom. Vaccine passports are a means of doing this.

Joe Talkback: Thanks for your question. Caller number two, what's your question?

Caller 2: Doctor, you are making my blood boil. I'm a nurse at the downtown hospital and I refuse to get vaccinated. The hospital tells me if proof of vaccination becomes policy, and if I don't get vaccinated, I'll have to quit my job as a nurse or else take a lower-paying clerical job away from the general public, probably in a basement somewhere. The result? I won't have the same opportunity to advance in the hospital than nurses who are vaccinated. Aren't we supposed to have equality of opportunity in America? How on earth can you defend this?

Dr. Cortez: I'm not going to deny the fact that when the policy is put into effect, the vaccinated and unvaccinated, at least in some areas, will not have the same opportunity. They won't. Even though there'll be attempts to accommodate the unvaccinated as much as possible, they are not going to have the same opportunities as others. But I do defend the policy. In times of a pandemic, just as with the value of freedom, some loss of equal opportunity can be justified on grounds of public health. A deadly virus is spreading across the state and across America. To combat this virus, we need to encourage vaccines, and a way of doing this is a policy of proof of vaccinations. I hope I've made my position clear. Thanks for raising the issue.

Joe Talkback: Yes, it's a big issue. But I'm afraid we're out of time now. Thank you, Dr. Cortez, for coming in. As always, we appreciate your time and your comments.

54

Grumpy Bill turns off his radio with a groan. Enough, he thinks. *Dr. Cortez is a well-meaning guy and he's a straight shooter. But he's too idealistic. He needs to be more like I am, more practical and down to earth. He needs to understand that the perfect is the enemy of the good.*

Grumpy Bill gets back to what he was doing before the interview—putting up a new display of baseball gear in his store's front window. It's late morning and he is expecting a visit from the mall manager.

When Michael arrives, Grumpy Bill motions to his assistant to watch the store. He invites Michael to his back office. Both remove their masks and sit down. Michael wants to know where the business association stands on vaccine passports for the mall. Grumpy Bill explains, and concludes, "Like masks, it's divided. Best to wait it out, wait for the Governor to take action."

"I'm thinking about going ahead anyway," says Michael.

"What! Yer thinking of what!" Grumpy Bill jerks his head violently to his side several times, startling Michael.

"You heard me. I'm considering passports as a requirement for entry into the mall, or at least parts of the mall. Seems very likely they're coming to Wolfville anyway. Rumor has it that the Mayor is going to require them for the city, the Governor for the state. The public is getting more and more on board. So I'm thinking about getting ahead on the issue, introducing them for the mall."

Grumpy Bill jumps up from his chair. He looks alarmed. "Dagnabbit, you've got to be joking!"

"No, I'm not joking. I'm not saying I'm definitely doing it. But I'm thinking about it. Look, the public is becoming more supportive. The Governor is probably going to act soon. Why not get ahead of the curve? Obviously, some people are opposed. There's Marv and his gang of crazies, there's our own security people. But they're in the minority. Most people appreciate that the passports are a necessary means of fighting the virus. Did you hear the interview Dr. Cortez did this morning? People hear things like that and they realize vaccine passports are a good idea. So, acting now would be the right thing to do."

"Dr. Cortez is too dreamy, and so are you if you think that interview would make people support passports." Grumpy Bill sits down. "Good golly, Michael, why stick your neck out? Maybe the public is getting behind the idea, even though I don't support it myself. And, as you say, the Governor probably will act, just like she did with masks. But my lordy, why not wait 'til she does? It worked out for you before. It worked with masks and the pharmacy issue. Why not wait?"

Michael puts his hands under his chin. "You know, Grumpy Bill, sometimes a person should do the right thing. It's not always about being strategic and pragmatic."

"Heavens to Betsy, chief. You better think more carefully about this. I'm telling you, it's not a wise thing to do." Grumpy Bill goes over the many disadvantages, including the mall losing business and the stores being billed more for more security. "Brenda whatever-her-name-is at Sunrise Mall has made it clear she's going to reject any requirement for passports, unless forced to do so by the Governor or city. This would mean losing more business to

Sunrise. And if the Governor doesn't go ahead with passports, you—everyone at this mall—is out on a limb. The idea is a loser for everyone, including you."

"You make a convincing argument," says Michael. "I certainly don't want business to suffer. Tell you what. I'll give it some more thought."

"You should listen to me, for goodness' sake, you really should." Grumpy Bill looks at Michael with amazement. How did this guy, he wonders, ever get to be a mall manager? He should have joined the priesthood or ministry.

Michael scratches the back of his head and sighs. "There's something else to discuss." Michael pauses and clenches his fists. "We have a threat to deal with in the mall. I didn't tell you before, GB, but now I think I should. It's weighing heavily on me."

Michael shows Grumpy Bill the note. As he reads it, his eyes open wide and his face turns white. He looks like he's been struck by lightning.

"Oh, my lordy! This is serious, deadly serious. We've got a psychopath in the mall. Jeepers! What have we got happening here! And yet another reason—you hear me, chief, another reason—not to go ahead with the passports."

"Actually, this is the third note."

Grumpy Bill gasps. "Third?"

"Yeah. There were two previous ones before this, one against masks, the other against the vaccines. I decided to keep it quiet, worrying it might cause fear or panic in the mall. Might harm business. Nothing happened. But this note has a more specific threat. I thought you should be aware, and I wanted your thoughts. Please keep it to yourself, at least for now."

"Don't worry, I'll keep it quiet." Grumpy Bill stands up, looking agitated. He wonders who it would be. Who would have so much anger, and so much hate. To threaten to throw sulfuric acid into somebody's face! Unbelievable, simply unbelievable!

"So, what do you think, GB? Should I alert the mall? Should I bring in the police? Or should I just ignore the note, keep it quiet as I did before."

Grumpy Bill paces the tiny office with his hands on his hips, and returns to his chair. "Gosh, it's a tough call. A really tough call. I'm simply flabbergasted. I think it would be prudent to ignore it, at least for now. We don't want to lose business. But ... I'm not sure. If I come up with anything more definitive, Michael, I'll let you know. In the meantime, and you've probably done this, you need to strengthen security. More guards, more monitoring, that sort of thing."

"Yeah, I've talked to Wally and instructed him to do just that. Thanks for your thoughts on this. Tell me if you think of anything more."

As Michael leaves, Grumpy Bill watches him, and considers the hard decision Michael will have to make. If Michael decides to do nothing and an attack happens, it'll be terrible for both Michael and the mall. On the other hand, if he alerts the public and nothing happens, that hurts the mall too.

Grumpy Bill speculates who might be a target. Dr. Cortez would be an obvious one. Or it could be random. But it's more likely someone who has spoken out on the issue. Somebody like ... like Si-Woo. He doesn't want anything bad to happen to her. Or ... Michael could be the target. He's the one responsible for policy. If Michael decides to go ahead with the passports, he'd be putting himself in danger. Has he considered this?

55

The next morning, Michael arrives at his office with a macchiato from Starbucks. As he is about to take a sip, he notices a message on his office phone. He sits down and listens to a familiar woman's voice.

"Mr. Manager, it's me again. I've got another message for you. Listen up. Your daughters are having a lot of fun this summer, playing with their friends, going swimming at the Golden Ears Pool. Be a shame if this got all messed up, wouldn't it? If you don't want to see Brandy or Bobbie traumatized, make it clear you won't introduce vaccine passports in the mall. Announce it. Spell it out. Your daughters are so innocent, so sweet. We wouldn't want to see anything nasty happen to them, would we? You have yourself a great day."

The call ends. I can't believe it, he thinks. This woman, whoever she is, is trying to intimidate me again, trying to force me to do what the anti-vaxxers want. *What'll I do? Will I just give in? I've got to protect my girls.*

He calls Cornelia and tells her what happened. She screams into the phone and shouts obscenities. Once she stops, Michael suggests she keep the girls at home, never letting them out of her sight. He then suggests that, as before, she should arrange for the twins to go down to Georgia and spend time with their grandfather. It's still the summer holidays and they're not in school. He also tells her it would be a good idea for her to lay low, keep the doors locked, and keep out of sight.

Cornelia agrees. She asks Michael how he plans to respond to the woman's demand. What is he going to decide about the passports? He tells her he doesn't know for sure, he's going to have to mull it over. Cornelia pauses. Then she says, in a calm voice, "You'd better think it through carefully. You've got to do whatever it takes to protect your family."

After ending the call, he stands up, rubs his hands together, and paces around his office. He has two big decisions to make, one on the note and the other on the passports. They are really the same issue: do something or do nothing.

He goes over to his laptop, sits down, and opens a new Word file. He names it Options. On one page, he types: Option #1: Do Nothing—Do Nothing About the Note, Do Nothing About the Passports. On the second page, he types: Option #2: Take Action—Warn the Public, Bring in Vaccine Passports. He prints off the two pages and pins them up on his bulletin board.

For several minutes, he stares at the Do Nothing option. This would probably be better, he thinks, for the mall's business, his chance of promotion, and his relationship with Cornelia. But there's a chance things will turn out badly. If he does nothing about the note, and if there was a deadly attack, it would be a disaster. His career would go up in smoke. And if he did nothing about the passports, and if the virus continued to get worse, it would be bad not just for public health, but also for the mall's long-term business. Still, all of this is unlikely. The more prudent course would be to sit back and just do nothing. Grumpy Bill would heartily approve.

He then looks at the Take Action option. He walks around his office and contemplates the possible outcomes. This, he reckons, would probably be worse for him. Business in the mall could suffer,

Pacific Gold might turn down his application for promotion, and Cornelia could get extremely angry and send him packing. She might end up divorcing him and moving back to Georgia, and he'd have to endure a painful separation from his girls. But there is a chance things will turn out well. Maybe the writer of the note would get caught, and the passports would be welcomed as a wise action. If all this were to happen, he'd be a heroic figure, his career could advance, and his family could stay together and thrive. But if he takes action, the odds are for a bad outcome.

Michael remembers his mother, many years ago, urging him to be more decisive in making decisions. Stop being like Hamlet, she'd always say, or it could end up in disaster. Stop being equivocal, she'd tell him, be strong, be resolute. He also thinks about his dad calling on him to do the right thing, even if you might suffer for it. Isn't it time, Michael thinks, to do the right thing, to put aside all the possible consequences and implications? Isn't it time to actually listen to his father? You've got to stop dithering, he tells himself, you've got to stop weighing everything so much, you've got to stop looking at things from every possible angle. Follow your principles, do the right thing.

Michael goes into his office washroom and looks at himself in the mirror. He sees sweat on his forehead, he sees wildness and turmoil in his eyes. "Well, well," he asks himself, "what are you going to do? You can't dither around forever. You've got to make a decision. And in the future, you've got to look at yourself in the mirror again, and again and again, and you've got to feel good about what you see." He hears his dad's voice: Do the right thing, put your principles above what's expedient. Finally, Michael says, "Yes ... yes ... yes ... this time, I *will* do the right thing. We can never be sure about what's going to happen down the road. We've got to do the right thing in the present moment."

As for Bobbie and Brandy, he doesn't want to endanger them. But he can't be intimidated by a phone threat. He can't allow a despicable anti-vaxxer on the phone to control him. Besides, the girls will be fine in Georgia. Their grandfather will take good care of them.

Michael makes his decision. First thing tomorrow morning, he'll send out an alert to the public about the threatened acid attack in the mall. He'll contact customer services and have them put up posts about the threat on the mall website and on posters throughout the mall. He'll notify the police and issue a press release. And he'll arrange for announcements through the PA system.

As for vaccine passports, he'll initiate a policy similar to ones he's read about in malls in California and New York. It will go into effect in three weeks, giving the public time to prepare for it. It will be a targeted policy. Not the whole mall, just places where the risk of spreading the virus is greater: the two restaurants, the movie theater, the gym, and the food court. Some shoppers may be angry, and there may be a protest. But, over time, he hopes they'll come to support the policy. He'll have the information made known in the morning through the PA system, the website, and posters around the mall.

56

"We're having beef bourguignon tonight," says Cornelia, as Michael comes in the door. "Might not be up there with Julia Child's cooking, but I think you'll like it."

"Fantastic," replies Michael, going into the kitchen. "One of my favorite dishes." Michael gives Cornelia a hug, knowing she's trying to be upbeat to hide being scared. He's going to try to be supportive and stay cool.

"To go with it, I've got a nice Italian red, a Sangiovese from central Tuscany. It's a Chianti Classico DOCG, 2014 vintage. We had one a few months back, remember. It's got that exquisite plum and earthy aroma, and the taste of sour cherries and dried oregano. It's positively voluptuous."

Voluptuous? She's got to be joking. "Uh, oh yeah, I remember it now. It was really good. So, princess, where are the girls?"

"They're upstairs in their rooms packing. I'm going to take them to the airport tomorrow after lunch. Daddy says he's really upset by the whole thing, but not to worry. He'll be glad to see them, and he'll keep a close eye on them."

"Yeah, it's upsetting for us all. Listen, I'll change, then we can try the Chianti."

"No, no, it's Chianti Classico. You've got to get it right. There's a big difference between Chianti and Chianti Classico. They're made differently, you know. In Chianti Classico, the wine's got to be made from at least eighty percent Sangiovese grapes; in Chianti, it has to be only seventy percent. Got it?"

"Okay, okay, I get it. I'll be back in a couple minutes."

Michael leaves for the bedroom to get changed. He reminds himself he's got to stay cool. He can't react to Cornelia's snootiness. She's having a really difficult time with the threat. They both are.

Back in the kitchen, he watches Cornelia add pearl onions to the beef bourguignon and stir them in. He assumes she finds that cooking a fancy meal is a good distraction.

"I'm back, princess. I'll open the Chianti—sorry, the Chianti Classico—and we'll go into the other room and have a nice pre-dinner glass of wine."

"Yes, let's do that. I'll leave the beef simmering. It'll be fine."

"It smells marvelous."

Michael follows Cornelia into the family room with the wine, and they both sit down in front of the fireplace.

"Okay, let's try this voluptuous wine," says Michael. He pours a glass for each of them, then samples his. "Mmm, this is awesome. Nice and dry, wickedly good!"

"Wickedly good, yes," says Cornelia, slowly taking a sip.

They spend a few minutes in silence. After a few more sips, Michael is ready to talk to Cornelia. "Princess, I've got a couple things to tell you."

"I hope it's not more bad news, Michael. We've had enough of that, don't you think?"

"I'm afraid it is. There's been another note. A third one. And it's crazier and more ominous, and more specific, than the other ones. It says an acid attack will happen in the mall, and it'll be in a week's time, meaning it could happen this coming Friday."

Cornelia jumps up from the sofa and shouts. "What the hell is going on, Michael! All these damn threats! It's unbelievable, simply unbelievable. What are you going to do about it?"

Michael braces himself for Cornelia's reaction. "Princess, I've made a decision. I believe the note is really serious and it just can't be ignored. Ergo, in addition to beefing up security, first thing in the morning, I'm going to notify the public and the police."

"Michael, are you sure this is the right thing to do? I can phone Daddy and see what he thinks."

Call Daddy? She's got to be kidding, Michael thinks. Why does she have to bring up dear old Daddy? Like he's some kind of deity. He doesn't need to live with the decision. "No need, princess," he says. "I've thought it through. This is the right course of action."

"But what about the fallout? How's this going to affect your business in the mall, and your chances of a promotion?

"It's hard to say, Cornelia. Could be bad for me. But if I ignore the note and something happens, if an acid attack actually happens, that could be worse. I'd get blamed and my career with Pacific Gold would come to a screeching halt. So, it seems to me I should err on the side of safety, on the side of protecting people in the mall from violence. Who knows? I might get some credit for this."

"Hope you're right, Michael, hope you're right. But if you're not—"

"Cornelia, there's one other thing I should tell you. I also made a decision to go ahead with vaccine passports in the mall. After some careful thought, I decided it's the correct thing to do. I have to give priority to the safety and health of our customers and workers. So, beginning in three weeks, a new policy of passports is going to go into effect. Mind you, it's not for the whole mall, only for selected locations where the risk of Covid is high."

Michael braces himself again for Cornelia's reaction. *Is she going to flip out?*

"Michael, are you sure about this? Remember that awful phone call you just got. Remember about our daughters. Do you really want to put our girls in jeopardy?"

"They'll be fine with your father in Georgia. We'll bring them back once this all blows over."

"Michael, what you've decided is really risky, reckless even. You don't have to do this, you don't have to stick your neck out. You didn't do this before—with the masks, with the vaccine issue. Why are you doing this now? Daddy is going to go wild!"

Daddy, Daddy! There she goes again, bringing up her dear know-it-all father. "You're right, Cornelia. I didn't do this before. I was always being super careful, super pragmatic. But sometimes one should just do the principled thing, which is what I'm doing now."

"The principled thing! You've got to be joking. If you want to talk principles, Michael, your first principle should be to look after me and your family. Why in the world would you want to risk your job, your promotion, your family? I can't believe you'd do such an idiotic thing. You really are a fool!"

"It's not idiotic, Cornelia. Proof of vaccination is coming to Wolfville anyway. It's being discussed by the city, the county, and the Governor. I'm just jumping ahead a bit, that's all. Malls in California and New York are already doing it. You know, Cornelia, I could get some praise for it. There is going to be criticism, that's for sure. Marv and his gang of loonies are going to be having a fit. But over time, I think most people will be supportive. Some may even applaud me."

"Applaud you … applaud you? Have you lost your marbles? In your dreams, Michael, in your wildest dreams. I don't want to talk about this anymore. It's the dumbest decision you've ever made. I just can't believe your idiocy. You can get your own dinner. I'm not hungry. I'm going to go upstairs and phone Daddy."

Cornelia throws her glass of half-finished red wine at the wall next to the stone fireplace. The glass shatters. What looks like blood streams down the wall. She storms out of the room, leaving Michael to stare at what looks like a crime scene.

57

I'm steaming mad now. Never in my life have I been so mad, never, ever. This morning, as I was getting my coffee, there was an announcement that the mall will be requiring vaccine passports in three weeks. And not just that. She also warned shoppers that there's been the threat of an acid attack against people who've been urging passports.

I'm so mad I'm shaking. I just can't believe it. The mall is actually going to go ahead with the passports. I thought the mall might do this. There's so much political correctness around these days. But another part of me figured it wouldn't happen. What the mall usually does is cowardly wait for the Governor or the city to act first.

So, I guess I have to go ahead. I haven't decided who my victim will be, or maybe victims. But high on the list, is Michael McQueen. He's deliberately chosen to cross me, piss me off, and require passports.

There's no question he deserves the acid. But there's others too. The doctor certainly would qualify. So would the old Morellato lady, the crinkly old hag with the walker. And so would the Asian lady, Si-Woo. I know she's been badgering the mall about requiring passports. I'd love to squirt some acid into her ugly face.

Next Friday. I'm gonna go hunting for the people on my list, and I'm gonna go after whoever's in the mall at the time. It'll be in the late afternoon, the perfect time because the mall will be busy, busier than usual for a Friday. There's a new phone being released, and a new superhero movie opening at the multiplex. It'll be the perfect time to strike. Can't wait!

58

Carole King's *I Feel the Earth Move* is playing in the mall. It's early morning and Sofia is walking, humming along to the song. But she's troubled. She got a call from Tina earlier this morning. Tina's voice was cracking, and she wanted to talk, in person. That's all she would say. Despite Sofia's anger at Tina for cutting her off from her granddaughter, she agreed to meet her at Starbucks for coffee.

Sofia could have retaliated against Tina for her cruelty by severing all communications. But this would have hurt her also. And it would have hurt little Brianna. So, she stayed connected with Tina, hoping that things would change, that Tina would allow her to reconnect with her dear Brianna. She knows that Tina has not got vaccinated and never wears a mask. But she's willing to risk being around Tina to visit Brianna.

Sofia sees a bright poster on the wall and goes over to read it. It's a notification about vaccine passports and a possible acid attack. She's glad Michael has done this. The poster doesn't say when the attack might happen, but she recalls the note—after a week passes, unless the mall refuses to bring in passports. The week is up today.

She wonders again if Tina might be the one responsible for the note. There must be other people who use the same paper and typeface. Her thoughts are interrupted by familiar voices. She looks over and sees Michael in deep conversation with Mary Barker. It looks like he's trying to comfort her. Her eyes are red and her face is wet, indicating she's been crying.

Sofia approaches them. "Is there anything wrong?"

"Afraid so," says Michael. He glances at Mary, and she nods. "Richard's coughing got worse overnight and now he's got a fever. He went to the hospital early this morning and ... well, he tested positive for Covid."

"Oh, no! I can't believe it, Mary" says Sofia. "That's terrible, I'm so sorry, really sorry."

Mary clears some tears away with a tissue. "Thanks, Sofia. I'm really stressed out, I'm so worried about Richard. I don't know what I'd do if anything happened to him. He's been my rock. I just don't understand ... I don't understand ... why he got it and I didn't. I asked Dr. Cortez about it a while ago, and he said it's unusual, but it can happen. Why ... why did my Richard have to get it? We always were so careful. Always."

Michael puts his arm around Mary. "Richard's condition is stable," he says to Sofia. "He's under observation but he's not in the ICU."

Mary again wipes some tears away. "He's having trouble breathing, but at least it's not getting any worse."

"I'm hopeful," says Sofia.

Sofia looks around. "But I'm not so hopeful about what's going on here in the mall. People have been warned about an acid attack. Yet they're carrying on as usual. Seems to me they're not clued in. Maybe they think the threat's an exaggeration or it just couldn't happen here."

"Yeah," says Michael, "everything seems normal, eerily normal."

"I've got to go now," says Sofia. "I'm meeting my daughter in a few minutes upstairs for coffee. Tina says she's got something urgent to tell me."

"But Sofia," says Michael, "you should have somebody with you when you're in the mall, especially now. If you send me an email or a text, I can have a security guard walk with you, or watch out for you, when you are in here. I can go with you now."

"Thanks, Michael, I might take you up on that. But I'm okay right now. And I think Tina might drive me home. Stay with Mary. Goodbye. Arrivederci."

Sofia heads for the elevator to go up to the food court. Power Walker speeds by and gives her a warm smile. A few minutes after that, she catches sight of Dr. Cortez coming out of his office, walking quickly. He waves and she waves back.

Finally, Sofia arrives at the elevator, maneuvers her walker inside, and goes up to Starbucks.

"Hey, Mom," says Tina, waving her hand. "I got you a latte, the way you like it."

"Thanks honey," replies Sofia, removing her mask and taking a sip. "You don't look so good. You don't look good at all. You've been crying. What in the world has happened?"

"Marv's got Covid!"

Sofia's eyes widen. I can't believe it, she thinks. Suddenly two cases of Covid, happening to people I know.

"Marv? Covid? Did I hear you right?"

"You did. Marv's got Covid," Tina repeats, nodding her head and looking up. Tears are streaming down her face. "I'm pretty sure he got it at the rally. He wasn't feeling good that night. He had a sore throat, a cough, a fever. Then it got worse through the night. The next morning, he couldn't smell anything, couldn't taste anything, his fever got worse, his cough got worse, he had trouble breathing. So, I took him to Wolfville General."

Sofia quickly puts her mask back on, thinking Tina might also have the virus. "This is terrible, Tina. I'm really sorry to hear this. Must be hard on you, and hard on our little Brianna. Is she okay?"

"She is."

Sofia wishes she could see for herself. She considers asking for that, but Tina continues.

"Yeah, it's hard. Marv was hospitalized right away. And that afternoon, because of Covid, he was diagnosed with ARDS. I think I got it right, ARDS or acute respiratory distress syndrome. Often goes along with Covid. Basically, means serious inflammation in the lungs."

"What are they doing for him?"

"They gave him some kind of prednisolone for the ARDS. But his breathing is getting worse. I'm really worried."

"What are they saying about his recovery?"

Tina's lips tremble. "One of the doctors told me it's really a serious case, really serious. They said he could die ... he actually could die." Tina is sobbing.

Sofia stands up and puts her arms around her daughter. "This is unbelievable! I'm so sorry, honey."

"It's so horrible. I love Marv. I hate to see him in this awful state. It's just so horrible, horrible, horrible!"

"I'm sorry, Tina. It's all so hard to believe."

"I can hardly believe it myself. I had to tell you in person. By phone or email, it wouldn't seem real." Tina looks at her phone. "I have to get back to the hospital and check on Marv. Visiting hours will be starting soon, if they'll let me see him. Can I drive you home?"

"That would be great."

As they leave Starbucks, Sofia's coffee barely touched, she wishes Marv had never got caught up in all that nonsense, that anti-government extremism. His life could have been so different.

59

"Come on in," says Michael, hearing a knock on his door. It is early Friday morning, and he is in his office, sipping his first coffee of the day.

"Hi, I'm Sue Sarkissian," she says, coming into his office. "I'm here to see Wally Waller, your head of security. No one seems to know where he is."

"He's off for a few days." With the mall under threat and security needing to prepare for vaccine passports, it was not a good time for Wally to be off. But he'd apologetically requested a few days off to deal with an urgent family matter. Michael wasn't happy about it, and wasn't entirely sure Wally was being honest, but family is important. "I'm Michael McQueen, the mall manager. Can I help you? Please, have a seat."

Sue sits down and takes off her mask. Short and slim, she's wearing a jean jacket and has long silver earrings, which match her long graying hair. "As I said, I'm Sue Sarkissian and I'm a security technician. I'm a specialist in the software you use. I was here in March, and got everything working, but after that Wally reported more problems. He said the feed from several cameras was missing."

"Yes, Wally told me about this. Do you want some coffee?"

"That would be great, thanks. As I said to Wally, the problem's not in the cameras, it's in the software that runs the monitoring system. Your monitoring system hardware is ancient, but I appreciate it's costly to replace everything. Unfortunately, it's not uncommon to have software problems with older systems. However, I should be able to get it going."

"Good. Anything with your coffee?"

"No, I'm good with it black."

As Sue drinks her coffee, Michael realizes he has an opportunity. Wally is not around to make things difficult. If Sue can get the software fixed, get all the cameras going, and retrieve footage from the archived files, Michael can see for himself who's been leaving the notes.

"If you can direct me to the monitoring room, I'll get to work."

"I'll take you there," says Michael.

The security guard on duty, Jim Hill, lets them in. Michael introduces Sue to Jim, and asks him to give her whatever help she needs. Jim agrees, and returns to his seat in front of a bank of monitors. The largest one, in the center of the bottom row, shows four camera views, changing cameras every fifteen seconds. Most of the others also show four camera views, but some are blank.

"Sue," says Michael, "you can see the blank screens for yourself. It's a large area of the mall with no coverage at all."

"You've tried system resets, and are sure those cameras have power?" Sue looks between Michael and Jim. Michael looks at Jim.

"Yes, and yes," says Jim. "And we checked the camera video cables are still connected. Traced most of the lines to make sure they weren't cut anywhere. Everything looks good until the main control unit." He points to a large cabinet in the corner of the room.

"Thanks. Okay, I'm going to get working on this. Michael, this might take some time."

"Good luck." Michael turns to leave, then stops. "One question."

"Go ahead."

"Once you've got this fixed, you can go back into the archived files and retrieve footage, right?"

"Yes, assuming the cameras were functioning and this issue is related to getting the images onto the screens here. That's the likely problem."

"There's some old footage I'd like to see."

"Sure. Your system has a huge archive capacity. Let me check." Sue taps on the keyboard of the corner cabinet and reads text on a small monitor there. "Your video is archived for sixteen months. So, we can go back to … let me think, now … back to May of last year. Upgrading all that data to a new system would be expensive, unless you scrap it. Not sure why your retention is so long—almost looks like someone forgot to set the retention property, or maybe there was a legal issue in the past…maybe not paying attention to online storage bills."

Michael isn't paying attention to Sue's speculations on the archive. He's wondering why Wally told him they couldn't go back far. *Was he trying to throw me off the trail?*

"We can go back sixteen months?" asks Michael.

"Apparently," says Sue. "I can confirm that for you, if you have a camera you want to check."

"Jim, what's the camera above the bulletin board."

Jim checks a chart beside him. "Thirty-five." He points to one of the blank monitors.

Michael turns to Sue. "If it's possible, from the archived files, I'd like to see the footage from three particular mornings."

Michael gets out his phone and taps on the notes icon. "These dates: June 4 and December 13 of last year, and August 12 of this year. The times on each day are between 8 and 10 AM. Sue, we had a serious security problem on those days, and seeing the footage might really help us. If you can retrieve it, and I really hope you can, can you put it into separate file I can view, and show it to me?"

"If it can be done, I'll do it. I'll try to have it done by the end of the day. It all depends on exactly what the display issue is."

Finally, Michael thinks, things are coming together. Maybe I can find out who pinned up the notes. "And one more thing, Sue. What about this camera?" he says, pointing to a screen with no images, and the text UNISX LAV ENT. "Can you also retrieve footage from this camera? It's for," he checks his phone again, "June 3 of last year, same hours."

"Sure, if it's possible, I can also do that. I'll store a copy with the others."

"Thanks," says Michael. "I'll keep my fingers crossed. Here's my card. I'll write the dates and times on it. Please give me a call or send me a text later in the day and let me know how you're doing. I'll be in my office or in the mall somewhere."

Michael returns to his office, anxious about whether the video can be retrieved and what it might show. He's also anxious about Cornelia. She's hardly spoken to him since the night she refused to serve dinner, and she's been on the phone with her father more than usual. Some of that might be talking with the girls, now safely away, but Michael wonders if she is making her own plans to leave. The last note really upset her. That last note said an attack would happen after a week—which is today!

60

At the same time as Sue Sarkissian knocked on Michael's office door, Tina knocks on her mother's apartment door. Sofia opens the door to see Tina shaking and crying.

"Mom, it's Marv. He's on death's doorstep. His breathing has gotten worse. They put him in the ICU and he's on a ventilator."

"Oh Tina, oh honey, I'm so sorry. Come on in and sit down over here." Sofia points to a sofa and Tina sits down. "I can't imagine how much you're hurting right now. I've got some coffee on in the kitchen. I'll get us each a cup."

After a few minutes, Sofia returns with the coffee.

"Thanks, Mom." She takes a sip. "I found out about it a couple hours ago. A doctor at the hospital phoned me. I was really shattered. Sort of expected it, you know, but when I the doctor told me ... I was just ..."

"I understand. It would be so incredibly difficult to hear." Sofia recalls the devastating morning when she heard that her husband was dying.

"Mom, the doctor also told me Marv had a message for me. He wanted me to know—and it shocked me when I heard it—but he wanted me to know he'd been wrong about things. Covid, he said, is not a hoax. He said, if he had the chance to go back, he'd accept what the health people said. He'd wear a mask, he'd get a vaccine."

"Tina, I'm so sorry, for Marv and for you."

"Marv also said, according to the doctor, that he wished he'd never got involved in the movement against vaccines and masks. It was a wrong turn in his life. It was the worst mistake he'd ever made."

A mistake, Sofia thinks? Really? We all make mistakes, but Marv's mistake was enormous. It hurt him and many others. "Anything else, Tina? Did the doctor say anything else?"

"Yes. The doctor told me that Marv said it was his hope I'd quit the movement, that I'd listen to the health professionals, get vaccinated, wear a mask, do whatever it takes to protect myself and others from the virus. He said to tell me Covid is real, it's not a hoax, that his being on a ventilator is proof of it."

At least that's one good thing, Sofia thinks. It's late in the game but Marv is trying to make amends, trying to get Tina on track. "That's so sad, Tina."

"It's not just sad, Mom, it's breaking me apart. For the last three hours, I've just been sitting in my apartment crying and crying. And when I haven't been crying, I've been thinking and thinking."

Sofia's mind turns to her granddaughter. "Is Brianna okay? She must be confused by all this."

Tina takes a sip of her coffee. "Oh, she's okay. She's with the sitter right now. Don't worry, she's doin' fine."

"Honey, you said you were thinking and thinking. What about?"

"Well, I just don't know how to respond to what Marv said, that I should quit the movement. Part of me says no. I dedicated myself to the cause, just like Marv did. I put my heart and soul into it, I really believe we need to prevent tyranny, that we need to fight the elites, that we need to push back against the medical establishment feeding us false information."

Sofia wonders how her daughter can possibly think this, after what's happened to Marv. "But Tina, doesn't Marv's situation show you that the medical people got it right, that Covid is a real problem, a huge problem. Didn't Marv say it himself? Didn't Marv say he made a mistake?"

"According to the doctor, he did say all of that. But it doesn't add up. I've read online that when doctors say somebody's got Covid, it's not true. It's just flu or a cold instead. And I read that when doctors treat what they say is Covid, they give people medication which makes them even worse or can kill them. I also read that doctors even give patients drugs that can make them say things that aren't true. They say things like, 'I've got Covid, I should have listened to the doctors, people should get vaccines'. Well, that got me thinking. I think Marv might have got brainwashed."

Brainwashed? Has my daughter gone completely off the rails? "Oh, honey, isn't that far-fetched? The doctors at the hospital have a good reputation, and the hospital itself has a good reputation. Does it really make sense that the doctors would mislead people like this?"

"Yeah, I know, Mom. On one level, it rings true. What the doctors say rings true. But on another level, it doesn't make sense at all. It's hard for me to believe Marv would really want me to reject everything he's been fighting for. I wish I could ask him about it. But I can't do it because the doctors won't let me see him. The excuse is Covid restrictions, which lets them hide all sorts of things."

Sofia has a sip of her coffee. "Might take some time to figure it out, Tina."

"Mom, as I said before, part of me wants to continue Marv's work, work with the black coats, continue the movement for freedom. When I'm part of the movement, it really makes me feel alive, I feel like my true self, I feel like I'm contributing. But another part of me wants me to honor Marv's last wishes, if they are real. If Marv really got sick from Covid and it's not a hoax, I need to make a break from the past, and maybe we can get back to the way it used to be. I know how much Brianna misses you, and how much she loves you. And I know how much you love Brianna. I don't know what to do."

"Honey, I'm here to support you, regardless."

Tina gets up and gives her mother a hug. "Mom, thanks for understanding. I should get back to Brianna."

"Okay, Tina, we'll talk later. Ciao."

After Tina leaves, Sofia feels a headache coming on. Tina's news, and confusion, and the possibility of seeing Brianna again soon has her mind whirling. The humidity isn't helping. She's out of pain pills at home, and if the headache doesn't get better, she'll have to go to the mall pharmacy and get some. Not that she wants to go the mall with a dangerous person running around. Could that dangerous person be Tina, she wonders, again thinking about the paper and typeface that she's seen Tina use. But no, it couldn't be. As mixed up as Tina is, she's not so addicted to the movement as to attack someone with acid. Sofia hopes she's right about that.

61

Later that same morning, Si-Woo is in the bakery putting out fresh apple Danishes on the shelves. Grumpy Bill comes in with two cups of Starbucks coffee. He gives one to Si-Woo, and asks if he might have one of the Danishes while reaching for his wallet.

"You don't have to pay for it, GB. Fair trade, don't you think? Coffee for a Danish?"

"Good golly, girl, it's a deal."

"So, anything new?" asks Si-Woo, sipping some coffee.

"Well, you must have heard what the chief did," he replies.

"I heard it on the PA, and I'm so glad he did it. The public needs to know about any threats in the mall, and it's in our interests to have the passports. Hard to argue with any of this, don't you think?"

Grumpy Bill raises his eyebrows. "I don't think passports are such a good idea. I talked to Michael earlier and, in fact, I advised him not to do it."

Si-Woo is surprised. Frowning at him, she asks him why he'd ever do that. Grumpy Bill is about to reply but his head jerks to his side several times. Embarrassed, he apologizes, and explains about his tic. Si-Woo nods in sympathy. Grumpy Bill explains that he urged Michael to wait until public opinion gets more solidly behind the idea of passports, and wait for the Governor or the city to act, which'll probably happen soon enough. "Why stick your neck out and take unnecessary criticism?," he says. "And why jeopardize business in the mall?"

"That's being a way too pragmatic, don't you think? I realize you have to pick your battles and not get caught up in every controversy. But sometimes you need to take a stand, especially on something that's really important. You have to do what's right, not think about all the possible repercussions. No?"

"Gosh, I'm just saying you need to be prudent. You can appreciate that, can't you, Si-Woo?"

Si-Woo shakes her head in disagreement. Changing the subject, she asks if he could watch the bakery for a few minutes. She wants to take some of yesterday's muffins and croissants to a couple of men that she saw earlier by the main door. They looked hungry.

Grumpy Bill asks her to be extra careful, given the threatened attack. He worries Si-Woo might be a target.

Si-Woo puts on her mask, leaves, and finds the men sitting on a bench by the door. They are older males, both poorly dressed and thin as rakes. One is tall and has long scraggly hair, the other is short and almost bald. Both look grim and neither are wearing masks.

"Gentlemen, here's something from the bakery. I thought you might like them."

"Thanks lady," says the tall one. "Got any coffee to wash it down with?"

"Sorry, I don't. But there's a drinking fountain just over there by the clothing store. You can see it from here."

"I see it," says the short one. "Thanks. And thanks again for the grub."

"You're welcome," says Si-Woo. "With all the Covid that's going around, we all should be wearing masks indoors. You should get vaccinated too, if you aren't yet."

The tall one gives Si-Woo a mean look. "Listen lady," he says, with anger in his voice, "I don't like being told what to do. Neither does my buddy here. We like our freedom. We won't wear masks and we won't be getting vaccinated. Who knows what's in those damn things anyway!"

"I'm only trying to help. These are difficult times, and we all need to care for each other."

Si-Woo limps away, disappointed and shaking her head. As she comes back into the bakery, Grumpy Bills asks if she is okay. She tries to keep her composure, but she's almost in tears. "I'm feeling let down," she says. "I said to the men they should be wearing masks, and they need to get vaccinated. But they got defensive and angry. I just don't understand it. Why do so many people—not just them, but so many people—refuse to do what's for their own good? And what's good for their community? Why are they so determined to put their own freedom above the well-being of other people?"

"Gosh, I don't understand it either. Some of them are ignorant, I suppose, some are selfish as heck, and some are plain mean. And they dress it all up in the language of freedom."

Si-Woo looks up at the ceiling in exasperation. "Yeah, I guess you're right. Though I suppose some of them genuinely believe that their own freedom is more important than anything else."

Grumpy Bill swats a fly going by. "But it seems to me they conveniently forget about the freedom of other people."

"I don't disagree. But you're starting to sound more like our idealistic doctor, Dr. Cortez, and less like Grumpy Bill, the pragmatic business tycoon."

"Idealistic? Goodness gracious, no. I just try to be practical and cautious. But if we're going to get along in this world, it seems to me we need to think about our social responsibilities and obligations, not just our freedom."

"Couldn't agree more."

A booming female voice from the PA system interrupts. "Mornin' folks. Shoppers are reminded that vaccine passports will soon be required for some areas of the mall. Masks are currently required in all areas. And please be vigilant for suspicious behavior. Extra security staff are on duty, and anything suspicious should be reported to security staff or the mall office. You have yourself a great day at Wolfville Mall, and God bless America."

"Scary stuff, isn't it?" Grumpy Bill says to Si-Woo. "Michael showed me the note. This guy is really angry. Imagine throwing acid into somebody's face, disfiguring them, for just urging passports in the mall. Gracious sakes, this is hard to believe."

Si-Woo agrees.

Grumpy Bill considers how he should phrase what he wants to say. "Si-Woo, an attack could come at any time now. I'm thinking about everybody's safety, but I'm especially thinking about your safety. You've spoken out in favor of the passports. Which means you're in danger."

"Thanks for your concern, GB. I get it. I'll try to be extra careful."

"I care about you." He takes her hand.

"I care about you too," says Si-Woo, pleased to realize their relationship is moving beyond friendship.

62

It is late in the afternoon and Michael is sitting at his desk, nervous. He looks at his watch. It is almost four-thirty. Shouldn't Sue Sarkissian have phoned him by now? She's been in the monitoring room all day. It would be so great if she could retrieve the footage. He could find out who this monster is.

He decides he'll go for a stretch. He needs to walk off his anxious energy. *Wouldn't it Be Nice* by the Beach Boys is playing in the mall. The first thing Michael sees is a security guard escorting an intoxicated man out a side door. They are being particularly attentive to who is in the mall today. The man looks angry and mean. Michael's mind goes back to the notes. It's still a possibility, he thinks, the notes were written by a man like this, somebody with grievances.

It's always busy on Friday afternoons, but today it's extra busy. He sees the line for a new phone. And he recalls there's a new movie opening today. But don't these people know, Michael asks himself, that despite the new phone and an exciting new movie, Covid remains a problem? People can still get sick and die. You'd think they'd be more cautious and stay home. He wonders how Richard is doing. Mary hasn't been in the mall.

Michael also wonders about the effectiveness of the warnings he's made about the threat. No one seems worried. Maybe they don't believe it. Maybe they think if it did happen, it wouldn't happen to them. At least he tried to warn people. But if people don't listen, what can he do?

He notices one of the black coats, the one with the Hitler-style mustache, rush by. The man is scanning the crowds, searching for somebody. Would it be Tina? Michael also notices Si-Woo and Grumpy Bill having a chat inside the bakery. They're together a lot these days. It would be great if they got together. They're both lonely and deserving of some happiness. As for him and Cornelia, Michael isn't sure their marriage will survive. Each night, when he gets home, he wonders if he will find his suitcase packed and sitting in the driveway?

Up ahead, he sees Sofia heading toward the pharmacy. As usual, she's struggling with her walker. Michael easily catches up and walked alongside her.

"Hi Sofia. I'm really surprised to see you here."

"Good afternoon, chief. Ciao. I didn't want to be here, what with that acid-thrower on the loose. But I have a terrible headache. It started this morning and has been getting worse all day. I need to get some extra strength pills at the pharmacy."

"Your daughter, Tina, couldn't she have done it for you?"

"No, she had to stay home with Brianna. Besides, she's really upset."

"What happened?"

"Marv got sick. He got Covid, and Tina is shattered. He's on a ventilator at the hospital. It's really serious."

Michael's jaw drops. "Jeez ... that's, well, I don't know what to say, that's ... hard to believe." Michael tries to digest this news. *Marv on a ventilator?* He can't picture the dynamic speaker and march leader reduced to that.

"Marv's not a nice person, that's for sure. But I didn't wish him ill. Not like that. It's a terrible thing for anybody to get Covid. And I'm really sorry for my poor daughter. Tina's in such bad shape. She's sad, and also confused. Marv sent a message to Tina telling her that Covid is not a hoax, that he was wrong to oppose masks and vaccines, and that he hoped Tina would quit the movement and take precautions. But Tina doesn't know whether to believe the doctor who passed on the message. So, I don't know what's going to happen with Tina. But I'm praying she listens to what Marv said."

"Sofia, I'm really sorry to hear about all this. This must be hard on you."

"It's hard, but I'll get through it." Sofia starts to tear up, stops walking, finds a tissue in her purse, and wipes her eyes. "And Michael, I want to thank you again for your decision about the notes and passports. I know you were hesitant, but you are doing the right thing."

Michael puts his arm around Sofia, and thanks her for her kind words. He tells her that with the threat in the mall, she really shouldn't be walking by herself. He will walk her over to the pharmacy himself, and when she's finished there, he'll arrange to have a security guard walk with her back to the main entrance.

After texting the security office and walking Sofia to the pharmacy, Michael heads back to his office. He thinks for a moment he sees Wally moving through the crowd up ahead. But it couldn't be Wally, he's out of town. There's a ping on his phone, a text from Sue. When Michael looks up again, he can't see Wally or anyone that looks like him.

Sue S: Hey, Michael, everything working now. Got the footage from the dates u wanted, copied it onto local file in sec office. Ready for you to view. Sue.

63

Michael rushes to the monitoring room and knocks on the door. Jim Hill, still on duty, lets him in. Sue is at a desk on the side, staring at a computer screen. All the monitors show images now. Michael goes over to Sue and she shows him the files for each date.

"Terrific! This is great news. So glad you could do this, Sue. Thank you, thank you so much. I'm going to go through each of them now, and try to find what I'm looking for."

"It'll take some time. But you can increase the speed in the file player to go through them faster. Remember, these aren't true video, but a series of still pictures, so a choppy view is normal at any speed. There's an option to print once you pause the playback."

"Great. Thanks again, this really helps."

"Glad I could take care it. The patches I put in place should keep this old system going for another year or two, but you do need to be looking at replacement. I just need a signature here." She holds out a tablet to him, and he signs. "Thanks. My office will send the invoice. Hope you find what you are looking for in the recordings."

Sue leaves the room. Michael checks his watch and sees it's nearly five-thirty, which means he won't be home until late. He sends Cornelia a text, explaining the situation. She doesn't respond. He starts reviewing the footage of activity around the bulletin board, beginning with the June 4 file.

Time ticks away. Michael is getting impatient, but realizes he is only a third of the way through the file. Then he sees a familiar figure approach the board and pin up a note. Michael hit pause, and yells, "My God, here it is! Here it is!" Jim comes over to have a look.

"Jim, check the live feeds and see if they are in the mall now!" Jim hurries back to his bank of monitors.

Michael checks the other two videos, faster now that he knows what he is looking for. "I found them again! It's the same person!"

"I don't see them in the mall," says Jim, "but it's crowded. Did you know there a new phone out today? I don't know how people afford them new."

Michael checks the footage from above the unisex washroom entrance, and soon calls Jim over. "Here's the old guy going into the washroom. And see who comes out? What do you think? Same person?"

"Hard to say," replies Jim. "The angle is different, so we can't compare height. Could be the same, but this person's wearing a hoodie. Can't see their face in this camera. We might find them on a nearby camera, but which one depends on where they went."

"Right. Still, we know who is putting up the notes. You don't see them anywhere?"

Jim glances at the monitors again. "Nope."

"Could be here, though. Alert the other security staff. Tell them to detain our friend, if they can, but to be careful. Then call the police, email them an image, and tell them we've identified the person we think is responsible for pinning up the notes. I've got to go."

Michael rushes into the mall to look for the suspect and warn others.

64

While Michael is reviewing the videos, Si-Woo and Grumpy Bill are leaving the bakery. Si-Woo has just finished her shift and is walking with Grumpy Bill back to his store through the crowded mall.

"Si-Woo, can I ask you a question?"

"I'm listening."

"I'm wondering if you'd like to join me next Tuesday night for dinner. I have in mind a new Italian restaurant that's just opened downtown. I hear it's darn good."

"Is this a date?"

"Gosh, I suppose it is."

"Well, I suppose I should accept. Happy to join you."

"Glad to hear it. I don't know much about the restaurant except it's supposed to specialize in northern Italian dishes. I hear the risotto dishes are fantastic. Of course, I'm most interested in the desserts, especially if there's tiramisu."

"I'm sure it's all great, Grumpy Bill. I'm looking forward to it."

"Okay, it's a date. I'll pick you up at your apartment, say around seven. You'll have to tell me the address, but, of course, I'll see you before that, here at the mall."

"You will. Thanks, and have a good evening. I'll head home from here."

Grumpy Bill takes her hands. "Listen, Si-Woo, be careful. Be extra careful. And please be sure to keep alongside others as you walk."

"I will."

As Grumpy Bill heads into his store, Si-Woo limps along toward the nearest exit. She follows the suggestion to walk alongside others and tries to keep an eye on the people around her, but she's thinking how happy she is to be asked out. With her early marriage, she never dated, but she imagines this must be how teenagers feel when they start dating—full of energy and hope.

Near the exit, by the pharmacy, Si-Woo spots Sofia Morellato coming out of the pharmacy, and a security guard meeting her. Si-Woo approaches Sofia and asks her why she's still in the mall. Sofia explains that Michael had arranged for a security guard to walk her out to the main entrance.

"Smart thing not to walk alone," says Si-Woo, smiling at the guard.

"Yes, it is. And I'm so glad Michael arranged it. He's a real angel. I've got a terrible feeling an attack could happen at any moment. I just can't believe how crowded it is in here. Don't people ever listen to warnings? And Si-Woo, I'm so surprised to see you walking by yourself."

"Well, I was walking with some people, but they've gone ahead. And I'm almost at the exit. With that heavy rain, though, I'd rather leave out the main entrance, and not be outside as much. Do you mind if I join you and your security friend?"

"Not at all. Please join us."

As they walk along, Si-Woo tells Sofia about her date with Grumpy Bill, and how much she is looking forward to it. Sofia shares her news that Marv has Covid but that he seems to regret his anti-mask and anti-vaccine ideas, and is encouraging Tina to take precautions.

Si-Woo is quiet for a few minutes. "Wow. Marv has been such an awful man. He hurt a lot of people, including me, but I am sorry he's got Covid. We're all human and he doesn't deserve that. I feel sorry for Tina too, but it's good she's considering giving up her opposition to masks and vaccines. We both have hope for a better future. Hope is important."

They pass by the line at the phone store. "Everybody wants the new thing," says Sofia.

Si-Woo checks the pockets of her jeans. "I don't have mine." Sofia looks at her.

"I don't have my phone. I must have left it in the bakery. It's not far from here. You carry on and I'll catch up."

"Okay, see you there. But be careful."

Si-Woo limps back to the bakery. The crowding makes her progress through the mall slow. She realizes having a security guard with her, or maybe a person with a walker, made people get out of the way.

She finds her phone where she left it, on the back counter. Back in the mall, the going is even slower. It looks like a movie just ended. She has a hard time getting around people, and gets frustrated about her slow pace. She wonders if she'll be able to catch up to Sofia.

Despite the crowd, she senses somebody is following her. The feeling is intense, more than it was last December. She looks back, but doesn't see anyone paying any attention to her. She tries walking faster, but her injured leg slows her down. Her heart races as she thinks about the note. She has chest pain and shortness of breath.

She is about to yell for help, when someone beside her pushes her to the floor, rips her mask partially off her face, and sprays something hot, again and again, into her eyes and face. She feels her face burning. She tries to protect herself with her flailing arms. She feels she is drowning in hot liquid. Someone is yelling. Michael. There's a scuffle. Her chest hurts.

Michael yells for water. Almost immediately, two bottles of water are handed to him by onlookers. He gets on his knees and pours water over Si-Woo's face, trying to rinse the acid away. He keeps pouring until there is no more water. Another bottle is handed to him, and he again uses the water to flush away the acid.

"Quick, call an ambulance and get Dr. Cortez," Michael yells to a nearby security guard.

Within minutes, Dr. Cortez arrives at the scene. He encourages Michael to continue the water, while he checks her pulse and listens to her heart.

Onlookers continue to pass bottles of water, while others use using their phones to record the scene. More security guards arrive and move people back.

"Did anyone get them?" asks Michael.

"No," a guard replies. "Ran by us."

"I wish I'd been able to hold them," says Michael.

"Better that you're treating her," says Dr. Cortez. "She's got signs of myocardial infarction. She's having a heart attack." He begins CPR.

Grumpy Bill, puffing and out of breath, pushes by the guards keeping the crowd back. He kneels down and gently puts his jacket under Si-Woo's head, then takes her hand. "Is she going to be okay?"

Paramedics arrive and take over the treatment. They put her on a gurney, and security helps clear a quick path to the exit and waiting ambulance. Michael, Dr. Cortez, and Grumpy Bill look at each other in stunned silence.

65

THE WOLFVILLE NEWS

Saturday, August 21, 2021

VICIOUS ATTACK AT WOLFVILLE MALL

A woman was viciously attacked at Wolfville Mall late Friday afternoon. She has been identified by the Wolfville Police as Si-Woo Lee, age fifty-five, an employee of the Diplomat Bakery at the mall. She was attacked in the mall after her shift.

According to witnesses, a man wearing a hoodie pushed her down and sprayed her with a water gun containing acid. Intervening in the attack was mall manager, Michael McQueen, who pulled the attacker away. The attacker ran off and disappeared into the crowd.

Police arrested a suspect two hours later at a downtown location. He will appear in court Monday to enter a plea to a charge of aggravated assault. Prosecutors are considering additional charges of attempted murder and with assault based on hate. The suspect has been identified as Power Walker. Born Tom Burns, he legally changed his name to reflect a nickname he had acquired at Wolfville Mall. He was known in the mall for his eccentric exercising and speed walking.

The police are now investigating Power Walker's background and motive. It appears Power Walker and Ms. Lee only knew each other through occasional meetings in the mall, but police are investigating if there was any other relationship.

Someone had posted notes in the mall threatening an acid attack. While acid attacks are not unusual in India and other parts of south Asia, they are rare in the United States.

Police report they were greatly assisted by the diligent work of Michael McQueen, the manager of the mall. Through retrieving and reviewing video from surveillance cameras dating back to last June, Mr. McQueen was able to identify the suspect and connect him with the earlier notes.

Police also report that Mr. McQueen deserves high praise for his valiant effort to save Ms. Lee from further harm. His quick intervention to remove the attacker and rinse away the acid probably saved Ms. Lee's life.

According to local physician Dr. Juan Cortez, Ms. Lee had a heart condition, and the attack triggered a heart attack. She was taken by ambulance to the coronary care unit at Wolfville General Hospital, where she is being treated. She has responded well to the treatment, but her recovery will be lengthy.

According to Dr. Cortez, she will require facial surgery, and one side of her face will likely be scarred, as well as part of her nose and upper lip. She also faces permanent hair loss and has lost the sight in one eye.

66

POLICE TRANSCRIPT: INTERVIEW WITH POWER WALKER

August 28, 2021

WOLFVILLE POLICE HEADQUARTERS

In Attendance: Detective Cyndy Parks, Detective Viraj Sharma.

Detective Parks: Good morning. You go by the name of Power Walker. But I see your original name was Tom Burns. Why the change?

Power Walker: I had my name changed a couple of years ago. People at Wolfville Mall called me Power Walker, I guess because of my speedy walking. I got to like it. And so, I changed my name.

Detective Parks: I see. We'd like to thank you for your cooperation in speaking to us this morning. We see you've waived your right to a lawyer, at least for this interview.

Power Walker: Yeah, I've got nothing to hide.

Detective Sharma: Power Walker, you have been charged with aggravated assault. Later, the DA may decide to add another charge—the attempted murder of Ms. Si-Woo Lee. And the DA may also add racially-motivated assault. Do you understand this?

Power Walker: I'll be pleading not guilty to any charge.

Detective Sharma: Power Walker, there's something else. Do you know anything at all about the murder of Mr. Jason Sommers? Strangled in a washroom at Wolfville Mall, last year in June.

Power Walker: I can't help you with that. I heard about it at the time, a guard told me. Terrible thing to happen, and I'm really sorry for the man's family.

Detective Sharma: What about Ms. Lee, Si-Woo Lee?

Power Walker: The old Asian lady. I certainly didn't try to murder her. My intention was only to hurt her a little, just to send out a message to people in the mall not to support vaccine passports. My cause was honorable. If I committed a crime at all, it was one of necessity. I think lawyers call it the defense of necessity. Look, I had to do it. I had to do it to try to prevent a greater crime from happening, the crime of requiring people to show proof they are vaccinated. That's un-American. Treasonous. I had to set an example.

Detective Sharma: You could have attacked anyone, but you chose to attack an Asian woman. Why did you do this? Why do you have a special hatred for Asian people?

Power Walker: No, that's not true. I don't hate them. I only wanted to go after anybody who was pushing for vaccine passports. I know the Asian lady did this. I heard her mouthing off. But it could've been somebody else.

Detective Parks: So, would you describe yourself as an anti-vaxxer, someone who is opposed to vaccines for Covid and to policies of requiring proof of vaccination?

Power Walker: I would. I absolutely would. I'm proud of that. And I also oppose the requiring of masks. All of this is un-American.

Detective Sharma: You previously admitted to pinning up not just this last note, but three notes in total, all with threats of an acid attack in Wolfville Mall. Why did you do this?

Power Walker: Well, if you wanna know the truth, at the start at least, I only wanted to scare people. I never meant to actually carry out an attack. I only wanted to scare them, get them not to wear masks.

Detective Parks: Why did you want to scare people?

Power Walker: It wasn't my idea. I got paid to pin up the notes. I got paid by my aunt. Her name is Brenda Mills and she's the manager of Sunrise Mall. She's a competitive person. Good business skills. She wanted to build up business at Sunrise and draw customers away from Wolfville Mall. She had the idea for the notes. I was short of cash and liked the idea of scaring people.

Detective Sharma: But you ended up not just trying to scare people but also getting a water gun, loading it with sulfuric acid, and squirting the acid into the face of Ms. Lee, blinding her in one eye and leaving her with ugly scars for life. She had a heart condition, and you could easily have killed her.

Power Walker: As I said, my plan was just to scare people. But they kept the notes secret. Nobody got scared. So, I had to be serious. People don't take you serious unless you do what you promise. I learned that when I was a kid.

Detective Parks: Well, I think that's enough for today. We'll talk again.

67

POLICE TRANSCRIPT: INTERVIEW WITH BRENDA MILLS

August 29, 2021

WOLFVILLE POLICE HEADQUARTERS

In Attendance: Detective Cyndy Parks, Detective Viraj Sharma

Detective Parks: Good morning, Ms. Mills.

Brenda Mills: You can call me Brenda.

Detective Parks: Okay, Brenda, thanks for agreeing to see us. We see that you have waived your right to a lawyer, at least at this point.

Brenda Mills: I have.

Detective Parks: So, you are an aunt of Power Walker, previously Tom Burns.

Brenda Mills: Correct. I have known Tom, sorry, Power Walker, ever since he was born. We both come from Seattle, you see. My sister is Power Walker's mother.

Detective Sharma: Later on, Brenda, you may be facing charges for instigating the crimes committed by Power Walker. We don't know yet what the DA has in mind. Probably aiding and abetting. But for now, we'd like to ask you some questions about Power Walker. We'd like to try to understand his background, and what led him to carrying out the acid attack.

Brenda Mills: Okay, I'll try to help.

Detective Parks: Can you describe Power Walker's childhood and teenage years, when he was growing up in Seattle?

Brenda Mills: Tom—I mean Power Walker, sorry, I have a hard time getting used to his new name—anyway, he had a terrible childhood. Tom's father was an alcoholic and beat him regularly. Tom's mother, my sister, she was—I'm afraid to say—emotionally distant from him, often cold. I lived down the street and tried to help Tom, show him some affection and warmth, to kind of make up for his parents. But you could tell he was suffering from the abuse.

Detective Sharma: How did this abuse show up in his behavior?

Brenda Mills: Well, he didn't do good at school and he got into trouble a lot. Other kids picked on him, and he fought back. It got so bad that social services had to intervene and, eventually, he was taken out of his home and put into foster care. He had several foster care homes and things got worse for him. Lots of fighting with other kids.

Detective Parks: And his teenage years?

Brenda Mills: He dropped out of school. I think it was grade 11 or something like that, and then he got a job working for a moving company. But he lost that job and just drifted from job to job. I really felt sorry for him. But I kept in contact with him. I knew he saw me as a kind of surrogate mother.

Detective Sharma: Did he get into any serious trouble during this time? We know he had three charges of assault and two kids had to be sent to the hospital. But apart from that, any other kind of trouble?

Brenda Mills: No. You might think he'd have a long juvenile record. But he didn't. It was just those three charges. He got probation and community service, never juvenile detention. Maybe he did things I'm not aware of, and maybe he did things and just didn't get caught. We were in touch, but I don't know what he did day to day. But you could tell he had a lot of inner anger. He was often on a short fuse, and he could easily get offended and mad.

Detective Parks: How did he end up in Wolfville?

Brenda Mills: Well, after I got my degree in business administration, I was offered a job with the company that owns Sunrise Mall. I worked my way up and became the manager of the mall. Tom moved to Wolfville a few years back, I'm pretty sure it was the fall of 2018. Yeah, that's when it was. He rented a basement suite in my house, and I helped him get established. I paid for him to take a bartender course online, which he then used to get a job as a bartender at a pub. And while doing this, at my urging, he got his high school equivalency diploma through online courses.

Detective Sharma: During the time he was with you, Brenda, anything unusual in his behavior?

Brenda Mills: For the most part, no. We got along great. Tom was always polite, friendly, and often charming and entertaining. As I said before, he saw me as a substitute mother. He appreciated my support, and he treated me well. But I found it odd—very odd—the way he did his exercises and fast walking in the mall. It was so weird. But you know, when I think back to Tom as a teenager, he always liked being a show-off. So, I suppose his weird walking in the mall was not so out of character, not so surprising.

Detective Sharma: Anything else odd about him?

Brenda Mills: Well, yes, I also found it weird when he got this big water gun and would go out to the park and practice squirting water at things. He even bragged to me about it. I just didn't understand it. A grown man doing this kid thing. I figured maybe he was trying to have some happy kid memories.

Detective Parks: But Brenda, didn't you know he was practicing for the acid attack? You paid him to pin up the notes. Did you pay him or encourage him, in any way, to carry out his threat of an attack?

Brenda Mills: No way! I've admitted I paid him to put up the notes. It was a stupid thing to do. My ambition got the better of me. I feel bad about it and I'm really sorry I did it. But my intention was only to scare people, get people to stop shopping at Wolfville Mall, get them to come over to Sunrise. I created this psychotic character on paper to make threats. But that's all. I just wanted to frighten people. It got out of hand. I had no idea Tom would take it further, and actually do such a dreadful thing. I still can't believe it.

Detective Sharma: One other thing, Brenda. Did you see any signs of racism in Power Walker? Did he show any feelings of hatred toward Asians or any other minority group? We'd like to know if his attack in the mall was motivated by hate.

Brenda Mills: His father was a terrible racist, and he would say a lot of racist things in their house, in front of Tom. I know this from my sister. I also know from my sister, and from other people in the neighborhood, that when Tom was bullying other kids, he would be especially hard on Asian and black kids, hurling racial taunts and insults at them. I think it was a case of 'like father, like son'. And this kind of attitude didn't stop as he got older. In conversations I had with him, when no one else was around, he sometimes would use racist language.

Detective Sharma: There's one thing I still don't get. People in the mall said Power Walker was polite, charming, and likable. And yet he pinned up those vile notes, and he carried out that foul vicious attack on Si-Woo Lee. Sort of like Jekyll and Hyde.

Brenda Mills: Yes, there is that quality to him. Most of the time, he is fun-loving, pleasant, and friendly. He can be really nice to people. But he can also turn dark, get mean, get nasty. Not to me. But to other people. That's what I've been told. I suppose it reflects his early years.

Detective Parks: That'll be all for now, Brenda. The DA will contact you about any charges that may be made against you. We will tell her you've been cooperative in answering our questions.

68

"I'm home, princess," says Michael, as he comes in the side door.

"In the family room," replies Cornelia.

"Girls get back from Georgia, okay?"

"Yeah, I picked them up at the airport after lunch. They're fine. They're still out with their friends. Should be back soon. Hey, we need to celebrate your big promotion. I've got something special for you, really special."

"What have you got?"

"Champagne, and the top of the line—Dom Pérignon! Only the best for my successful husband. It's on ice in the kitchen. Let's celebrate."

"What a great surprise! Okay then, let's do it. I'll go and get it." Michael goes into the kitchen, opens the Dom, and brings it into the family room, along with two flutes. He happily pours the champagne.

"A toast to my wonderful husband," says Cornelia, grinning ear to ear.

"Thanks princess," says Michael, tasting the Dom. "This is so great, isn't it? It's been a long haul, trying to get this promotion. I've earned it." Michael feels relaxed, happy. He hasn't felt this way for a long time.

"Yeah, it didn't look so good before, did it?" Cornelia replies, taking a sip. "But thankfully, the stars came into alignment. I'm so happy for you and for us, sweetie."

Michael looks through the window at the birch trees in the backyard. He sees some yellow leaves on one of them and wonders if fall is going to come early. "Yes, it's all good. Pacific Gold was extremely happy with the way things turned out. So happy, they made me senior properties manager. Not only did they give me a big pay increase, but they assigned me an office at the corporation's glitzy building downtown. For sure, I'll miss my old job as mall manager, and the company of the mall walkers. They're great people. But I'm happy to move on."

Cornelia asks him to tell her, in more detail, why Pacific Gold finally decided to give him the promotion. Michael explains. "The Board of Directors was very pleased with how things unfolded. There was good publicity gained from the capturing and charging of the person who posted the notes and attacked Si-Woo Lee. The police told the media their success in catching Power Walker was due in large part to my wonderful detective work and evidence gathering. They also told the media that my quick thinking was responsible for helping Ms. Lee and preventing a worse outcome for her. All this publicity, the board said, reflects well on me and the mall. It will be very good for business."

Michael wonders if he's being too pragmatic, thinking about the business benefits. He also wonders about Power Walker. He will be charged with aggravated assault and likely spend a good chunk of time in prison. Apparently, the DA didn't think there was enough solid evidence for attempted murder or racially-motivated hate. And the murder of the poor bookstore clerk remains unsolved. Power Walker denied having anything to do with it and the video evidence wasn't good enough for identification. Michael thinks that Power Walker probably did do it, but unless evidence is uncovered, he's probably going to get away with murder. It's not fair to the old man's sister. But then again, there are so many things in life that are unfair.

Michael realizes he is drifting. He apologizes to Cornelia and continues. "And while it wasn't anything directly to do with me, all the negative publicity for the Sunrise Mall manager has been good for business. Some of the board thought their manager saw me as tough competition." Michael wonders again how Brenda Mills could she have possibly come up with such a devious idea? Blind ambition? Her competitive spirit gone wild?

"Finally, there was the Governor's announcement yesterday about vaccine passports for the state. In making the announcement, she referred to the me and Wolfville Mall as one of the great pioneers of the policy in the Pacific Northwest. A bit overstated, perhaps. But everybody was impressed, including Pacific Gold. So here I am, a senior manager at Pacific Gold."

Cornelia claps and gives Michael a huge smile. "Well, I'm certainly impressed, sweetie. So is Daddy. Oh, and he sends his congratulations. He told me he always thought you were going to accomplish big things."

"Thanks princess," says Michael, raising an eyebrow. "Still, a couple of things upset me. It's so sad about Si-Woo Lee."

Cornelia nods.

"Her friend, Grumpy Bill—you've met him—he's really shaken up about it. He talked to me today and said he can't sleep at night. Says he's feeling really miserable about it. Everyone at the mall does. Such horrible results can come out of extremism and hate."

"And the other thing?"

Michael takes another sip of the Dom. "Someone I know died from Covid. It was on the news this morning."

"Hmm. Was it Richard somebody? I think you mentioned he had got Covid."

"You're thinking of Richard Barker. No, he hasn't died, but his situation isn't good. He went into ICU yesterday and he's on a ventilator. Dr. Cortez told me he probably won't make it. His wife Mary, as you can imagine, is out of her mind. She still has hope ... but ...."

"So, who was it that died?"

"Leader of the anti-vaxxers, Marv Hammar."

"Wow." Cornelia drinks some more Dom.

"He was a mean character, and sometimes cruel. And he did a lot of harm through opposing vaccines and masks. Many people have suffered and died, needlessly suffered and died, not just because of Covid but because of people like Marv. But he was doing something he believed in. Sad that it killed him. He had a death-bed conversion to the view that strong government action was needed to fight the virus."

Michael looks out the window again and takes another sip. "At least his girlfriend changed her mind. Do you remember Tina Morellato?"

"Is she the one with those horrible tattoos—skulls and things. Yuk!"

"Yes, that's her. After she found out Marv died from Covid, she decided, at least according to Dr. Cortez, to quit the anti-vaxxer cause and get counseling—"

"Counseling? Counseling for what?"

"For withdrawal from the anti-vaxxer movement and from her obsession with conspiracy theories. Hopefully it'll work. Tina's mother, Sofia—you might have seen her with her walker—has been hoping Tina would cut ties with the movement and get back to her previous self. If that happens, Sofia will be able to see her granddaughter again. Tina, if you can believe it, had actually blocked her from seeing her own granddaughter, blocked her for over a year."

"That's terrible! Amazing she'd do such a nasty thing. Hard to believe any parent would do that." She finishes her Dom. Did you ever find out who made those nasty phone calls?"

Michael looks uneasy. "Nope, I never did. I don't think we'll ever know. I didn't even bother reporting it to the police. People who do this hardly ever get caught."

"Hey, let's talk about something else, something more positive. We're supposed to be celebrating. And let's have some more champagne."

"Yeah, let's do that." Michael pours them more of the Dom.

Cornelia rubs her hands together and smiles. "I think you'll be happy to know, sweetie, that I've been checking out some real estate listings. A couple new and impressive properties have just come on the market and guess where they are? In Blue Mountain Heights! Isn't this great? And now that you've got your new position, we can afford it. I'm really thrilled about it, Michael. I've already told my yoga friends. I told Alexandra, and she was blown-away. Maybe we can go and have a look on the weekend."

"That's great, Cornelia, I suppose we can."

"It's a deal," she says, taking a large sip of the Dom. "Listen, I hear the girls coming in through the back door. I'll collect them and we'll get ready for dinner."

As Cornelia leaves the room, Michael wonders what the future will bring. They'll move into that fancy new house in Blue Mountain Heights, they'll have a higher social status, maybe the girls will go to a private school. But will Cornelia be happy? Perhaps. Her love for him, however, seems to be conditional on his income. What if he hadn't got his promotion? Or, what if he doesn't get the next one?

69

THE WOLFVILLE NEWS

Tuesday, August 31, 2021

PLANS FOR NEW HOMELESS SHELTER

Plans were announced at a news conference last night for a new homeless shelter in the city, a short distance from Wolfville Mall. The project was made possible through buying the Quiet Night Hotel, which closed last year. The hotel will be converted into a shelter of 40 to 60 beds and be at least partly operational this winter.

Funding for the project will be provided primarily by local businessman William Massey, known around Wolfville as Grumpy Bill. He is the owner and operator of three sporting goods stores in the city, the largest one situated in Wolfville Mall.

The shelter will be called Good Karma Shelter. It will be managed by Si-Woo Lee, who is currently recovering from a vicious assault at Wolfville Mall on August 20. Ms. Lee was attacked with sulfuric acid by a young man known as Power Walker, who is being charged with aggravated assault. She faces a long and difficult recovery but is expected to be able to take on her management position sometime late next year.

Asked by reporters to explain his generosity, Grumpy Bill said there currently is no shelter in the area and one is badly needed, given the large population of unhoused people. "The purpose, as a wonderful woman once told me," he says, "is to give people who are down on their luck food, warmth, and counseling, and a sense that somebody cares. This provides them with hope, until they can develop the strength to move forward in life."

Acknowledgements

The writing of this novel was inspired in part by my observations of mall walkers at the Richmond Centre, an indoor shopping mall not far from where I live in Steveston, British Columbia, during the worst years of Covid-19. I wondered who they were and how they were being affected by the virus. I was also influenced by what I saw on the news. Almost every day, it seemed, there were reports about the incredible spread of Covid, among the deadliest pandemics in modern history. There were dramatic accounts of death, fear, anger, hate, protest, and heroism. Reflecting on this while walking in the mall, I conjured up a story about how a group of different people at an imaginary shopping mall reacted to the crisis of Covid and what it revealed about their character. The outcome of my journey of the mind was *The Mall Walkers*.

I have several people to thank. Jan Hancock read an early draft and made a number of very helpful suggestions, which I incorporated into the novel. My marvelous partner, Katherine Covell, read several versions of the work and proposed adjustments that I happily accepted, knowing they were on the mark. I greatly appreciate her support in all that I do. Anonymous reviewers associated with *Somewhat Grumpy Press* also made comments that were invaluable in moving the project along. They made me rethink several things that led to adjustments. Finally, I thank Tim Covell for his conscientious work in editing the book. Exacting and giving careful attention to detail, he helped make this story what it is.

ABOUT THE **AUTHOR**

R. Brian Howe has published a variety of academic books and articles on human rights and the *UN Convention on the Rights of the Child*. A professor emeritus of political science, he is internationally known as a leader in the field of human rights and child rights education. Now retired and living in Vancouver, he's written his first novel, *The Mall Walkers*. Set in a northwestern American mall during the arrival of Covid, Howe explores themes of human rights, the dangers of angry populism, and the clash between the values of individual freedom and social responsibility.

Contact the author through the Somewhat Grumpy Press web site: SomewhatGrumpyPress.com

Help independent authors and small presses by leaving a review at your favourite online retailer or review site, or sharing on social media.